DONNY AND URSULA SAVE THE WORLD

BY SHARON WEIL

Hank—
M. Earth & I thank you!
Sharon Weil

PASSING 4 NORMAL PRESS | LOS ANGELES

Published by Passing 4 Normal Press
passing4normal.com

ISBN 978-0-9889071-9-5

Library of Congress Control Number: 2013901610

First Edition

Donny And Ursula Save the World is a work of fiction and a product of the author's imagination. Any resemblance to actual events, corporations, locales, or persons, living or dead, is entirely coincidental.

Cover and text design by Valerie Madden
Interior layout by Rey Howard
Cover illustration by Yogy Ikhwanto
Author photo by Natalia Knezevic

To order, visit Donny and Ursula Save the World at donnyandursula.com.

5 2 1 3

For my three daughters.
And for M. Earth and all the creatures who love her.

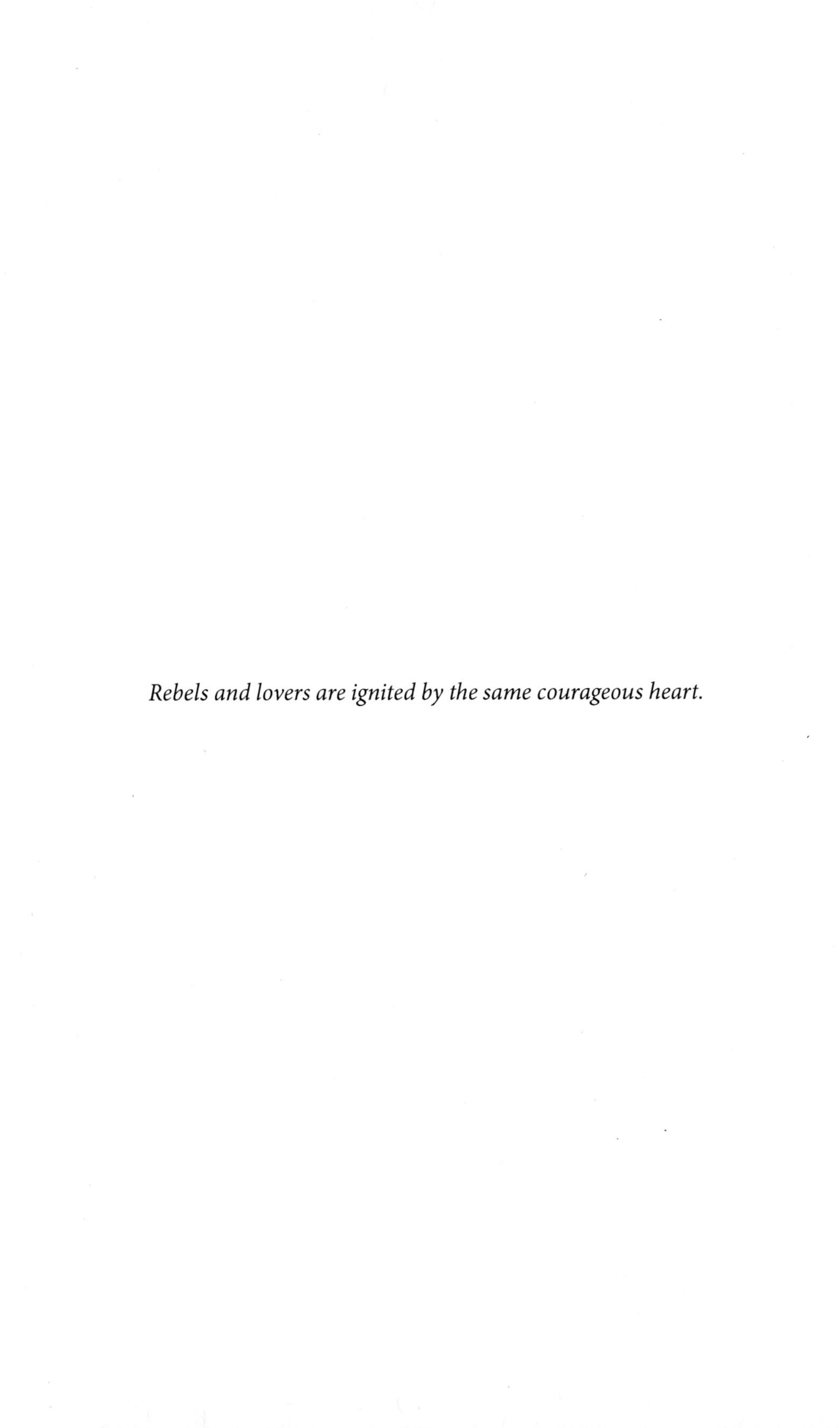

Rebels and lovers are ignited by the same courageous heart.

PROLOGUE

THIS is the story of an orgasm.

Or it could be said, this is the story of an orgasm that never was, and then was, and once it was, it's the story of all the ripples it set in motion. It's the reiteration of the total fecundity slam dance, Big Bang Explosion that created the world.

Or something like that.

If you told the creation story from the point of view of the orgasm, not only would it not be allowed in schools, it couldn't set foot in the Church. *And God said, was it good for you?* The answer would be yes.

Since the beginning of time, the world has turned on the O.

> Entire Empires have been built and fallen...
> All wars...
> All resolutions...
> When it comes down to it... all motivation for human
> endeavor has been in pursuit of that unparalleled pleasure.

It's what compels us and juices us up.

But even before recorded history, and ever since, the Earth Herself has always liked to have a good go at it once in a while, building to some heaving, panting, outrageous seismic climax, shrugging off a million people or more in her post-coital sigh.

Everyone has their own form of ecstatic release—this is hers.

This whole thing started because Ursula wanted an orgasm, and never had one. And because Donny wanted to be in love, and didn't have the first clue that's what he wanted. First he had to care... and well, that was already too much to ask. And she had to take the MUTE off her entire system, and couldn't even find the button.

Strange, the odd attractors that magnetize us into orbit.

If Donny and Ursula could have their first orgasm together, the egg and the sperm of their desire might meet and set in play their own creation story of big things yet to come.

They might both have an awakening.
They might both become fearless.
They might laugh all day long.
But this is too much speculating.

One thing is certain: Pleasure opens many an unexpected door. The pursuit of pleasure is our prime motivator, for nothing feels as good as feeling good.

The power of Eros, surging like a glistening snake upriver, moves mere mortals to rise above their tiny neurotic existences and do phenomenal things they never dreamed they could do. Like saving the world, for instance.

At the very least, Eros is a scent worth following—like how the intoxicating fragrance of night blooming jasmine pulls you out into a warm Los Angeles summer's evening… looking for something you have no idea how to find.

This story is written as one possible scent.

1 | THE BEGINNING

The world's a perfect place, Donny thought to himself as he sat behind the wheel of his '04 Camry, waiting for the light to change. The sun was out, traffic was moving, and the last half of the New York Giants game was playing on the car radio. They were still his team. "Sports," he would say, "is the only drama left where you don't know the outcome," and therefore something you could still care about. He didn't care about much, but he did care about the Giants.

His vehicle had long given over from the sporty sensible car it had been, to a tattered and worn room addition to the Hollywood-bungalow apartment Donny occupied when he was home, which he rarely was.

Between his car and overcrowded trunk, he had all the necessaries for spontaneous participation in any number of the activities he deemed important: today's newspaper, a basketball, football, and most importantly, golf clubs, a hat, another hat, several books at various stages of completion, a half pack of cigarettes, a three pack of condoms, black and white cookies from the deli, wrappers from other cookies, his most recent TV script with annoying notes in the margins, a hairbrush, a cell phone, three vintage baseball cards in their protective packets, two comic books in their original plastics inside a padded envelope, a beard trimmer, and some mints. Except for the cell phone, the cookies, and the cigarettes, all the necessaries were closed in the trunk. His father always stressed, "Never leave anything exposed in the car; it's an invitation for a break in."

A commercial for the Center for the Cure of Hyperhidosis came on in the time out. "A fancy name for sweaty palms," he grumbled, cutting the ad short with a flip of the dial. He was aware of the perspiration on his own sweaty palms as his wet fingertips slid across the buttons.

He'd always had sweaty hands and sweaty feet. Dry as a desert in the middle. All his anxiety, all the urgency and consternation that he was unable to bite back behind the butt of another cigarette leaked out of his palms. There was no hiding.

He thought for a moment of all the things that had slipped through his wet hands: jobs, ideas, friends… and wondered if there was any connection. But not given to deep thinking, he let the question drift by.

And here they had given it a medical name and were asking people to call an 800 number for help. He would not be calling that number. As much as Donny despised his "condition," he hated being part of a trend even more. Once they made you part of a trend, they'd overlap you into other trends, and try and sell you crap you didn't need. Thanks, he already had plenty.

He was headed for Ursula's house. She was a woman he'd met at a party a few nights ago and wanted to go out with her because he liked saying her name. "Ursula." He'd never had a chance to say that name much before, never known an Ursula. But now he found himself saying her name out loud in his car, playing with the emphasis. "Ursula, Ursuuula." Doing a Stanley Kowalski thing, "Urrr-sula." She said she was a travel agent who was studying belly dancing. How bad could that be?

No one would call Donny a lady's man, though he liked to think of himself that way. There was nothing suave or elegant about him. He was handsome enough. Trim enough. But mostly, he was a big Italian guy from Queens, which is to say, he was good at survival. And he'd be the first one to tell you a man needs a woman in order to survive—otherwise he backs up and becomes congested in the gonads, which leads to festering thoughts and a decay of the mind, and dulls all sense of direction. A man needs a good circulation of fluids to keep his GPS on the mark.

He told himself he was merely following his nose, like any dog does. But there was something about this "Ursuuula" that stirred him in a curious way. She was shy and forthcoming at the same time, different from the others… or was she?

Donny prided himself that for a guy who seemed not to care about much, he had managed to become convincing to those females who were looking for the right signal… in other words, for a man with a very low commitment factor, or because of it, he had perfected the key. And being so convincing, he had also perfected all the excuses and back door exits he needed to skip out in the nick of time.

What would he have to tell this one, this time? It's the hard work that men must do. Even when she wants him, she makes him work for it. Oh, sure, the ones who want it will signal, pretty clearly, to the male what it is he needs to say or do to enter her sweet garden. Say it, do it, and *sprong*, the gate unlocks and swings wide open. It's those others who confound. Either they make their message so obscure, or they genuinely don't want you. Donny has run into more than his share of those, he'd have to admit.

Which one would Ursula be?

He was on his way to Ursula's to find out. Even though she had laughed at his jokes and laughed even more when he gave her a rundown of his latest TV comedy pilot, she did not give him her phone number. She said if it were important enough to him, he'd find her.

It wasn't hard. It never is, for him. How many Ursulas were there anyway? He found her last name on a registry of travel agents, Google Earthed her, and here he was, a mere few blocks away.

There has been no mention yet that while driving with his left hand, Donny was finishing the last of a two-pound Whopper with his right, which we have already established was slippery with sweat. Out of nowhere, two huge, hideous looking insects, big red eyes and lacy wings, flew in through the open car window and buzzed around his head. Though Donny was not native to these parts, he was familiar enough with the various bugs that splattered his windshield to know he'd never seen anything like these monsters that were now buggy-fornicating on his arm. He swatted the damn things with the burger…

"Fuck!" he exclaimed, as ketchup dropped from between the patties and plopped onto his neatly pressed pants. He gobbled down the rest of the burger, pulled his car over to the side of the road, and chased the little fuckers out. Riffling though his trunk, he grabbed hold of some balled up, sour gym trunks and proceeded to change his pants right there on La Brea. He noticed his black loafers would now not go with the shorts, so he changed into sneakers.

Donny told himself that showing up "casual" was the way to go with these things. Like he'd just been in the neighborhood shooting some hoops and happened to stop by… so as not to appear too wanting, or eager, or even intentional, for God's sake. Besides, it was less embarrassing to tell himself this. One of the benefits of "not caring" is you do save yourself a lot of embarrassment.

However, while he was changing, Donny noticed a homeless drunk, out cold on the covered bench at the bus stop, wearing a soiled and ripped Giants t-shirt. The guy's shoes had no soles, and his feet, blistered beyond recognition, had worn right through his socks. Donny tucked his black loafers up underneath the guy's bedroll. The Giants were up by two touchdowns. Go Big Blue.

Returning to his car he wondered, would Ursula be happy to see him? Surprised? Questions like that just clutter the mind and impede action. A pursuit is a pursuit. The outcome is something all together different, and often, as it turns out, not the point.

2 | URSULA

When Ursula turned off the music, she heard a very loud, very insistent banging. Peeved at whoever it was who needed her so urgently he had to nearly break down the door, she chinga-chinga-chinga'd and swish-swished across the floor of the living room to answer whoever the bejeezus it was. She had taken up belly dancing as a way to locate her misplaced feminine, and every sparkly coin that hung from every angle or mound of her jangled as she walked—part shuffle, part float.

She didn't notice that she was twirling her hair around her finger the closer she got to the banging door. She wore her dirty-blonde hair in odd little ponytails that stuck out in irregular directions from the globe of her head in a sort of post-modern Farina do. Some were shorter, some longer—all this hiding a tiny bald spot on the side of her head where she habitually pulled hairs out from excessive twirling.

Before she opened the door, she stood before it, palms out, eyes shut, to see if she could "feel" who was on the other side. Even when the banging turned into that overly cutesy *bum-bum-pa-bump*, she still couldn't tell. So she opened the door to find Donny examining the paper taped over the doorbell that read DO NOT RING BELL.

"Oh, hi, it's you," Ursula said, relieved that it wasn't some fanatic trying to sell her the all-purpose cleaner of religion. She didn't know how she felt about Donny standing at her door, although she was a bit impressed that he was able to find her, or cared to. It showed initiative. Cleverness. She liked good survival skills in a man.

"Is your doorbell out of order?" he asked.

"No," she said flatly. She just stood there.

"I guess maybe you're surprised to see me," he said, filling in the awkward space between them.

"Come in," Ursula said, finally. "I'd offer you something to eat, but I'm only juicing right now." She walked a few steps ahead of him into the house. "Something to drink?"

"Coffee or Coke," Donny replied, following her in.

As they stepped inside, he was assaulted by the piercing, acrid smell that captured the air. People's houses always have an odor particular to them, and frankly he was not one to judge... but yeesh. Was she pickling some dead animal?

Ursula, aware of his awareness, quickly swished off to the kitchen. She didn't want to be gone too long. Donny held his ketchup-scented fingers up to his nose until he acclimated to the foul air. He casually inspected all the books, artwork, and figurines in her living room, looking for some commonality to bring up in conversation. She seemed to be a world traveler. And she seemed to like figures of cats. That's good. He liked cats. He noticed the orange tabby sunning in the corner. Maybe that was the stink, though he was familiar enough with unattended cat boxes to know it wasn't. She had a lot of healthy looking plants growing by the windows. Not something they had in common.

She returned in no time, placing a frothy, fluorescent green drink in his hand. "I usually use spinach," she said, "but apparently it's all tainted with bacteria, and it's been pulled off the shelves at the co-op, so I'm using lots more wheatgrass. I only buy local."

This nuance of ingredients mattered not to him. He'd eaten all manner of disgusting things on a dare—tequila worms, menudo, prairie oysters—but he'd never put anything in his mouth this color *on purpose*. If it were radioactive, it would melt the glass, right?

Who is this woman? he asked himself, as she leaned over to place the frothy devil-drink on the coffee table. She was odder than he expected, and certainly more unexpected than any woman he had known. But he liked odd. And even though she had not much in the way of breasts, those jangly coins at her ankles were a real turn on.

"Chew your juice, and juice your food," she told him. She demonstrated masticating each mouthful 40 times. "This stimulates the digestive juices

to break down the meal, while at the same time giving your organs a rest. According to Sheerah. She's my teacher."

This woman is out of her mind, he thought, holding his breath against the green fumes. But he just smiled and nodded.

"Cows contribute over 20% of the methane gas of the world, and it takes 167 pounds of grass to feed each cow. Wouldn't it be a whole lot simpler just to eat the grass?" Ursula offered.

"I've read that it's actually the methane gas from all the dinosaur poop released from beneath the defrosting tundra that's going to do this planet in…" he replied, rattling off anything to avoid putting the sludge to his lips. "And a medium-sized dog has a larger carbon footprint than a Toyota Land Cruiser."

She couldn't help but laugh. "That may be so, but Americans eat 20 million burgers a day. Between clear cutting the forests to create the pastures, and the industrial farms that grow the lettuce and tomatoes… if we all just stopped, we might save our planet in time."

Donny nodded, glad he'd left the ketchup stained pants in the trunk. He kept on nodding like a stupid bobble-head until there was nothing left to do but take a drink. She looked at him encouragingly. Something about her look, hopeful and sincere, set off a twinkle inside him—more like a rush of a twinkle—and suddenly he found himself raising the glass up to the air, toasting.

"To the planet," he said, and tossed it back.

He smiled, nodded, chewing at nothing, which was really just him biting the stuff back from being projectile vomited all across her living room. She watched him intently for his reaction. He continued to chew, his throat refusing to take it down.

He's thinking, *I must look like such an idiot.*

She's thinking, *He's really savoring it.*

Nothing he tells himself will get his throat to open to this crap. And the longer he waits the worse it gets, the vile drink just sitting there in oral constipation, contaminating his taste buds. He'd rather be sucking on the dinosaur poop.

She's never seen a man appreciate the subtle flavors of his food in this way before. She beamed a smile of admiration at him that caught him off guard; and, for just an instant, his face softened in response, creating the opening he'd been looking for. Down it went. His eyes bugged open and flared. My God, that's bad! Oh, what he wouldn't do for the burn of scotch right now!

"You like it?" she asked. "Not many people can handle that, believe me. I think it's better with the spinach."

"No, this was good." The words squeezed hoarsely through his constricted throat.

"I honestly didn't think you were that kind of guy." She smiled.

So he knew he had to finish the whole damned thing. Which he did. Shudders convulsed through his entire body, but he tried not to show it. He slammed his glass down hard, in a big finish.

"Well, thanks for stopping by, but I really have to get back to my practice," she said abruptly, getting up from the couch.

She couldn't have said that before?

He asked her to go out the next night. "Out," he said with emphasis. She said she had this sort-of-a-class she went to.

"Maybe another time?" he asked.

"Maybe," she said.

After the door closed behind him, he wrote down the number 3 on a small piece of paper he pulled from his pocket—which represented the number of weeks he thought it would take to get her to bed. He smiled at how easy this odd one would be, but resolved never to go to her house hungry.

On her side of the door, she stood there, twirling her hair, thinking, *I like this guy*. Then she stiffened. *Oh, no, not again.*

3 | SPINACH

"I hate spinach," the President of the United States blurted out. "Not the least bit sorry to see it happen." He spoke these candid words in a hush-hush, closed-door meeting with a "special advisor" from agribusiness giant, AgriNu.

"Hate it." The President went on, "You know what else I hate? Peas. Despise peas… and there's so many of them."

Edwin Edwards (why do parents do that?), otherwise known as Mr. Ed, leaned back with a sly smile. "What if I told you there was a way to get rid of spinach? And peas? And, at the same time, break open this damned European block to our special genetically modified seeds, allowing us to finally take control of the world market?"

The President settled back in his seat, indicating for him to go on. Despite not liking vegetables, the President liked a man with a big appetite.

Mr. Ed hadn't fully developed a big appetite, but he was learning how. For you see, just last week—over his usual breakfast of grapefruit, oatmeal, and dry toast—he'd read in the newspaper about the E. coli outbreak in spinach crops coming from California; and the light bulb went *bling* in his head.

His wife, Bitsy, was already out playing an early round of tennis—though she had all but told him she was having an affair with his boss, the head of AgriNu, and this was just her excuse to get out of the house. She told Edwin he needed to get some balls and move up in that company. She sure knew how to motivate a guy.

Mr. Ed had an important job as Senior VP of Acquisitions of Technological Development at AgriNu, but apparently not important enough. He was a mid-sized guy in every way, hands, feet, and all that implies. But he had a big Rolodex and a cloudy moral compass that allowed him to move in whatever direction was necessary—and now, a highly motivated ambition.

It should be noted that Mr. Ed descended from a family of early Ohio settlers—most of whom perished in the early years of settling. But those who remained came to cultivate the land, beating back the wild, and all the hellish uncertainty that came with it, in order to survive. That fear of the wild ran through Mr. Ed like a wood-hewn raft on the river of his gene pool. That determination to conquer it—he inherited that too, which made him the perfect company man for AgriNu.

So here he was, the very next day, sitting in the office of the President of the United States, discussing this very tasty idea, the two of them having several former cabinet-member friends-in-common who now sat on AgriNu's board.

And they formed a plan—in exchange for Mr. Ed's promise to the President that spinach would be eliminated from the food palate of the United States (that, and stock in the company placed in his children's name). Since AgriNu was close to controlling virtually all the seeds of this country and most countries around the world, spinach could just… disappear. The only ones who might miss it were a couple of Italians and Popeye.

"This might just be the greatest accomplishment of my administration," the President said out loud. *Now I'll be appreciated* is what he was really thinking. He knew in his bones there were a whole hell of a lot of folks out there who hated vegetables as much as he did. And besides, he had the authority to do it. Finally, for once, he could use his executive powers to do something that actually benefited *him*, instead of all those fanatic constituents and special interest lobbies.

On his exit, as he was shaking the President's hand, Mr. Ed was thinking that if he pulled this off, he could dump Bitsy and go for that cute blonde from legal who smiles at him in the elevator.

4 | WHAT SHE MEANT BY SORT-OF-A-CLASS

Ursula was loath to admit it, but her first attractions to Sheerah's belly dancing class were the jangly coins, and a fascination with how her very own slim, boyish hips could produce those elaborate sounds.

As it was, the class turned out to be like Miss Suzi's Dance School back in Oklahoma, when she was a kid—a little ballet, a little tap, and some baton twirling in shiny, sequined tutus. Only here, it was a little belly dancing, a little tantra instruction, and some ayurvedic beauty supplies sold at the end of class.

Sheerah was the only supplier in Southern California of these magical creams manufactured in the dark caves of Sri Lanka, but she sold them to her students at cost. They smelled ancient and exotic, each one unlocking an entire spice cabinet with one whiff. Ursula was fond of the apricot oil that smelled like cinnamon buns.

But just as it had been with Miss Suzi's tutus, it was the costumes that drew her in. The rich, vivid colors of the flowing skirts, the gold coins and bangles off the hips, and the skimpy tops, also with sequins, transported her to a world of feminine possibility of a completely different order. It was the outfit that led Ursula exactly where she needed to be. What held her there was something else altogether.

Something was missing, Ursula suspected. She wasn't sure she'd know what was missing until she'd found it, but she did have some ideas. Though she cared about many things, she lacked a fire, a hunger, a zest, a zeal. She was muted in every way. You might not know it from the outside; she could be lively and confident with her clients and friends when need be. But inside, she couldn't feel much of anything. She thought if it weren't for mirrors, she couldn't locate herself, at all. And here was Sheerah. Well... Sheerah was ripe. Like a red fruit burst open, dripping with juicy feminine generosity. And these other women in the class, they were a diverse expression of the wonder of the female body, Persian, African-American and coffee-colored mixed races. And then there was Ursula. Sheerah knew secrets. What did Ursula know? But still, even in her struggle, Ursula kept coming back for more.

That first class, after a rigorous warm up of abdominal undulations in every which direction, the twelve or so belly dancerinas gathered on colored cushions and sipped spiced tea. Sheerah announced bluntly to the group, "Lovers remain in each other's energy fields for 21 days after intercourse. Renewed with each act. Do the math. Choose wisely… otherwise you're carrying that stink with you for a long time."

More than one woman rolled her eyes in a knowing way.

Sheerah continued, "Stop having sex right now!" She had a flair for the dramatic. "All of you. Until you know you're not giving yourselves away."

While this statement gathered a few gasps from the other students, this was not really much of a problem for Ursula, since she wasn't so keen on sex in the first place. Many of her past relationships had ended out of sheer *his and her* frustration due to sex, or the lack of it. She couldn't see what the whole big deal was about, to the point where now she couldn't really be bothered.

"And how will you know when you're not giving yourself away?" Sheerah questioned. "He will hold your heart sure and gentle. Take pleasure from pleasing you. Ravish you with his full being, for your sake, not his. And, in return… he'll dissolve into explosive pleasure like he's never known." She took a long sip of tea. "And don't elevate him into something he's not, out of your own loneliness. He is who he is, and a lover must earn the right." She continued, "Not with goats, and camels, and fancy trinkets, but with acts of personal bravery and kindness. A man must prove himself to enter your gates… and you, in turn, must lay out the garden. Receive him with sweet nectars and sensual delights. In there, he'll find union with that part of himself he seems to have lost, and keeps poking into every hole he can to find… a union with the Divine. It's a little different than hooking up on Facebook for a quickie."

Ursula's jaw dropped. This was a conversation she had always wanted to have but never dreamed of. Perhaps this was the reason she was so muted inside, why she herself never really felt the passion in any kind of physical intimacy. There was never a proper preparation, no sacred courtship to speak of. Just her throwing herself in for the sheer velocity, vainly hoping the momentum would hurl her down the slide into the pool of arousal and excitation.

Ursula bought three lotions, four oils, and a balm that had more uses than household vinegar; and charged them all on her Visa card whose limit was already maxed. She walked to her car—*jangle, jangle*—and drove home in what appeared to be a stupor, but really was the brightest clarity she'd had in a very long time.

5 | THE NEXT TIME

Ursula had only started out with one. But then she did the multiplication. One became two. Two became four. Four became eight, but really eleven because the original mushrooms continued reproducing as well. She lost a few along the way, so it was not so easy to keep track. It's understandable how this whole thing got out of hand very quickly.

It seemed harmless enough when she accepted Sheerah's offer of the single Kombucha mushroom that promised a lengthy list of curative properties: eliminates wrinkles, aches and pains; cleanses liver, gall bladder, kidneys; soothes colitis; lowers cholesterol; reduces insomnia; prevents cancer and constipation; helps burn fat; enhances the immune system; decreases the craving for alcohol; and has a shelf life of about 100 years.

Ursula saw the offer of the mushroom as an extended gesture of acceptance and belonging that she so desperately wanted from Sheerah, who seemed to know everything about everything that still eluded *her.* Little did Ursula know she would become a servant to the reproductive life force of this organism. She knew it would reproduce, but not at such a rapid rate. And, she thought she'd be able to pass the offspring off to others, but it seemed she was at the bottom of the pyramid. The people she knew had them, were finished with them, or never wanted them in the first place.

It was good to be of service, Ursula told herself; it's good to have a purpose.

She had read somewhere that scientists believe that fungi were the first life forms on Earth. We may actually be their descendants. If they're family, you have to treat them well, right?

There was a particular way Ursula had perfected of carefully removing the baby from its parent so as not to upset one or the other. Placing the glass bowl on the table directly before her, she steadily edged the side of a large, flat, slotted spoon into the living juices of the Kombucha mushroom and surgically slid the utensil in between the two.

She could feel their threads of connection sever, and the communication between them spill out into their surrounding waters. Oh, she hated this part! Hated to be the one to cause such a cut. But over time, she found that if ripe enough, like a loose tooth dangling by one thread, the connection was very thin; and the parent was ready to offer up the child for its own destiny. In this case, its destiny was to occupy its own bowl and immediately fulfill its role in the perpetuation of the species.

She had played around with the best times of day to perform her deliveries. The morning, before work seemed too bright, like the babies were recoiling somehow from the daylight. She had to be at work all day, so mid-day was out. No, she found that nighttime, around 9:00 or 10:00 p.m., was the best time to tend her colony. It was quiet, and the mushrooms seemed to orb together in the darkness, gently pulsating with the moonlight. Sometimes she found herself talking to them—a little bit simple and silly, the way you talk to babies, but encouraging, speaking of their purpose and mission, and what they were going to do for this world. Sometimes she felt she could hear them talk back.

"Don't you ever call first?" she asked Donny, though the answer was apparent. She sighed and slipped out onto the porch, quickly pulling the door shut behind her. She was happy to see him, but this was definitely not the right time.

Donny stood there, earnestly, with three roses and some baby's breath wrapped together in cellophane that he had purchased from a small Mexican man on the corner. In bad-miming Spanish he'd asked the small man to choose a bunch for him. What did Donny know from flowers? The man handed him red ones, and patted his heart with a big smile. He gave the man an extra dollar.

He then made a quick turn into the drive-through lane at McDonald's; ordered a double cheese burger, fries, and a Coke; and finished them at the long left turn signal at La Brea and Third. His tank *topped off*, if she offered, he'd only accept water.

But at this point, he wasn't sure she'd even offer that.

"I was hoping you'd be home," he said, angling for a better reception.

"I am. I was in the... middle of something... which most people are when they're home."

"Next time I'll call first."

She noted to herself that he thinks there'll be a next time.

He handed her the flowers. She accepted them with an awkward smile, but did not make a move to open the door. "I'd ask you in, but I'm... in the middle of something, as I said, and... my place is a mess." She started twirling her hair.

Donny laughed. "There's no mess too scary for me."

"That's not the scary part," she muttered to herself. "I think it'd be better another time."

Donny's grandfather had been an encyclopedia salesman who'd always impressed upon his grandson that the first thing you must do is get your foot in the door. Just get in the door and you are more than halfway there.

"Can I use your bathroom?"

Ursula cringed. "That's the biggest mess of all..."

"Please," he asked urgently, doing a little anxious hopping for effect.

Ahh, jeez. "Wait a minute..." She slipped through the door, closing it in his face, and rushed to the hallway, where she quickly shoved all the bowls she could find into the dining room, shutting that door tight. She opened the front door, slightly out of breath. "Just the bathroom."

Sometimes he couldn't believe how simple things can be.

Or not. His first step inside, he was practically knocked over from the sharp sting in the air. "Whoa!" he exclaimed, nose curling in protection.

"The bathroom is over there." She pointed, ignoring his bodily response.

He went gladly, splashing water on his face as soon as he was near a sink.

Immediately, Ursula ran to remove even more bowls from the hallway and put them in her bedroom. All the while, she listened for him with one ear. When she came out, the bathroom door was open and Donny was… standing in the kitchen. Large glass bowls occupied nearly every inch of the counter space. Each was covered by a cloth. He had lifted the cloth on one and was staring down at a thick, slimy disc bathing in brown liquid. The smell was stronger still.

Ursula came around behind him and replaced the cloth. "Shhh, it's making a baby."

"A baby?"

"A mushroom baby," she replied. "It makes a new one every week. I don't have the heart to kill them. It seems so unnecessary."

As she was talking, Donny looked past her to the dining room where every surface, including the floor, was covered with cloth-covered bowls. Every surface.

"How many?" he asked with trepidation.

After she finished hatching this batch, she said, she would have 178. "Only I ran out of people to give them to." Tentatively, she offered, "You can take one if you'd like."

No fucking way! his voice screamed inside. Outside, he just smiled and nodded. He's thinking this could make some kind of whacked out horror movie pitch. But more than that, he's thinking he's going to have to revise the number he wrote down in his pocket.

"Sheerah said the tea made her gray hair return to black," Ursula blurted out, "and it gives her the stamina for some 'very late nights.' Sheerah also has a sister who planted her placenta beneath a young peach tree to celebrate the birth of her peach of a daughter, and the tree produces an awesome amount of fruit several times a year, so she should know. Would you like to taste it?" Her eyes were wide with invitation.

"Would I like to taste it?" he repeated, stalling for time. His foot's in the door, more than halfway there. That number in his pocket… he'd like to hit it. *OK, what's it gonna take?* He knew the answer definitely included new taste sensations. He smiled at her, and shrugged, "How bad could it be?"

His acceptance delighted her. She giggled as she dipped a small cup into the tea beneath the mushroom and offered it to him. He closed his eyes and quickly downed it like a shot. The vinegar taste clenched up his throat, and he gasped for air. Seriously. Worst thing he's ever tasted! Worse than the moonshine his college buddies once tried to make, worse than that green drink from the other day. Worst thing ever!

He was coughing and gasping so hard he couldn't nod, or smile, or fake his way out of this one; nor did he want to, lest he'd have to drink it again.

She knew the tea was an acquired taste. She handed him a glass of water. He gulped it down in desperation.

"You know, a lot of people are afraid of mushrooms," she said.

"That's because they're always poking out of something decayed and disgusting," he cracked, barely able to speak.

"But get this, I hear some mushrooms can actually ingest toxic oil spills and bring the soil back to health."

"And a medium-sized dog has a larger carbon footprint than a Land Cruiser..."

She laughed. She knew she had a tendency to take things too seriously.

"Come play a game with me," she said as she led him to sit down on the couch. She thought it best to change the subject. She'd let him stay after all, as a bit of an apology. She could relax more, now that her secret babies had been discovered and he didn't freak out. When she sat, her red polished toes peeked out from beneath her silky skirt as she curled her feet underneath the hem. His attention followed them like a raven after shiny things, and his respiration returned. Seemed the wackier she was, the more his interest piqued—and she was plenty wacky. Her cat Kitty Boy tucked up into her lap. "I like to guess where people have traveled." She took a good look at him. "Cancun, Las Vegas, Amsterdam. Am I right so far?"

He nodded yes, amazed. These were all places he had visited.

"I've sent a lot of people to Amsterdam, mostly as a place to start in Europe. But some folks get stuck there and don't go any farther."

Donny shifted in his seat. She was describing him—smoking hash, day and night until he used up all his time and money.

"Go on," he said, interested.

"You're from New York, so all those beaches… Long Island or the Vineyard…"

He shook his head. "Not really."

"Coney Island? Atlantic City…"

He nodded yes.

"OK, you're that type."

What type was that, he wondered? Whatever it was, he had to admit, he was that type. Was she some kind of mind reader?

"You like to do stuff," she replied kindly.

"If by that you mean immaturely squander away precious time on nonsense… then yes."

She laughed again.

She's laughing. This is good. Donny knows a man has to make a woman laugh or she won't put up with him.

"I've pretty much been everywhere I could go," she said, "The perks of being an agent. My favorite trip was to South America, and the Galapagos. Those baby sea lions are the cutest things ever. I love islands. You can completely orient yourself wherever you are to the water. It's either over this shoulder or that one."

Donny wouldn't know. Coney Island is not really an island.

"And where is it you'd like to go next?" she asked.

"Road trip," he answered. "I like to go see weird stuff. Or I was thinking of doing a Diners and Dives trip; in search of the best hot…" he suddenly remembered his company.

"You are what you eat," she said, simply.

Then I'm a big fat-fried, cream-filled, mile-high meatball sandwich the size of my head, was his thought. But he just smiled and nodded.

6 | THE DECREE

Speaking of what you eat, Donny was sitting in front of Noah's, downing a salt bagel with lox schmear, and a black coffee. He was here this morning because he had too many dishes piled up in his sink at home, and couldn't find a plate encrusted with less than three days of fossilized food.

The news item did not even appear on the front page of the *New York Times* but was buried on page 13. Only because Donny is in the habit of reading the news sections from cover to cover did he see it at all—though he would certainly have heard about it by the end of the day from his friend Paul.

By the time the President made the announcement, the deed was already done. Who knew for how long, or what the reach of his decree would actually be.

What Donny read was this:

> *(AP) By order of the President of the United States, all spinach production in the United States is to be quarantined, and all spinach crops destroyed. In addition, a cautionary warning has been placed on food grown on organic farms. "The health risk to our nation is of epidemic proportions. E. coli is just one possible threat. Organic farms do not protect against bacteria or pests with FDA standard and approved chemicals, and therefore put everyone in harm's way. If we allow these tainted foods to come to market, there's no telling what damage they could bring to the unsuspecting public. Above all, it is the government's job to protect the people. We are at war... and will not make ourselves vulnerable... not at the food table where we eat."*

Of course the congressmen from the food belt were up in arms, writing bills and counter bills to no great effect, because basically they were all in agribusiness's pocket.

Normally, Donny would not even have noticed an article about organic anything, as it had no direct impact on his own diet. But now he found himself considering this eccentric woman Ursula, and surely this was something she would want to know.

"Damn." He got a little shiver of frustration at the thought of courting her for two weeks now, and not even a kiss. This might help.

Donny suddenly thought of Paul, his best friend since childhood who used to work as a news researcher, but now, news being what it is, devoted himself entirely to compiling evidence. For what? Anything really. Everything. Mostly conspiracy theories. Paul was especially engrossed in the Kennedy assassination. His tiny apartment was filled with files and notebooks of articles clipped and pieced together.

Donny felt the JFK thing was so over, but for Paul, the time when Kennedy was shot marked the turning in our country's belief in government, which has completely deteriorated since then—with good reason. Paul was into uncovering secrets, and there was still a big stinker there. Needless to say, Paul hadn't had a girlfriend in several years. Still, he could find out about anything, especially when the government was to blame. He did work, as his time would permit, as a freelance researcher for book authors and movie producers, always supplying more information than was needed.

Paul had a blog—which was basically a rant, a personal outlet for his rage against the machine. He used it as a place to test out his theories of conspiracy and such. So far he had four followers, each equally "engaged" in their own theories, which only sometimes converged. It so happened, he was just wrapping up his latest post when Donny phoned him, asking if he'd seen the article, or knew anything about it.

Paul said, "I'll know even more by the time you get here."

Donny didn't want to go over there. Paul's apartment was the cave of a man who gave no attention to his surroundings, or their smell. Donny truly wanted his answer over the phone, but Paul's sense of urgency about everything left him no choice.

When Paul opened the door, he shook his head ominously. Rushing Donny inside, he closed and double-locked the door in his usual paranoid manner, and shoved a pile of papers and pizza boxes off a stool to offer Donny a seat. Paul said only, "AgriNu." Donny nodded, as if he knew what that meant.

"I know they're behind this," Paul continued. "Those bastards have been doing this all over the world for years, pushing their genetically modified seeds that can't reproduce themselves past one season. AgriNu owns the patents on practically all the seed now: corn, soy, rice, wheat. Thousands of years, farmers have been saving and replanting their own seed, but now they have to keep buying it year after year from AgriNu. If they do, they go way into debt. If they don't, they get shut out of the system, and don't get our government's foreign aid. AgriNu owns the patents, they own the seed, they set the prices… they own the farmers. Looks like Big B and our Mr. P" (he liked to talk in code) "are trying to squeeze more of *our* farmers into that trap. It's all about the money. Power and money."

This was the kind of absolute conspiracy shit Paul thrived on. And he was just getting started. Donny could tell by the way his breath quickened and he started to pace, pointing sharply at the air.

"The organic movement has caught on too well," he said. "People actually see diversification and going back to earlier practices of farming as the only answer to food safety. It's giving the big boys steady competition they hadn't counted on. Anyone who wants to be healthy, and not become some mangled mutant from these untested GMOs, is eating organic. Now, all the food giants want to have an organic brand to get into these markets they used to think of as 'fringe.' And these organic types are strong cuz they've also got a philosophy. Their hearts are in it. To them it's a way of life, not just grow and sell. So Big B's got to take it down." He proceeded to babble on and on about what Oswald was given to eat after he was arrested. "They were trying to poison him then and there…"

Donny had heard this story, or one very much like it, many times already from his friend. Even before JFK, Paul was equally obsessive about all the games they played as kids in the neighborhood, whether it was running around as caped avengers, endless arcade games, or the Xbox. To this day, there was nobody Donny would rather battle to the death in a full on role-play on Xbox. Worthy adversaries, they knew exactly how the other thought and could anticipate his every move. But knowing that, they were clever enough to trick each other. It was like Donny could get inside Paul's mind, so when he started in on his rants, it made Donny's own head hurt.

Donny jumped up from his chair suddenly, pulling his cell phone from his pocket, pretending to have received the shock of a vibrating signal. He placed the phone to his ear, "Unhuh, Unhuh. Right. OK." And he hung up. "She needs me," he said with a half wink, and quickly unlocked the door and let himself out.

As he got in the car he thought, *Maybe she does need me,* and set off in her direction.

Paul logged onto his blog and started writing frantically.

7 | WHEN NO ONE IS WATCHING, AGRINU...

Paul wrote:

> While people are trampling each other at Walmart on Black Friday, agriculture giant, AgriNu, is buying up all your food. Oh, yeah, there's plenty on the shelf, so you won't know it. But they've been buying it up all right, seed by seed—AND THEY MEAN TO OWN IT ALL. As long as it's on sale, we don't care, right?
>
> WAKE UP PEOPLE!! All through history, farmers saved the seed from their crops to plant the next year. They planted lots of varieties to make sure the crops would hold up to the changes that come down—weather, insects, disease.
>
> But all that history CHANGED in the 1970s when the Agriculture and Oil industries copulated in the dark to produce their lovechild, AgriNu, and some other sniveling mongrels like them. "Agribusiness" was going to do it bigger and better, and feed the world. What they SAID was that more people could be fed with their "increased yield" hybrid seeds, but REALLY, it was just a way to create a hungry market for petroleum products. AND REALLY... it was about something else...
>
> Hey, Henry Kissinger said it himself, "Control oil and you control the nations; control food and you control the people..." GET IT???
>
> Farmers, all over the world, threw out their "primitive" methods in favor of newer, hybrid seed technology. AgriNu, and its evil siblings, just HAPPENED to own the seed patents.
>
> It all got rolling when GMO (Genetically Modified Organism) seeds were engineered to withstand the accompanying herbicide that

would annihilate any living vegetation that dared stick its little leaf up from the earth—except the plants that grew from these special, resistant seeds. What farmer wouldn't want to trade away weeding? It's a backbreaking, expensive **PAIN IN THE ASS.**

But when farmers saved those seeds, it didn't put any money in AgriNu's greedy pockets, so they created the mighty Terminator seeds (Genetic Use Restriction Technology or GURTS) whose plants die off after **ONLY ONE SEASON.** With no chance to reproduce—which is the mission of pretty much everything here on earth—they have to be repurchased and replanted each year.

But even that was too hard to control, so they developed T-GURTS or Traitor Seeds that grow only when a particular chemical is present to trigger their growth sequence—a chemical that had to be purchased from AgriNu.

By the 1980s most family farms were driven off their land to make way for more efficient corporate Factory Farms planting "high yield" GMOs. It got even worse in the 1990s. And, while no one was looking, AgriNu **ATE THE OTHER CHILDREN,** and bought up pretty much all the seed companies in the United States and Europe—with the complete sanction of our government, I might add. All in the name of profit, under the guise of the feeding the world.

Oh, well.

Did anyone catch the finale of American Idol?

According to our government there is "no difference" between natural seeds and GMO mutants, therefore they don't have to be identified or labeled differently; and thanks to the World Trade Organization, there are no measures, nor can there be, to protect humans or animals from them, or to prevent them from being spread throughout the world. Hah!

So by the time people woke up from their Starbucks coffee break with the Red Bull chaser, just about the time they put down their People magazine with Brangelina's latest baby on the cover, pretty much all the seeds were owned by one company, all the seeds were meant not to work past a season—and no government could stop them.

ARE YOU SCARED YET??!!

The Europeans aren't taking these shit seeds. They're still powerful enough to refuse them, and they hate us enough to stick to it.

Plus, in certain pockets of the USA, organic farming has taken hold and is expanding. Most of these farms are family run, and they're throwing a monkey wrench in agribusiness's big machine...

AND NOW OUR GOVERNMENT IS SHUTTING DOWN ORGANIC FARMS???

Oh, I hope I'm not disturbing your nap...

When he finished, he was so heated up he posted his entry on any number of other radical blogs, under a pseudonym of course.

8 | WHEN NO ONE IS WATCHING, DONNY...

It turned out Ursula didn't need him. She wasn't even at home, he discovered, having called first as he promised. So he went home. It was a shabby place, but it was his sanctuary, his hide-out where no one kept an eye on him, and that's a necessity for a guy like him.

When no one is watching, Donny will watch every sports game on the dish, back to back, while lying half-naked on the couch. He will scratch his balls. In truth, he will unconsciously hold his balls nearly the entire time, except when he is lighting up a cigarette.

He will eat off the same dirty plate more than once. He will read two newspapers while watching the games. He will flip around the TV with the remote during all the commercials; unless he decides, for his own sport, to flip around to *only* the commercials, and see if he can guess the product in the first two seconds. He might jerk off if the score spread gets too wide and the game gets too slow—or if it's baseball, which by definition needs a little jerking off to keep your interest. He loves baseball.

And then, still naked, he might go over to his computer and put the keyboard on his lap, and bang out the idea for the TV pitch he promised to deliver tomorrow. Ideas came easily to him. Like many writers, he was in the habit of mining his own life encounters for his next story. *A man watches sports all day long, and is witness to a murder in the next apartment during the commercial.* Why not?

The reasons why a person chooses a particular career over another can be greatly romanticized. That person receives a "calling," or demonstrates an extraordinary talent at an early age. They're obsessed with certain activities like digging, or building, or squeezing blackheads. Or have an unwavering fascination with fashion or reptiles. Or the desire to journey to places like Indonesia, or Antarctica. Or to eras like the Golden Age of Greece, or Paris in the Twenties. Or to reach to the farthest realms; the oceans below, outer space, or down the center of the volcano...

Donny simply needed to choose a job where he would not have to be constantly shaking hands. This threw out the possibilities of sales, hospitality, or any field where he would have to meet and greet with a sweaty palm. This meant no meetings with people he did not already know. Preferably no meeting anyone at all.

He could not work outside. He could not work with precise tools. He could not work in an assembly plant where he would have to pass his part on to another, unless he wore gloves. He could wear gloves, but he hated gloves. Gloves only made the sweating worse.

He could not handle food. He *could* wash dishes, but as has been pointed out, he was not prone to cleanliness. And while he could work in water, he did not have the ripped physique or the stamina to be a lifeguard, nor did he have the patience to be a swim instructor. He did have a short-lived job as a dog groomer, but there was an image problem that gave the wrong message to the wrong gender.

He needed a job where he didn't have to touch anyone or anything of consequence, so he eventually became a writer. A TV writer. He wasn't really a good writer, just a surly one. He had developed a bit of a reputation for his sarcastic wit, as a way to capitalize on his pissy outlook on the world. Good thing it worked.

Sometimes Donny would care about his work, and be quite successful. Sometimes he wouldn't give a shit, and be even more so. Sometimes he would give a shit and fall flat on his face. It was not something he could ever figure out. Just luck, dumb luck, or shit out of luck. And he never knew which it would be.

Donny supposed if a comedian like Jimmy Durante could shape an entire career behind a nose, he could shape one out of what he could, could not, and would not do because of these sweaty palms.

More than a writer, Donny was a reader. He devoured books—several at a time, but nothing too literary. Dark detectives and political conspiracies; pulp fiction in any form was his favorite. But he learned to read on comic books, and they were his first love. Some people would say it's because he's never grown up, which would be true, but deep down, Donny was an old fashioned kind of guy, and he liked the classic heroes.

His favorites were: Captain Marvel (the wanna-be Superman); Batman; Flash; and Hank Pym, the psychotic fuck-up of the super world. These were simple heroes in an increasingly complex world. They were mythic figures translated into their times, with transformative powers, improbable resurrections, and a strict moral code, be it their own. They rescued readers from their fears, and from the mundane limits of every day life.

His real heroes, of course, were baseball players, and his real team was the Yankees. Was, is, and forever will be. Say no more.

He collected their cards—Mickey Mantle, Roger Maris, Whitey Ford, and he could always trade up on a Reggie Jackson—all preserved for eternity in their individualized plastic wrappers, away from the icky-stickiness of his own life.

When no one is listening, Donny will sing Frank Sinatra in the shower. He's another hero. He's got Frank's phrasing down just right. Sometimes he dances, but he doesn't dance, so it's an approximation of a dance one who danced might do.

However, when no one is watching, what Donny will do most often is invite the neighbor's cat in, pet him and give him some Sheba, which is a delicacy food to cats, or some liverwurst if there's no cat food around. This usually attracts all the strays in the immediate area; so he'll feed them, too; bat a little ball of string around in a kind of group play; and then throw them back out.

9 | WHEN NO ONE IS WATCHING, URSULA...

When no one is watching, Ursula will sit spinning her globe around and around, contemplating all the places in the world where people live. She'll wonder what they're eating right now. She'll think about who they are talking to on the telephone, if they have a telephone; and if they don't, who they are thinking about. She'll think about how fast the world is turning and why it is we don't fall off.

As long as she can remember, she's had an amazing affection for globes. She had a collection of globes as a child, but in the several moves since leaving her parents' home, Ursula had given them all away, except for this one, her first one—a metal globe from the 1970s.

It had been given to her by a cousin who was moving with his family to live in another country, and wanted Ursula to know where he was, and to think about him by looking at his tiny new country of Dubai before she went to sleep at night. Ursula did just that… and she looked at Portugal, and at New Guinea, and South Africa. She added a new country each night, memorizing its location, continent, and surrounding bodies of water. This is how she came to know the world.

And this is where her first dreams of travel began.

Though her cousin left Dubai after about six months to return to Oklahoma, Ursula always thought of it as the center of a new world, for it was the first place where she knew that she knew someone living outside of her own neighborhood, city, and state.

Ursula still consults this globe, often. She likes how it represents the world as it was at a given moment in time—countries that no longer exist, borders that have changed and changed again, carrying new names that erased the old. This globe held the solid belief that the way things were is the way they would always be. Otherwise, it would've been made from Play-Doh, something soft and stretchy, with the lines all drawn in chalk, to acknowledge that nothing stays the same.

And, of course, it never does. Rivers twist and take new turns, changing national borders. Continents drift, reforming themselves over hundreds of millions of years, until maybe one day they'll get it right. But for this moment, frozen in metal and paint, the earth stood still.

At one point, Ursula had 27 globes. She had collected them over time; birthdays, allowance money—it was her request from Santa five years in a row. Some lit up from the inside, from the outside, spoke the country's capitals when touched with a magic pointer, showed ancient mariner chartings. But all those impermanent renditions of Planet Earth were eventually moved along except for this one that was her original love.

Before Ursula went raw, before she went juicy, she would stock up on the little organic chocolate balls covered in foil printed like globes of the earth. She'd pop at least two or three of those little worlds daily, satisfying her sweet tooth and her longing to belong to something much larger.

Now that chocolate was no longer part of her diet, she made mobiles out of them, stringing them at odd lengths from the dining room chandelier.

Yes, Ursula was in love with Planet Earth, and always had been. Mother Earth, Planet Earth… it's all the same thing.

Her work at the travel agency was a natural extension of her interest in all the places of the world, not just visiting these places herself, but the certain joy she felt in sending others. She only asked one thing of all her clients, to go up to a local stranger, give them her card, tell them "Ursula said hello and if you're ever in Los Angeles, please look her up," and take a picture together.

Some of her clients thought her silly, or were too embarrassed to do such a thing. So Ursula would give clients a hefty rebate on hotel and car rentals for doing so, but only after they returned with the photo.

Ursula kept these photos pinned to a giant map in her travel office. The map covered the entire wall, and covering the map were scads of photographs of happy looking strangers, together, smiling.

Ursula is always tickled when she gets a call from someone from Japan or Nigeria or Finland just passing through. She'll invite them down to the travel office, take their picture together, and give them a map of the city with a packet of free discount coupons.

It's her own small way of bringing the world a little closer together, and bringing us all closer to Mother Earth.

When no one is watching, Ursula will take each picture down one by one, and see in the strangers' faces how they've been changed by the new surroundings.

These days, when no one is watching, Ursula will put on all the creams she's purchased from her class, stand in front of the mirror in her jingly skirt, and wiggle her hips. Their movement is stiff and jerky, like a car with a rusted gearshift. She pictures, instead, what it would be to spin her belly bowl like one of her globes, circling around and around, stopping someplace wondrous and new each time.

10 | WHEN NO ONE IS WATCHING, MOTHER EARTH...

When no one is watching Mother Earth, and most of the time no one is, she sings softly to herself.

Certainly no one is watching *after* her, to the point where she's now calling herself M. Earth, using her first initial only, like the early women writers who did not want their work to be automatically dismissed because of their gender disadvantage.

Though she is grand, M. Earth is feeling, perhaps, overly feminine, and therefore vulnerable. Don't even mention the word *Gaia*; it's such a projection! She thinks she could benefit from a more macho profile, a little kick-ass to make her point. Perhaps a little masculine detachment would be helpful, or a thicker skin. Because, frankly, she's been trampled, poisoned, stripped bare, robbed blind, and blamed for just about everything that's come down the pike. And like all mothers, everyone just assumes she'll always be there for them with open, loving arms, and a cup of hot cocoa. That it will be her pleasure to feed them, lick their wounds, and clean a load or two of their dirty laundry. She's looking for a little more respect.

Believe it or not, one of the ways M. Earth watches over her dominion is through Google Earth. Loves that this was invented. Loves the Internet, and how it mimics her intricate networks of bio-intelligence already in play. It helps her hold the whole zoomed-out picture of the whole ding-dang thing. It also helps her zero in on one species, or microclimate at a time—because, it's a very big picture to hold. The micro and the macro are not always tracking together. Well, they are, but her attention can only be split in so many directions. So as long as the technology is there, she'll use it, alongside teen-aged boys, stalkers, and minor league spies. She may be ancient, but she's cool.

If we *were* to watch M. Earth, we'd find her playing Sudoku to keep from getting bored. She's been at this so long, she bores easily. And when she's bored, she starts mindlessly moving things around to keep it lively, like plant forms and animal species, and entire continents. She's sneaky. Tends to do it slowly so no one can notice—as if anyone were looking, which only a few are, and those crackpots get institutionalized as quick as you can say "Global Warming," so really, what's the problem? It's simply for her own amusement.

She works hard to keep it all in balance. So much of it has to do with food. Simply put, it's *eat or be eaten* in her world. The Big Guys eat the Littler Guys, and the Littlest Guys—insects, fungi, and bacteria—eat all the rest. Everyone is food for somebody. Otherwise we'd all be knee deep in decaying bodies and leafy refuse, and she'd end up having to do all the clean up…

So she employs allies. Lots of them.

And they all have to eat.

11 | YOU ARE WHAT YOU EAT

Even though Ursula was quite slim, not too long ago, she wanted to lose weight. *I am poochy in the middle* is what she repeated to herself daily. Since no matter how slim, svelte, or gorgeous a woman actually is, she will always think of herself as *fat*... Ursula resolved to go on a diet.

She said it had nothing to do with Sheerah's influence; belly dancers are revered for their curvaceous fullness. But Ursula had enough sense to know that something wasn't getting through "down there," and maybe she could feel some tingle if she wasn't feeling all this bloat.

At the time, the Western World was eating Atkins, then South Beach, then Zone... and then ballooned up again after they stopped. Weight Watchers and Jenny Craig were too public. High fiber had appeal, but you'd spend too much time chewing. Every woman's magazine was selling a different answer. She left the newsstand frustrated and confused.

Walking back to work a different route than usual—the way that would pass the Coffee Bean and Tea Leaf, instead of the Starbucks—took her right past a new restaurant that had just opened, serving nothing but raw food. That seemed extreme enough to catch her interest.

When she sampled the ground almonds with three radish sprouts wrapped in a cabbage leaf she thought, *What a silly excuse for a cuisine.* When she saw the lithe and defined shapes of all who were in there, including the staff, she thought, *Not one ounce of fat in the entire joint.* She then decided, regardless of the taste or lack of it, she would join them.

She had never viewed eating as much beyond a tedious necessity, anyway. She ate a narrow palette and picked convenient foods she could tolerate that gave her enough nutrition to her keep her going. That five of those foods included something to do with bread could have explained her pooch. That the other five included something to go on bread really held her to the ground. That she considered coffee with milk and sugar a food group unto itself gave her license to include it in every meal.

Her staples included:

Bread w/
Butter
Cream cheese
Peanut butter
Jelly
Tuna salad

Bagel w/
Butter
Cream cheese
Peanut Butter
Jelly
Tuna Salad

Crackers w/
Butter
Cream cheese
Peanut Butter
Jelly
Tuna Salad

Croissant w/
Butter
Jelly

Muffins
Plain

When Ursula had her first bright green bowel movement after eating three days at the raw food restaurant, she knew she was onto something completely different. Now she mostly juices. That may be taking things too far.

Regarding Donny's relationship to food, he would say:

"Heartburn is how I recognize myself. It's how I know I feel like me." He equates preserving the bad way he eats with preserving his own personal freedom, and he's a man determined to be free.

If the President of the United States had his druthers, he'd never eat anything green again. He's doing what is in his power to make it so. Paul would actually say *Amen* to that, if he didn't hate the government more than broccoli.

Sheerah drinks her Kombucha tea on the rocks, mixed with vodka, a little cherry juice, and some shavings of antler horn. Her students mistakenly think of her as a purist, but she's a mixologist of a magical order. Whether an adventurer, glutton, or picker: a person's relationship to food is the same as their relationship to all of life.

Locusts live to eat. They became locusts because they got too hungry. When grasshoppers are starving for lack of food, something cues them to swarm and transform into locusts. Then they eat everything in sight.

The locusts are simply not interested in some food sources, and leave them alone. But the AgriNu grains… they love them. Just so you know.

12 | THE FIRST GUERILLA GARDENER

Johnny Appleseed dotted the plains with apple trees grown from seeds he planted as he walked westward along the trails. He had his sack of seeds over his shoulder as he walked for miles at a time. Sometimes he'd encounter folks in covered wagons, and ride along with them for a while until he came to a farm or settlement, where he'd offer seeds and some gospel in exchange for food and a bed.

We don't really know what motivated Johnny to take up such an adventure. Was he so in love with apples? Had he heard the voice of the Lord? Or did he need to leave town quickly, and this was a way out?

Ursula did not set out to be—but here she was, just like Johnny Appleseed—a guerilla gardener. Only Johnny lived in a time when the land, wild or welcome, was wide open, and every inch was not yet owned by somebody else.

For Ursula, it began with the radish sprouts that dropped out of her "sandwich" onto the patio behind the raw foods restaurant. (What is meant by "sandwich" is lettuce and seed cheese spread thinly between two dehydrated onion slices.) It would have been rude to pick the sprouts up and eat them, though they had constituted one half of what was on her lunch plate.

She was going to have to work late that night to be available to the cruise ship that was docking at Long Beach. Even she might be hungry later on after such a tiny meal. But the sprouts had already touched the ground, and she had already inadvertently stepped on them, attempting to retrieve them.

When she bent down, she thought for sure she could see the seed at the base of the sprout already reaching for the dirt in between the brick pavers of the patio. The urge to grow is that strong.

She decided that rather than try and recover the fallen sprouts and eat them, she would leave them where they fell and come back and visit them daily to see if they grew. She could always get a latte later.

Each day she returned to sit at the same table. She adjusted the table to create a protective canopy so no customers would crush the delicate seedling. She removed the umbrella from the center, lined up the hole so the sun would shine directly down. She gently poured out the contents of her water glass.

Within a few days, the sprout sent off new leaves, and began to establish itself as a plant. Ursula was flush with a deep sense of satisfaction—something a mother might feel, she imagined. Or a farmer. She was growing new life.

At lunchtime, Ursula began knocking her sprouts off into various window boxes and planters around the patio of the restaurant. She watered them, pretending no one was noticing what she was doing. But if they did, it really didn't matter. To be thought of as weird among this restaurant's clientele would be an accomplishment, indeed.

Weeks later, she delighted in seeing radishes among the geraniums, sunflowers in the marigolds, and neat rows of alfalfa cropping up underneath the tables.

What delighted her wasn't just the secret of the unexpected, subversive plants growing among the flowers, it was the verification that life could insist itself anywhere.

So, with her beaded pouch on her shoulder filled with a surprise mixture of sprouts and seeds, she began tossing them out into whatever patches of dirt she could find. Meridians on highways, unnoticed corners of parks, vacant lots…

She planted the easy growers—green beans for speed, zucchini for abundance, and tomatoes, the self-seeders.

She'd simply find a patch of dirt, sprinkle some seeds in when no one was looking, squirt water from her self-filtering water bottle, then see what happened.

This was her own experiment in spreading life. Toss something out there, and see what will grow. See what it needs. See what tries to stop it, or feed on it before it matures.

At first, she'd go around to visit the various places she'd planted, to check in, give a little encouragement and water. But soon she'd planted in so many places that she forgot where she planted, and so she just prayed for rain. Still, she started to notice that some of the places she had watered, or over watered, had sprouted little tiny mushrooms around the emerging plants, and she wondered what that was all about. She pulled up a few and saw the tiny threadlike roots of the mushroom's mycelium entwined in a matrix with the plants' own roots. Hummh.

13 | SEEDS

Now that Ursula was engaged in her experiment with seeds, she wanted to know more about them. Always a thorough investigator, she sought out every plant related documentary she could find on the Discovery Channel. She tivoed *The Secret Life of Seeds,* and watched it three times.

It began at the beginning. Dr. Morton Mulvane, an evolutionary botanist from UC Davis claimed the earliest fossilized seeds discovered by humans were said to be from the Late Devonian period, approximately 365 million years ago. They were found in West Virginia. Before then, who knows how plants reproduced?

He pointed out this was the same time that fish evolved legs and came crawling out onto land to get a breath of fresh air. "Seeds are highly adaptive," he stated. "Believe it or not, back then there was far less oxygen available, and the carbon dioxide level was even far worse than we have now."

After a commercial for Miracle Grow, Ursula was fascinated to learn that no matter what its shape or size, a seed kernel is actually a small embryonic plant enclosed in a hard shell for its protection and transport. "Carrying the spirit of its ancestors and the promise of its offspring," Dr. Mulvane said, "seeds are the agent of a plant's urge to perpetuate its own kind. The strategies for propagating are endless. They are perfect on their own."

He ended by saying, "Seeds occur naturally in thousands of variations. The fish with legs did not have the need to *improve* seeds, thank you very much. Only the crazy humans do."

14 | JUAN JOSE SAVES THE LAST POD

When the last plant from the last furrow in the soil was removed, when the last leaves were waiting to be hauled away, and all else was turned back under into the soil—Juan Jose pushed his tattered straw hat back off his sweaty brow, and shook his head again, and again at the shame of it all.

He wanted to let his family, and the families of all the farmworkers who worked under his supervision, gather the crops in baskets or in their apron skirts to put food on their tables. This food could last them for weeks. But the National Guard soldiers had moved in yesterday and stationed themselves every 50 feet at both ends of the fields to make sure the crops were destroyed. So instead of the farmworkers, thousands of voracious insects were already having their way with the rapidly wilting plants piled high in open trucks.

Spinach was now the #1 threat to America, and must be destroyed. This farm had nothing to do with the outbreak, and had been tested to be free of any bacterial infection, but Juan Jose was told no chances could be taken. Not on spinach, or beets, or lettuce, or any of their other crops. Spinach was the target, but the soldiers were forcing the workers to rip it all out. All the crops! It was crazy and unjustified.

According to Mr. Ed, it was brilliant. Having gained the confidence of his boss, the AgriNu board, and the President himself, his job now was to undermine the nation's trust in their food so they would accept any solution presented, no matter how dire.

Standing with the camera crew, Mr. Ed felt the intoxicating rush of real power. This campaign was his baby. He knew how to steer it, control it, and make sure the credit went where the credit was due. That's how you move from company man to architect. His task now was to supply video to the various news networks showing the swift attention being paid to this grave spinach situation. And while he was here, he would create footage for the next phase of his plan.

As he directed the camera to focus on the growing pile of the "tainted" crops, the spirals of insects buzzing on the rapidly rotting spinach disgusted him—the way they immediately took over everything. The Young Mr. Ed was the kind to pull the wings off butterflies, and he did. Every summer, growing up. He'd catch a bunch in a jar from his granddaddy's bushes—then lift them out one by one. He'd hold the butterfly in the center, and pluck the right wing off, then the left. He'd watch that creature teeter, struggle, and fall, before it bled to death.

It wasn't so much that bugs were the enemy; it's just that they're small, and he was bored. Bored to tears out there on his granddad's farm when all he wanted to do was spy on the girl who lived next door back home as she undressed in her window. But he was in the middle of Ohio—where his relatives had once carved out the wilderness, and now was fucking nowhere. So you'd better believe the middle of Nowhere California was going to take him exactly where he wanted to go.

Juan Jose looked at the whole scene in disbelief. He was not an American citizen, though his family has crossed the border repeatedly, and worked in these fields of Central California for three generations. Juan Jose was not an American, and perhaps that's why he didn't feel the least bit threatened by these rows and rows of spinach. And perhaps that's why he slipped the very last seed flowers into his pocket—where they might remain for another day.

15 | DONNY'S LITTLE PROBLEM

Donny was eager to see Ursula again, but he had a little problem where she was concerned. He was a smoker, and he could tell from the first time he entered her house that she would not approve. Oh, it was fine for her to completely stink up the place with the putrid odor of mushroom scum, but a little cigarette smoke, he was sure, would send him sailing out the door. She would say what they all said, that it was less about her than her concern for his own health. *Yeah, right.*

Not only did Donny live a life that proved he didn't care about his own health, he had a way of turning not caring into a righteous act. He has demonstrated this over and over again.

For example, as a kid, Donny could knock a baseball out of the park. He was always the one to hit the base runners home. In high school, he could pitch a curve ball no one could hit, but he wouldn't go out for the team.

Donny knew it would make his father proud, but his father had a job teaching at the junior college, and couldn't come to most of his games; so Donny didn't do it. He smoked dope instead, underneath the bleachers on the school field where the varsity team practiced. He'd comment, yes. Criticize, yes. But he wouldn't play.

This is what formed him, knowing his greatest power lay not in performance, but in withholding. His father yelled at him more often after that, about every little thing—leaving the dishes in the sink, running the bathroom water too long, the length of his hair. Though it aggravated Donny no end, each incident gave him the twisted pleasure of the recurring effect of his power.

It gave him a certain notoriety around school. Girls seemed to feel sorry for him and would try to bring out his *potential.* He was the one who could become a star, easily be offered a college scholarship, but wouldn't. They would try to heal whatever it was that was holding him back. What was holding him back was sheer will. Or was it? Sometimes Donny felt that his greatness was lying in wait for some catastrophic urgency to call it forward, but nothing less. (At least he hoped it was that.) Superman doesn't rescue cats from trees, ya know? So until then… withholding just became a habit.

Odd to feel your power through what you will not do. Donny's *potential* held local fame and interest for a while… but eventually the girls gave up. Even Donny, himself, had trouble caring after a joint or two. Even about the Yankees. His 1952 Topps Mickey Mantle, framed in Lucite was still his favorite card. Worth at least $25,000 in mint condition, and his was. Damn those Yankees, there was a team! Nothing like them since. Still, he tells himself he'd sell it, just like that. He tells himself he could be a hero like Mantle if only the bases were loaded in the last game of the series. He tells himself a lot of things, true or not.

He tells himself his interest in Ursula is not about caring, it's about pursuit. So in order to pull off pursuit, Donny has to smoke on the way over before he arrives on her block. He can't even smoke in his own car lest it reek, and that was that. He could suggest they take her car, but that goes against the manly code. Both women and men expect the man to drive, and to drive his own car. So he'd stop at a corner, get out and smoke several cigarettes in a row till he got light headed (try this several days into a juice fast), change his shirt, put the cigarette-smoke shirt deep in his truck, drink nearly an entire bottle of water, wash off his beard with the last bit, dry it with an old towel he wished was fresher, and pop some mints.

Who was he kidding? She had to know, right? But he had to keep up the charade because he was not, and I mean NOT giving up smoking. Not for his mother, not for this girl, not for anyone. It was enough that he gave up pot—coming to the conclusion that being a pot head did indeed make him lazy, and he already had quite a leaning in that direction on his own. He could only drink until his acid reflux kicked in, which was sooner and sooner of late—so really cigarettes were his only vice, and a man needs at least one. Otherwise, he's too passive, controllable, predictable, and what's the word? A "wuss."

What was he going to talk to her about? Oh, yeah, organic farms.

16 | THE PHOTO WALL

Ursula looked up from her desk and saw it was already eleven in the morning. She had been at work since five a.m. The cruise ship to Puerto Vallarta, where three quarters of the passengers contracted violent stomach flu, had stopped halfway down and aborted the trip.

She had two groups booked on that ship and had spent the entire morning re-routing each one of them home. Her ear was throbbing. Her head felt so tight it was squeezing out her brain, and she was in great need of water.

How could someone who liked traveling the world so much end up all day behind a computer? She had not become a travel agent for the joy of making reservations, though there was a small competitive thrill in getting the last two seats on a flight to Vermont in early October.

When she'd gotten the very last of the cruisers secured on an airplane equipped with extra airsickness bags, she tore off her headset, threw it down on her desk, and let out a sigh so strong it pushed back her chair.

She was grateful to her co-worker, Sid, who supplied her with the connecting cities, as she jockeyed these folks all over the continent to get home. Sid was awesome. He was some kind of idiot savant when it came to capital cities. Sid knew the geographies, topographies, imports, exports, and drug trades of every nation. He knew their rainy seasons, dry seasons, tourist seasons, and major festivals. He loved for you to test him. You'd give him a city, and he'd give you the best way to get there: airline, flight schedule, what hotel to stay at, and how much to tip the cab.

If only he weren't so annoying when he got going and wouldn't let you stop.

Needless to say, he was another guy who didn't have a girlfriend. He did have a dog though, which he brought to work; and it had this slobber ball. All day long, over and over, that dog would lay the chewed up ball with saliva strings hanging off of it at Ursula's feet, and expect her to throw it. It was not a very big office. They say we resemble our dogs…

"Hello," she heard Donny sing out as he came through the door, smelling rather minty. He was holding some overly expensive high-energy juice drink made from organic carrots, beets, and ginseng, with a power boost of bee pollen and kava kava. Her face lit up. Donny wasn't sure if it was the sight of him or the juice that switched on the light—but no matter. He was within days of his estimate, and he was not usually wrong about these things.

He wiped his moist hands surreptitiously before handing her the drink. Ursula was grateful in this moment for something wet and restorative. She told him all about the ship and the maladies of the passengers, and how she could barely move and needed this more than he knew. He just smiled like a good dog.

"So this is where you work?" he said, stating the obvious. His eyes immediately scanned the travel posters of gorgeous settings, and landed on the unusual map behind her, with the photos of smiling faces pinned all over. His eyebrow went up in question.

Ursula was too exhausted to explain. She had already been talking way too much today—and barfing people don't tend to be all that pleasant.

Fortunately, at that very moment, a tiny Japanese man and his tinier wife walked into the agency, checking the address from a piece of paper they held in their hand. Ursula immediately recognized why these people were here, stole a hard gulp from her juice, and sprang out of her chair to greet them.

"Tokyo Joe send us," the tiny man said in broken English.

Ursula knew exactly who he was talking about. She gave each of her clients a nickname based on where they were going, for moments just like this when they in turn sent someone back to Ursula to be photographed for the wall. The tiny woman held a photo of them with Tokyo Joe in Tokyo. They had been his "strangers" in that land; and now these two would be Ursula's strangers, and go up on her Wall of Strangers, along with Tokyo Joe. This was what truly delighted her about her job.

She handed the camera to Donny, since Sid had suddenly gone out to "take his mother to the doctor" or some other made-up excuse. Ursula stood between the two of them against the Wall of Strangers and asked him to snap. Say "Cheese".

She ran off and printed it while the couple and Donny mostly smiled and nodded at each other—occasionally saying a word like "Hollywood," or "Disneyland." She returned, handed them a copy, and placed one on the map, in a big sidebar adjacent to Los Angeles. Everyone was happy. She handed them coupons for a free meal at IHOP (even though she'd never eat there herself), some passes for Universal Studios, and a tour of movie stars' homes. They left as thrilled as if they'd won the lottery.

Ursula smiled after them. Donny looked at her, amazed. There didn't seem to be a cynical bone in her body. The woman took pleasure in the oddest things, he had to admit, but she did indeed take pleasure. He became distracted by the sensation of wanting to take pleasure in her. Maybe he could be more like her someday… nah. *Nature is nature*, he thought to himself. And he was stuck with his.

"Thanks for the juice," she said, taking the last slug, jolting him out of his daze. And then more shyly, "I like that you like to eat this way. I think people who eat alike are more compatible at a very basic level." Donny just smiled and nodded, which had become his best way of avoiding the truth.

"Enjoy it…" he began, "that may be the last juice you or I have for a while…" He proceeded to tell her about the quarantine on all organic farms.

17 | BUT WHAT CAN ONE PERSON DO?

Paul posted on his blog:

> **People should be out there OCCUPYING THE STREETS, but the truth is...**
>
> **NOBODY LIKES SPINACH!!!**
>
> **When the Government put a quarantine on the green leaves, people recalled how much they really didn't like spinach in the first place. Downright hated it. It brought back horrid memories of being forced to eat it as a child. So now they have the excuse—the adults as well as the children—to refuse spinach, demonize it, and ban it for life if they can...**

It was true. Except for a couple of health nuts, people were so delighted, that they celebrated with an extra heap of GMO corn to fill the space spinach had vacated on the plate. As for those who did care, they took the attitude that *this too shall pass.*

Spinach sales plummeted, as they were meant to, even for the spinach that grocery stores scrambled to import from Mexico, deemed "safe." The whole idea was to stop the spread of the tainted spinach wherever it might show up—organic or not. But the disappearance of spinach was pretty much taking care of itself.

"All it takes is the rumor," Mr. Ed said. "The danger itself is irrelevant. It's the *perception* of danger we're selling." The media, in the business of churning out a good scare, was happy to spread the word.

And because no one spoke out, Mr. Ed decided he would make good on his entire deal with the President, early. The next day, buried on page 21 this time, was this:

> *The presence of E. coli has been discovered in recent shipments of peas from certain organic farms in California. In light of this second dangerous outbreak, the CDC, along with the Department of Agriculture has determined more severe measures are required regarding organic farms. Traces of E. coli were also found on organically grown cabbage and lettuce. Other unhealthful organisms were found on the leaves of organic crops sampled at three California organic farms, and one farm in Hawaii. The practices of organic farming are deemed a danger to public health; therefore, sales of any crop from organic farms will be prohibited, and the crops themselves destroyed until further notice.*

The evening news played Mr. Ed's *phase two* footage. There went the peas… and a whole lot more.

Paul ranted in his blog again:

> **OK people… anyone going to get upset, NOW?!**

Though Ursula was completely alarmed, she was not the type to join in any sort of public protest. She didn't especially like crowds, and… what did it do anyway?

To her, the world seemed so large, even when broken up into its smaller geographic parts—so many people with so many different agendas, so many pairs of shoes. Just to tally up the shoes alone in this world… uncountable.

In the face of this vastness, she perceived herself to be but a speck. In fact, a speck on a speck. And what possible effect could a speck on a speck have on anything else at all? Even if joined with other specks?

When she thought about any possible action she could take, she felt so small and insignificant compared to the larger need. One could be slammed by the sheer weight of all the need, and never be able to get out of bed in the morning. Just reading the newspaper put Ursula into a spin. So she didn't.

Ursula always feared that calling too much attention to herself would get her in big trouble. She had some distant memory of being burned as a witch for expressing unpopular ideas. Or maybe that was just a movie she saw. But it made her skin crawl, along with any number of other fears she harbored—founded or unfounded. She feared embarrassment, shame, and at the other end of the spectrum, persecution. Those fears told her to remain anonymous.

She therefore told herself that her best actions should be small and local, caring for what or who was directly in her circle of concern. Her circle of concern included one cat and now 273 Kombucha mushrooms—well, that's how that goes. And now Donny was entering her circle of concern. Sometimes that was a bother. Certainly her food was within her circle of concern, but this issue of the farms was way too large. Surely, somebody else would find the answer. Somebody else would work it through. Or she'd learn to adjust and do without. What can one person do?

Donny, on the other hand, did read the newspaper. Two in fact. It helped him feel as if he knew what was going on in the world; therefore he was part of it. It helped him form an opinion; and he reasoned that if he had an opinion, it was the same as appearing to be involved. (And if those opinions gave him ideas for a screenplay, all the better.) The idea of actually taking a political action didn't even occur to him.

18 | EARTH: IT HELPS TO TAKE THE OVERVIEW

M. Earth's response to all this was less of a rise than you might think. She's seen it all before. Oh, maybe not this, where an entire species of "intelligent" life plots to annihilate itself—but she's seen so many come and go. She can't get attached. Otherwise she'd be crying all the damned time.

M. Earth has learned to take in the Big Picture with the necessary indifference that comes from too many disappointments. The closest we humans can get to the Big Picture is to get on Google Earth from a satellite, and even then we can't really comprehend the multiplicity of interplay that takes place in a given moment. But M. Earth always has her finger on the pulse… the pulse of creation, the pulse of destruction, and the pulse of extinction.

Yeah, that one. Where entire life forms and landforms disappear. Gone, done. *Sorry fella, your turn is over.* It's partly her way of clearing the decks from time to time; partly this sort of mixing it up she likes to do. But there's a recognizable rhythm to these pulses of extinction—at intervals of say, 3 million years or so—if anyone were around long enough to take notes.

Ursula used to have a globe that showed the Earth as it once was: Pangaea.

At one time, about the time the first seeds appeared, all we had was Pangaea—one enormous continent surrounded by one single ocean. It was the conglomeration of all the continents of the northern and southern hemispheres together before they separated and drifted out into the continents we now stand on today. That took a while. About 100 million years.

To M. Earth, that's just like waiting for the bus.

If you saw it drawn out, as the continents split off from each other and drifted apart, they looked like bodies that had been spooning each other, holding that memory like sleeping lovers do when they separate into their day.

The continental plates are still moving. They shift at the rate toenails grow. That could seem long or short to you, depending on how often you need a pedicure.

Right now, new continents are forming that don't yet appear on one of Ursula's globes. The Northern Pacific Gyre, for instance. A landmass of garbage and plastic debris the size of Texas floating out there in the Pacific, collected together in one spot by the swirling current. It's exciting. Only problem is the whole damned thing is toxic, and can't support a speck of life. At least not yet. Give it time. M. Earth is very clever.

She'll come up with enough biodiversity to take hold and populate that plastic land through symbiotic relationships and odd pairings. Perhaps some of the species that are disappearing from our more conventional continents might have a better shot on the plastic.

One difference between humans and M. Earth is that we have such a short attention span, and can't stand to wait. In the Late Devonian Period, a wiping out of species took place over 1-15 million years. In the Late Petroleum Period, we're trying to go for it in one giant POP. It's what the AgriNu folks are betting on. The Ultimate Ejaculation.

M. Earth, like all good mothers, has infinite patience for the childish behavior of her offspring. She says… "I can wait." She's shown she can.

Here's the thing though—it's just not a big deal for her. Regardless of what the humans do, M. Earth Herself will be just fine. There's always some form of life that will adapt and thrive under any given condition, lying in wait for their turn at bat. They may not even know they've been played yet. And she understands, as a default, she can simply back up a bit to a far earlier time—say like 365 million years earlier—start the whole damned thing over again, and give some rookie a try.

19 | HERE'S M. EARTH'S OVERVIEW

Scientists estimate that:

4.5 billion years ago: The Earth came together, somehow.

1.3 billion years ago: The first organisms appeared on Earth, and they may well have been fungi.

600 million years later: Plants arrived (mycelium was already here).

365 million years ago: Fossils provide evidence of the earliest seeds.

250 million years ago: Pangaea came together as one landform, and then began moving apart at the rate of toenails, though there weren't any back then.

250 million years ago (probably not on the same day that Pangaea formed): What scientists think of as an asteroid struck, causing great volcanic eruptions and colossal changes. The debris was such that it blocked out the sun, causing huge numbers of species to die in a colossal pulse of extinction. Only fungi survived because they needed no sunlight and could decompose and feed from debris. Fungi inherited the Earth.

65 million years ago: Another asteroid hit, and fungi inherited the Earth again.

60 million years ago: After all that drifting, Pangaea finally spread apart to the continents we know today.

Over the last 25 million years: Several pulses of extinction changed the balance of life forms on Earth.

68 years ago: The explosion of the atomic bomb created a mushroom cloud, but was not a real fungus.

23 years ago: The World Wide Web emerged.

23 years ago: AgriNu "improved" on the seed.

As recently as 10 years ago: AgriNu registered all the patents.

It's always good to know a little bit about where you come from.

20 | PAUL WAS BECOMING A SURVIVALIST

This news about AgriNu's latest shenanigans did not come as a surprise to Paul. Nothing surprises fatalists, which is one of their best protections. For that and other reasons, Paul was becoming a survivalist.

The evidence was all around him, piling up like the emergency lights, dehydrated food, and hand-crank-powered radios in every corner of his already cluttered apartment.

Even he had to admit that the whole JFK conspiracy thing had played itself out. It was time to move on. Nothing new had come to light that *could* come to light. One can only keep going to the same soup pot, adding one cup of liquid after another, before you realize you're just eating water.

Still, all his research and probing, uncovering and declassifying, left him with a very bad taste in his mouth for government—ours, theirs, or anybody's—but mostly ours. He knew too much about the revolving doors between mega business, agribusiness, and the government. Private sector and public sector, constantly trading places. Lobbyists at the highest level advocating for their special interests.

The vile, unconscionable actions of men and women full of greedy lust for power—full of shit and *Oh, shit, we'd better cover our asses here*—were the very foundations of government. Here the cream rises to the top, the crap falls to the bottom, and the whole barrel gets flipped over. These are the politicians—at the top at last and determined to stay there, no matter what the cost.

Oh, he could go on and on, and usually did if someone were around to hear him. But people mostly stayed away. He still only has seven followers on his blog, having picked up three since his recent postings about AgriNu. Paul tells himself it's because most people can't bear the searing truth. It upends their pretty little lives, and has them wading through the murky swamp of their own confusion. But Paul knows he's overbearing, tediously single minded, and repeats himself. He can't help any of it. He's burning to tell people the secrets he knows, and he can't remember who he's told what to. It all feels like one continuous loop. It seems like he's repeating himself, but in fact, the same damned things keep happening over and over again.

It's only a matter of days, weeks, months before the FBI/CIA/United Homeland Security thugs bash down his door and take him away in the dark of the night while his neighbors are all stoned and watching the Jay Leno monologue. So it's better that he doesn't have a girlfriend they could torture for information. This is, he tells himself, a heroic act of valor, and not simply pathetic.

He even gets these guys who want to own guns and form their own militias against the days when the government shows its true colors. Paul is not a gun nut. Christ, his parents were such hippie peaceniks they wouldn't even let him play with water pistols. So he doesn't even have a clue which end is up. But he tells himself he'll get there soon enough. It's coming to that, soon enough.

What he does have is enough food, water, and alternative energy supplies to last for three months—and an even larger stash at a public storage container out in Lancaster. He's working to get himself "off the grid." He means all the way off. No need for electricity, or gas, or public food and water sources. Solar ovens, cars that run on water, pedal-powered power packs for running the coffee grinder and TV; he's made files on all these technologies. He's bought kits, assembled prototypes—not just for money-saving measures—but necessities for survival if there is to be a future. The giant Energies are gobbling up the new technology so fast… if there is a future, they'll still own it. Still, maybe he can have his own small piece.

His friends call him an alarmist. They tell him he's being ridiculous and extreme. But it's in his nature to share, so he's made certain that he has supplies for at least three others. He figures if it's one man and two other women, it could be up to them to repopulate the world once it's been blown to pieces. Which is why he asked Donny to ask Ursula if she had a girlfriend who was in good reproductive health. It was for the greater good of mankind, not just some horny request.

Coincidental to all this, Paul was not only becoming a survivalist, he was becoming a vegetarian. More like a chip-a-tarian or a greasy-pizza-a-tarian. Which is to say he stopped eating meat. Not so much a principled thing as something that just happened of its own accord.

Paul rarely thought much about food, eating only when necessary. He'd eat the same thing over and over as if the thoughts he didn't waste on new food selection could be used for something else. He kept it simple, and liked foods that went crunch because they were supposed to, and not because they'd been exposed to the air for too long. To Paul, Cheetos were the perfect food.

What was totally weird was the synchronicity that this dietary change was occurring at the same time that Ursula had gone on juices only, and Donny was at least *appearing* to eat something other than lunchmeat and cigarettes. Paul had never discussed this with his friend, but it was like some turn in the Universe caused these simultaneous events to occur. A Tipping Point, like the discovery of fire, or tools, or repeats of the great floods that appeared at the same time in history in various ancient civilizations around the world. He was experiencing his own tipping point towards meatlessness—not teetering so far as broccoli, but recognizing that some form of vegetables might just enter his system. Anything was possible.

Paul wrote about it in his blog. He gained five more followers and two recipes for Spam, which some do not consider meat.

All this thinking gave Paul one of his headaches. When they got this bad, he had no choice but to go to the biofeedback machine his mother insisted he learn to use, and produce alpha waves with his stereo headset blasting Led Zeppelin. Focusing on a blue light, he alternated his brainwaves back and forth. All the thoughts and rattles of his mind, all the urgings and surgings of his body would crescendo to painful chaos until the fragments lined up to the constant light. Then something in his mind would go *pop*—and he would glide on that blue light for as long as he could and, eventually, fall asleep.

21 | ONE STRANGER WAS NOT A STRANGER

Ursula looked up at her Wall of Strangers. *So many smiling people,* she thought, *who do not know who they are smiling for.* All strangers, except for one… one of the strangers was not a stranger. She had placed his photo on the wall to hide him among the others.

It was a photo of Ernesto, the smiling poet-biologist tour guide she had tangled with in Ecuador.

He had sent her his picture after she returned from her trip to the equator. She guessed he had access to her travel records and information, him being a tour guide and all. She didn't expect to hear from him again—certainly didn't expect a photograph and the pubic hair he said belonged to her that he found in his bed. *Right,* she thought, *like he can tell the difference between mine and the seven other women he'd slept with that week.* Ernesto was so very charming and, oh, so very handsome. He would be hard for any gringa to resist. Must be this hair belonged to one of them. It was curlier and darker than her own. She did a match test—and did not see the similarity. Maybe he had plucked it from his own manly bush.

One of the perks of being a travel agent, besides free rental cars, were travel junkets—short excursions, mostly free, organized for the purpose of promotion. The intent was that the agents would become familiar with a place, enamored with a place, and refer their clients to the place. It worked out well for everyone.

Ursula had gone on one of these junkets over a long President's Day weekend well over a year ago, a quick four-day eco-tour in Ecuador. She went to the central city of Quito, the eucalyptus scented Highlands, boated in the rainforest—but what struck her strongest was the spot where she straddled the equator.

Maybe it was her lifelong fascination with globes, Ursula having at one time memorized all the countries and bodies of water that the equator crossed through. She loved the equator, how it remained in the center when she'd spin the globe, like it was holding the whole thing together.

When standing at the equator, one has four choices—stand on this side, that side, straddle the damn thing, or make your body as tight and compact as you can and stand right on the line itself. She straddled wide to include as much area as possible. She felt an incredible balance all throughout her system.

Ursula was anxious to get a cup of coffee at the adjacent Nifty-Gifty to try out that thing she had heard about the two hemispheres. She bought her coffee in the north, dumped in a teaspoon of sugar with a plastic spoon, and stirred till it dissolved. She lifted out the spoon—the swirl left behind went clockwise. She hopped over to the other side of the border; stirred again, and sure enough the coffee swirled in the other direction. She let out a yelp of spontaneous excitement, spilling said coffee down the front of her Protect the Amazonas t-shirt.

The tour guide, who had been watching her with hungry eyes, was right there with some crumpled napkins, "Cuidado, cuidado, Senorita," he said in a smooth concerned tone, offering to mop her up. He was dazzlingly handsome, with shining white teeth and dark coffee eyes. A country that wants to make a good impression puts its best foot forward. Ernesto was the name of that foot.

Ursula blushed light pink, and excused herself to go to the bathroom. She turned on the water in the sink. Sure enough, it also swirled down the drain in the opposite direction. She ran the water and stopped it several times, watching it reverse itself down the drain, giggling to herself. She then flushed the toilet three or four times, fascinated. All the natural rules were opposite, a reversed universe. She decided as long as she stayed in the south, she would do things opposite—or let them run their course to the left instead of the right.

That night, when the group went out to dinner, Ernesto found a way to sit next to her. He told her he was a poet-biologist on leave from his studies at the university where he was getting his PhD, trying to put all of nature into words. He wanted to read her his poems, he wanted to practice his English, he wanted her to come to his apartment and "see how the natives lived."

The more wine she had, the more deeply charming he became. She was dizzy in a way she had not known before. She said goodnight to the group at the hotel and followed the path outside to the left, as he had instructed. He was waiting for her at the corner of the plaza. They crossed together as he pointed out various important facts about the church that dominated the center. He gently slipped his hand into hers. She accepted it, having resolved to go the other way from her usual impulses.

At his door, she had four choices—to remain on this side, to straddle the middle, to perch on the razor's edge, or to go with this sparkling smile to the other side...

But now what did he want... mailing her this photo, all smiles and seduction? And this pubic hair, which, let's face it, is not something one ever wants returned. It's embarrassing to know that one is shedding, and discomforting to know that one has left parts behind.

Did he want to come visit? Did he want a visa? Maybe he wanted to come to the United States to marry a rich woman and write poetry, or meet Lady Gaga. They all seemed to want that.

He had shown her a very good time. They'd giggled over red wine and ceviche late, late into the night, swirling whatever liquid she could find in the opposite direction. Then, themselves spinning until they dropped dizzy on to the bed, he was upon her—hands up her skirt—searching for said pubic hair. Her thinking then had been that plunging herself into passion might land her into the current of release she had never really felt. And maybe that might free her.

Mostly she noticed the ceiling with its particular cracks in the stucco, and how it all seemed to be swirling in the opposite direction.

Since meeting Sheerah, she had to put aside the idea that it was the right guy who would thrill her so much as to push her over the edge. She was coming to see the problem and the answer resided in her... and therefore, was truly hopeless.

She had to admit, he was cute. And seeing his photo up there on the board gave her a little pick-me-up for the sense of adventure, if not the sensations, of love.

She didn't know that he later would become part of her plan. At this point she didn't even know she would have a plan. But something told her it might be a good idea to write him back.

22 | WHAT DONNY WANTS

1. Donny wants to sleep with Ursula so badly that he's been on a juice fast for three days now.

2. At this moment, he sits in his car in the McDonald's parking lot testing himself to see if he will go in. He remains there one hour and forty-five minutes. Ultimately, he breaks down and orders a small fries with ketchup, and eats half.

3. Donny throws up in the parking lot behind his car.

That evening they were making out on her couch. Finally. Having sat through any number of chick flicks over the past weeks, he felt he had more than paid the price of admission. Tonight's feature stretched the bounds into the overly cute animals genre, and he didn't know how much of *that* he could take.

The first kiss was so "at last" that Donny missed feeling the moment. It was so "oh, no, here we go…" that Ursula missed it, too. It was enjoyable if anyone had noticed, but at this point, there had been such a line to be crossed, that's mostly what it was.

As they continued, Ursula could feel the pressure in his probing tongue, and was hoping to stall the inevitable.

"Lovers stay in each other's field for 21 days." She tried to sound casual, but it came out as more of a blurt. Like all new devotees, she was perhaps taking Sheerah's words a little too seriously, but she knew the other way got her nowhere.

"And?" he inquired.

"And," she replied, "I barely know you, and certainly don't know if I want you in my field…"

"I've already known you four and a half weeks. That's longer than 21 days, so I think I'm already *in* your field."

She considered. *He's certainly been both persistent and consistent, and being with him has been fairly easy. He's smart, makes me laugh, and eats the right kind of diet… It's obvious what he wants. I might like it, too… but why would this time be any different?* She was so tired of feeling nothing and faking it just to make someone else feel OK, or to keep them around so that something different might happen, some day. *Yet, Sheerah talks of a communion that's beyond what we consider to be the body. She says there are portals that can open… powers to be unlocked…*

In her silence Donny whispered, "Let's go to bed." Of course that was coming. In fact, she was relieved that it finally arrived, so she could stop anticipating.

"OK, but you can't stick it in," she replied.

Whatever passion had been building in Donny's johnson from their heavy petting froze there in his pants. His palms started to sweat. He was already feeling weak and woozy from lack of food; and now, confused and very annoyed. "Not stick it in? What am I supposed to do with it?"

"I don't know," Ursula said, by way of apology, "It can just lie down there between us."

"It's not lying down!"

"Then I suppose we can fiddle around a little…"

Blue balls, blue balls! blared staccato in his brain.

Warning, warning! sounded the alarm in hers.

She's a prick teasing, belly dancing, sludge-drinking prude! No woman is worth this, no woman is worth this…

Don't throw it away, don't throw it away…

Ursula took a deep breath. "I just have to do things… differently. So things can go… differently. So I can feel something." She lowered her head in shame, and he really couldn't tell what was going on. She looked like she was about to cry. He hates it when girls cry. He hates it even more when they're on the verge, and he knows it's his fault, and in that very minute he could do something to turn it around—but so many times he doesn't catch it in time, or doesn't know what to do at all. And this was one of those moments.

Do something, he screamed to himself, *do it now!* And without thinking, he put his big arms around her, and drew her into his chest. It was warm there, and she snuggled in. Relieved. And much to his surprise, she didn't cry. And even more to his surprise, he liked this feeling—warm instead of hot, easy instead of urgent.

Ah, jeez. He was going to have to get out of there fast!

23 | SHEERAH PREPARES

Sheerah could smell a change in the wind. It blew warm from the east. It carried on it the sweet smell of night blooming jasmine, so full and fragrant it nearly knocked her out. The air brushed against her cheek in a way she knew well. She put down her book and stepped off the porch into the night, and let the moonlight stream down on her. The moon was nearly full, and the constellations were glinting all around it like an elegantly crafted diamond necklace. She felt a tug on her navel that brought a sly smile to her face. She knew it was time.

Sheerah went inside and pulled out candles, and placed them on every surface. Some tall and grand, with layers and layers of dripped melted wax, some scented, some carved. She placed tapers in elaborate candelabras, and spread tiny tea lights in votives in between. Nothing was lit. Not yet.

She stripped the bed, gathered up her laundry and put it near the washer to be done. Draped colorful shawls over chairs and hung blood orange fabric as a canopy over the posts of the bed. She brought out red silk sheets that had been packed in boxes, smelling of allspice and clove. She spread them carefully on the bed—pulling up the velvet covers, arranging all the pillows in a comfortable pile.

A satisfied grin spread across her face as she busied with her preparations. Creating the temple was part of the fun. It was one of the best things a woman gets to do. Courting all of the senses.

The farmers' market was tomorrow, and they always had the ripest, freshest produce—grapes, late figs, and early avocados. She would make her own clotted cream. And melt in your mouth chocolates, yes, especially the dark ones with just a hint of chili that burst open passages through the head, and exploded on the tongue. And red wine. Or maybe an effervescent prosecco. And enough of her special elixir to keep their strength up for three days.

Tonight she would draw henna designs on the insides of her thighs. Something like a fecund flowering vine reaching up from her ankles, and blossoming at the door of her yoni. Flame colors, to match the rich bedspread from India with its reds and hot oranges, deep yellows, and cobalt blue.

This was not a woman afraid of color—anywhere. Sheerah is wont to dye her pubic hair to suit her mood, his whim, and the position of the celestial bodies. She will also dust it with spices: cinnamon, and vanilla, smelling just like apple pie. She believes, after all, the way to man's heart is through his stomach—by way of his cock.

Sheerah says to her class, "I only want a man who wants to step away from the world with me, to get lost and found in each other for days on end."

Sean would be arriving soon. No one was going anywhere when that man came to town.

24 | SID

Ursula wasn't sure how she got talked in to it, but Sid had actually met a woman from Austin, online, and needed a ride home from the airport. Ursula had said no to dog sitting the slobber dog. So, he had to let the dog sitter use his car in order to take the dog to the dog park all day, because the dog was so used to going to the office, which is why he didn't just park in long-term parking, and needed Ursula to pick him up.

Ursula had to admit, she was very curious indeed about any woman who wanted Sid, and even more curious about what kind of woman could get this guy off his computer and on to a plane to come see her.

Ursula told him she'd meet him outside the baggage claim. When she got there, the curb was empty; and there was only a recorded voice to tell her "no parking." The closest cop was another terminal down, trying to straighten out some taxicab altercation. So Ursula parked and got out of the car.

She waited at the baggage claim doors until someone came through, then she slipped right in. There was no claim ticket lady at the door. Never had been any at LAX, guess there never will be. Upstairs, they were carefully checking, scanning, and x-raying each and everyone's identity, key chains, and tonsils on the way IN, but no one was checking anything on the way OUT.

Ursula thought, if I were a terrorist, I could walk right in with a bomb in a suitcase, place it on the carousel, slip out, and *Boom!* Or place the suitcase in the corner and then slip out, and *Boom!* Or dress up like one of these begging nuns who position themselves at the bottom of the escalator, and *Boom!*

She wondered what it really took to blow up an airport, or cause someone serious damage. She wondered how there could be so much guarding at one end, while having none at the other. She wondered if it were possible to board a plane "backing in" from the bottom up. She made a mental note.

This was all before she even knew she might have a reason to want to know this.

"Jesus Christ, Urs, what is that smell?" Sid's breath strangled in his throat as soon as Ursula opened her front door. Both of them, in that moment, were rethinking her invitation to come in while she grabbed a few things she needed for the office. Living with that smell all the time, Ursula barely noticed it, until she went out and came back in. She offered him a cup of tea, because that's the polite thing to do when someone is in your house, and went off to the kitchen. Perhaps the smell of the brew would cover the odor.

Uncharacteristically, Sid was anxious to share about his weekend. Shouting to her in the other room, he said, "All we did was fight and fuck. It was pretty hot at first, cuz she fought hard, and fucked the same way… but I was noticing some serious anger management issues that were raising a red flag…"

This was the best sex (come on… only sex) he'd had in a long time, and even though he had to reroute through Phoenix to get home, he didn't care. "It's not worth it. I'm lucky I escaped with my…" Sid interrupted himself, shouting even louder, "Honestly, it smells like something died in here. Can we open a window or something?"

Ursula shouted back from the kitchen. "Can't."

Sid rolled his eyes dismissively. He thought Ursula had always been impossibly peculiar, and now this proved it.

"I mean it, we gotta go to Starbucks or something," Sid said, standing up and heading for the door. "Where's your bathroom?"

He proceeded towards the back of the apartment, hunting for the toilet. Passing by a darkened bedroom, he noticed that every inch was covered by glass bowls with something brown and slimy floating in them. And there were more bowls lining the hallway. He gasped, feeling like a character in one of those sci-fi movies where the hero discovers he's stumbled upon an alien breeding ground.

"Urs," Sid said cautiously, "What's going on here?"

Ursula suddenly appeared. "Growing mushrooms," she said, trying not to sound defensive.

"Why?"

"Because I can't kill them," she replied. "And they just keep multiplying. As of this morning, 337, and it's like… I'm in service to them, somehow."

"Service?"

"They're very special… creatures. And the tea they grow in has all these incredible healing properties. It would probably cure that flaking psoriasis you have."

"Right," said Sid, not convinced in the least.

"Wanna see something incredible?" asked Ursula.

Sid had no response. Frankly, he was afraid to move. One of these things might jump out and ingest him on the spot. Ursula closed the doors at both ends of the hallway so it was completely dark—the kind of dark so black you can't even use your eyes.

"What are we doing here?" Sid whispered, cautiously.

"Look," Ursula whispered back.

"At what?"

"They're glowing. Like the fish that glow at the darkest bottom of the sea."

"I don't see it."

Ursula was honestly surprised. "You don't see that light coming off those bowls all along that wall?"

"No… I don't."

"Or over there?"

"No."

Sid was practically swooning from the closeness in the hall. He looked at Ursula, and down at the mushrooms, then back at Ursula, and said, "You know Urs, I'm starting to think that maybe I shouldn't have been so quick to leave Janeene back there. I mean, so what if she threw the TV out the window—it *was* her TV. I still have three more vacation days. I'm going back to the airport. Maybe I can go standby and be there before she gets home from work."

"I hope you don't expect me to drive you," said Ursula, annoyed.

"I'll take a cab." Sid ran for the door.

25 | BIG ED

Suddenly, Mr. Ed found himself receiving huge *atta-boys* all around the office. His idea to use the contaminated spinach as the excuse to get rid of those damn dirt-loving organics was sheer opportunistic brilliance.

Mr. Ed was even invited to lunch at the Club with the Big Boss of AgriNu himself. The Big Boss liked Ed's initiative, liked where he was going with this, and wanted to let him run with it. Sitting back in the huge soft leather chair, aged brandy in one hand, a perfectly rolled cigar in the other, Mr. Ed thought, *Can it be this easy, after all?*

Even Bitsy seemed impressed. She was no longer "going out" for her early morning tennis matches, or her evening Beautification League meetings. She bought new sheets for the bed, and a whole new wardrobe of skimpy lingerie (at least it was new to Mr. Ed); and made herself available and open for business.

Really? This easy? he mused to himself, as he assumed the position on top of Bitsy and banged her to kingdom come.

26 | PAUL GOES TO SURVIVAL CAMP

Sleep was a problem. Whether he slipped innocently into slumber only to be overtaken by the supersonic wild ride of the "munching rodent" dreams, or whether he was awakened, choking for air by his own fitful apnea, it didn't much matter. Paul's problem with sleep, at this moment, was that he'd had none.

For days now, no really, for weeks, Paul didn't sleep but an hour or two at a time with long, endless staring spaces in between. All his digging around about AgriNu, and this new threat to the organics, froze his warning lights on.

Ursula said it was his diet. Donny said it was because he hadn't gotten laid since the early Clinton Administration. But Paul knew it went deeper than that. Those munching rodents were trying to tell him something, and he didn't want to listen. Paul had this uneasy feeling about the erosion of the world, eaten to its core by millions of sharp little teeth—a frightening image even for a confirmed paranoid.

Staring up at the cottage cheese ceiling of his bedroom—he still had asbestos because he wouldn't let anyone into his apartment to replace the ceiling for fear of bugging devices—Paul decided, *I've gotta get away for some R and R!*

All those medical studies show how sleep deprivation can produce a type of psychosis, which in turn creates all kinds of strange behaviors, and affects choices—like the one he was about to make.

Turning on his bedside lamp, he opened the magazine on his nightstand to the ad he'd seen for Back to Basics Survival Camp. It was inexpensive, and he'd always liked to camp as a kid.

He tore out the coupon for the 10% discount. Then he typed one line on his blog:

GOING OFF THE GRID.

27 | SEAN IS COMING

Sean zoomed his high-end digital Nikon to catch a close-up of the underside of the luminescent green mushroom. It had to be a long exposure, since they were way deep in the darkened forest. Mesameyama Island, in Japan, was one of only two places where these glowing mushrooms appeared. The other was in the jungle of Brazil, where he had been just prior to coming to Japan. There is a short and delicate season when these mushrooms arrive.

He and his assistant had been at this for days, nights—who knew how long in the pitch dark—waiting for the full bloom of luminescence to arrive. But that's what it took to merge enough to be able to "see" it. Appearing in the dark were not only the glowing mushroom fruit, but he could sense the entire mycelial mat beneath the ground, the huge web of tiny interconnected thread-like fibers that was the real body of this organism. The mycelia's reach was vast, extending for unseen miles, connecting everything in that forest. It provided crosstalk between plant forms, transporting nutrients... Maybe he'd been there too long, because he could swear he could hear them, feel their *mushroom mind* pulsing as one. He was not on drugs, but he might as well have been for all the information he was receiving.

Sean caught a whiff of musty earth that made his nose tickle in just that way. Abruptly, he said, "I've got enough," and packed up his personal gear, leaving his assistant to finish up. Once he hiked out into a clearing, he looked up to the night sky, and he knew it was time. The constellation of stars formed an arrow, pointing directly to Sheerah's bed.

Sean Morrisey was a nature photographer, the tracker of unique and wondrous natural treasures in remote and hidden places. Which means he was prone to disappear for long periods of time. *National Geographic* considered him their boy—that is, when they could find him.

Sean has sat with lamas and sheiks. He's photographed in the Amazon rainforest, where natives say the Mother Tree stands at the center of the world. He's been in crystal caves and sacred burial chambers, but his favorite place on earth is inside Sheerah. That's the hidden treasure place he dreams about most. Even if he doesn't stay with her for long… that is his home.

Whenever he arrives, he is never surprised to find that she has already spread silk sheets on the bed, and laid the table with scrumptious aphrodisiac delectables and beautiful flowers. That's just the way it is with them.

He's known Sheerah for a long timeless time. They met in Bali, a place far more exotic than Los Angeles, and were lovers for that time. But years ago, Sheerah came back home to look after her mother, and decided to stay because she developed a clientele who needed her.

She lives in a canyon in Malibu where she can touch the stars. When Sean comes off the road, whenever he can, he comes to her. And no matter what, he'll always come at the full moon prior to the Fall Equinox. They met under this same moon, and when the time gets near, even if he's been out in the bush for weeks without a calendar or a watch—he can sense when it's time, and he'll simply pack up and come to her. They both just know when the moment has arrived.

Sheerah loves gifts, and he loves to gift her—the more colorful the gift, the better. Rich fabrics, curious artifacts, and cultural antiquities—she now has quite a collection, and he's proud to be its curator. That look of delight and appreciation on her face quickens him to the core, and makes him want desperately to be inside that smile.

Sitting in the airport with a fertility totem wrapped together with a glowing mushroom, he admits he is tired. At age sixty, he's getting older, and feels it in his joints and dry muscles. Too much desert time. But soon all this will change. Soon he'll be inside Sheerah, and she'll be wrapped all around him like a magic medicinal vine and…

The announcement of his flight, 1247 to Los Angeles, comes over the loud speaker. He leaps up and springs for the gate. Oh, yes…

28 | PAUL DRIVES THRU

Paul hadn't been on a road trip in a very long time. He'd barely been out of the apartment in the last six weeks. All his computer research and blogging on the Internet required that he remain right in his seat surrounded by stacks of grease-stained pizza boxes and empty Gatorade bottles.

His car was neglected. Hell, his entire health and hygiene were neglected. Anything offside of his computer screen was neglected. Hey, wait… didn't he used to have a cat?

So Paul didn't check his oil and stuff like that in his car before he took off for survival camp. Who wants to bother with that shit? And besides, though admittedly he was mechanically impaired, he was too embarrassed to ask for help and have another guy put oil in his car.

All that is to say that he left LA in a hurry, heading inland towards the desert. The sun was brutal, bearing down on a car low on oil and water. Ever since NPR cut out way back in Barstow, all he had to listen to was the spurting and struggling of his 1982 Volvo.

Maybe he could take an auto mechanics class at the camp, if they offered such a thing. Different people had different survival needs. He wondered what array of courses might be offered to the urban survivor.

He traveled a long stretch of empty hot road. Power line towers marked one mile after another.

Appearing in the distance—a small shopping center. Outlet stores: Samsonite luggage, Hanes underwear seconds, and a kiosk with a sign, *Free Bibles, Free Prayer, Free Water Bottles.*

As Paul rolled closer, the kiosk looked very much like an old Photomat booth; and, in fact, was still painted in Kodak's mustard yellow and black.

Paul's car needed water. So did Paul. Whether he needed that other shit—bibles and prayer—there was no question. The answer was no.

"Hello, brother," was the sweet greeting Paul received from the young woman seated inside the booth, as he drove up to the prayer window. "Would you like to pray together, today?"

"Actually I was interested in the free water bottles," Paul replied, trying not to get sucked in to her bullshit. "I'd like two if you don't mind. One for me and one for my car here."

Patsy Patterson had been sitting in the sweltering prayer booth for over three hours. Paul was her first drive-thru all day. She had been sitting there far too long to let this one get away. The booth was a project of her church high school youth group, and she was on the high noon trainee shift. What would she tell her pastor? That she couldn't even stop one man with the Lord's words of redemption?

"Then let us pray for this water," she began. "Dear Lord, you have made the Earth and all its inhabitants, made the food and the water to sustain us…"

"Excuse me, but the sign says, *free* water bottles," Paul interrupted. "If I have to sit here and listen to that crap—that's a higher price than I want to pay."

"Prayer and gratitude could change your life," Patsy offered sincerely.

"I'm about to change my life," Paul replied.

"But will it be for good?" She tried to bring some threatening urgency to her voice.

"Hard to know," he said, and he drove on through the booth.

Paul bought a couple of new undershirts and located a cold root beer for himself. He consented to let the old Pakistani guy at the gas station look under his hood. The attendant shook his head a couple of times as ferocious steam exploded from the radiator. After a while, he filled the car with all the necessary fluids, and Paul drove off into the sun's anvil.

Looking back at the prayer booth in his rear-view mirror, Paul thought, *Why is it the religious nuts are always the ones who look like they need saving?*

Patsy wondered if she didn't have these pimples on her forehead, would he have stayed for the prayer? She wondered how it was that a guy like that could even think he could do it all on his own, without the Lord? He was so clearly in need of help. The other kids in the youth group seemed to have much better luck. They'd come back with stories of entire families dropping to their knees right there on the hot asphalt, pleading to be received and showered in the waters of the Lord's true message.

It occurred to her that instead of praying with this man, she could pray *for* him. She could pray into the water, and then drink it herself. (She was getting thirsty.) And then she could show the pastor how much water she distributed by way of empty bottles. The Pastor might just place his hand on hers like he does with that fucking Jennifer Connell.

29 | THE LARGER FIELD

In class, Sheerah speaks of Eros as the enlivening force that flows through us. It's both the spark and the stream of pleasure, the sensation that radiates outward into our *fields of existence.* She says one can access fields of existence through shared resonance, and of course one of the easiest ways to experience this resonance is through sexual communion. Another is through prayer or meditation with other people. It's a communal hum that can be felt through the body—and not just your own body and your lover's body, but, as she calls it, in the *collective body.* Like particles shimmering. This field is expansive and limitless, and is another network of communication (like the mycelium).

Trouble is, even those who can find it, may not know the extent of its potency, or the extent of its reach. She tells her students, "Feeling the collective body will change how you experience yourself in relationship to others, in an instant. It's a mind re-set for sure. And our pea-brains don't want to admit they're not in charge of the show. They'll reject any notion that comes from the experience of this field consciousness, because they didn't think it up." And that's a shame, because in that field, a speck is not just a speck, it's a part of a functioning and potent whole. But Ursula doesn't really understand any of this. She hasn't experienced it. Sheerah does. That's why she's the teacher.

It's *this* field that Sheerah cautions can get all mucked up for 21 days if shared with the wrong person. It's this field she and Sean locate when they are together.

Mmmmmmmm, Sean. Sheerah lubricates her Eros with every breath, humming her own little tune, waiting for his arrival.

30 | SURVIVALIST CAMP

What Paul didn't know was that the survivalist camp he selected was a nudist survival camp. It said nothing about that in the ad, nor was it apparent from his conversation with the overly clothed guard at the gate who questioned Paul from behind the site of an automatic rifle. After a long interrogation, Paul was allowed to drive into the camp.

He parked his car alongside some other vehicles. He saw an array of temporary structures, everything from strung tarps to Quonset huts. He imagined these buildings served as classrooms, bunks, or a dining hall, perhaps? It was all pretty scruffy. There were no toilets in sight.

The real survivalist compound was top secret, and nowhere to be found. This camp was erected so they could take on a few students and show them a thing or two. Survival was a hot topic of interest, and they needed the extra income. With each natural disaster and "socialist" bill passed in Congress, their enrollment grew. More and more people were finally becoming convinced, or sufficiently afraid, that we were headed for complete social breakdown, and they'd better be prepared.

Paul saw a small, unclothed group taking apart a motor in one area; another group worked together filtering water from huge collection barrels. They seemed highly focused and detailed in their procedures. Muscular and fit supermen without capes, or tights or even underwear, for God's sake.

Papa John, the leader of the camp, met Paul at the center of the compound. As this large, naked man approached, it was easy to see why he had been selected as alpha male. Paul introduced himself.

"You people out there are finally smelling the coffee," Papa John began. "Sniveling around trying to figure out how the hell to G.O.O.D. when the S.H.T.F. You bet you're gonna need to know how to do it yourself—not this pansy-ass 'do it for me' excuse for a life you've been living. You've got to provide your own food, your own water, your own power. You've got to know how to protect yourself from the damned government trying to take over your life, and from your good neighbors when they all come running after what you've got. They may be all nice and friendly right now, but wait till you've got the only can of beans left on the block. You may have to shoot your own brother in the head." He laughed hard, amused by the picture.

Paul just stood there.

"I am your supreme commander," Papa John continued, "and if you want to survive survival school, you'll listen to what I say, and follow every order. Learning to survive means knowing who to listen to—or you are fucked. Am I clear, cupcake?"

Paul managed to nod, yes.

"Good. Stay awake, because in a very short time you're going to learn what you need, and how to build it: BOL, BOV, BOB, and PYS."

Paul clearly had no idea what he was talking about.

Papa John declared, "Bug Out Location, Bug Out Vehicle, Bug Out Bag, and how to Protect Your Shit. That's what you came for, right?"

Not exactly the R and R Paul had pictured. *Was this nudity really a necessary part of the course work,* he wondered, *or was it just part of the harassment?*

"Exposing yourself to adverse conditions will prepare you for when you are not prepared. Try digging a ditch in only what God gave you."

Paul let out a nervous laugh.

Papa John threw up his hands. "People think this is some sort of joke. You can keep your head up your butt and laugh all you want—but the joke's on you."

Paul knew it was sign up or shut up. He slowly dropped his pants. Papa John smacked him on his bare ass saying, "Thatta boy," and walked on.

Paul scanned the landscape. Everyone was busy rigging, repairing, and making provisions for "the end" that now seemed a whole lot closer than ever before. All Paul had seen so far were men, all seemingly more endowed than he. It takes a certain kind of man to commit to his own survival in the elements, and it takes a certain confidence in what you were given to parade around naked all the time. So, it was unexpected to see Lindey, standing by the fire pit, wearing nothing but Gore-Tex, high laced hiking boots. She was blonde and beefy, and could wield an ax like nobody's business. She had a tattoo of the state of Florida spread across her abdomen.

Paul approached her, awkward and curious. "I noticed there aren't many women here. Why is it you don't see many women survivalists?"

"Because," she replied in a post-feminist fervor, "women already know how to survive. They survive crippling high heels, panty hose, lower wages, childbirth, football, groping hands of smarmy stepfathers, and stupid questions that are transparent come-ons. What else ya got?" She brought the ax down right in the center, jettisoning the huge log into two flying parts.

Struck silent, Paul's only response was his underused, overexposed erection pointing straight at Miami.

31 | LIFE CYCLES AND RHYTHMS

M. Earth knows, any good courtship begins with a good song. Or at least it doesn't hurt. Ask pretty much any animal in the kingdom. Blue Whales each sing a signature ballad that's all their own. Dolphins learn the song-names of the others in their pods, and sing out when calling to them. Monkeys, wolves, birds; chirps, howls, squawks. Bees dance—and that's a good thing.

Insects, especially, fill the air with their crooning. Since they comprise multitudes and are short-lived, large numbers of couples are singing, courting, and mating all the time.

They live through cycles, court through cycles—all cued by M. Earth Herself. Humans think they are the choreographers of their own courtship song and dance, but their predictable, sometimes bizarre behavior is easier to explain if we understand that they are cued just the same as the insects, by a change in the weather, the smell of spring, the position of the moon, who knows really? It's all a mystery.

Take the 13-year cicadas in the southern regions of North America. M. Earth designed them to lay dormant in the ground for twelve years, eleven months. Then suddenly, on a cue we humans can't hear, they burrow up from the ground, beetle-like, crawling up onto the faces of houses, the doors of cars, ladders leading up to billboards, becoming the billboards themselves—an advertisement for mayhem. They crawl onto any available vertical surface and hang in wait for days. Then, on another signal, they crack through their casings, open black lacy wings, sprout red buggy eyes, and fly into the sky, showering down their empty shells like a burst jackpot piñata on the terrified people below.

Crunch.

New at flight, they bump into everything, buildings, street signs, flying into open car windows at stoplights, swirling the sky black. Yawners beware.

Within only a few days they will all take to the trees. A particular kind of tree that only grows in that region of the country. The male will make a swelling cacophonous sound to call the female, and she will sing a swell song back.

When they do mate, the trees are rockin'. Post coital, she will inject her eggs into the tiniest branches of this particular kind of tree; and those swollen and burdened twigs will fall to the ground below. The larvae, millions of them, will crawl back into the earth—some of them directly into the holes left from the emergence of their parents' generation—where they will rest in the ground, undetected for another thirteen years. Go figure.

Cicadas mate because it is time. Grasshoppers become locusts because of the times they are in. Both like to sing about it. Sean and Sheerah know exactly when the right time has come. Donny and Ursula are still off the beat. Paul, who does not sing, finds himself humming "Just give me some kind of sign, girl…" softly to himself. Does he mean Florida?

32 | SHEERAH AND SEAN PLUG IN

Sheerah's smile beamed softly across her face as she opened her eyes from her evening "beditation." She bounced up from the center of the bed and opened the door. Sean was standing on the other side. She said, "Yes," and he said, "Hell, yes!" And the two of them fell into rapturous embrace, him kicking the door with his foot—where it remained shut for the next three days.

Though there was so much to talk about, the two remained silent, with the exception of the occasional exhales of his delight and relief. She took him by the hand and led him to the bath. The bathtub glowed with the reflection of candlelight, warm water drawn with ylang-ylang flowers, and sandalwood. The tub was big enough for two, but right now she encouraged Sean to slide into the water while she remained outside. She cascaded the warm scented flow over his hair, face, and body from a purple cut-crystal goblet. The stress from his journey rippled out into the water, allowing him to come into his senses.

She began to hum. A tune they'd learned together one evening in Bali. He joined her.

When he felt restored, but not too relaxed, they traded places, Sheerah slid across him as she slipped into the water, closed her eyes, and rested her head back against a pillow he formed from a folded towel.

As he poured the water over her body, he could not resist running the back of his hand ever so lightly over her ripe breasts, mounded above the water's surface like enchanted islands.

"Mmmmmm," she purred, a delicious fullness spreading across her upper and lower lips. It doesn't take much to bring her to life. That got his attention. He continued to pour across her shoulders and chest. Then he lifted her legs out of the water one by one to let her feel the warmth trickle down towards her flame-orange, open smile.

That was it. He had to have her. He didn't want to be so rude as to cut her luxuriating time short, but the feelings were intensifying inside him. As long as he was closer to her, he could wait. So he slipped into the water, facing her from the opposite end of the tub. Making lots of soapy lather, he caressed her foot, working his way up her leafy vine, stopping teasingly short of her bloom. She did the same for him, but he was ticklish, so she went instead to his calves.

Finally she turned around and crawled on top of his thighs. His magic wand reached up to touch her magic lamp, rubbing gently to be given his wishes. He remained on the outside of her body, his hands gently cupping her breasts from behind, toying with her nipples. And without much ado—he gave her the first of the welcome home presents he had brought her.

They dried each other in warm towels, and wrapped up in Chinese silk robes. She lit all the candles she had laid out around the house—there were at least 20 in the bedroom. She brought out platters of sweets and savories; soft cheeses with figs and lavender honey, grapes coated in crystallized ginger and almond powder, and the ruby red drink she called "the elixir." She beckoned him to the temple.

"Sheeraaaaaaaahhhhhh," was his elated response at the sight of it all. The bed was ringed with colorful candlelight, one big circle of delight.

Propped up by all the pillows, they sat on the bed and fed each other. The Eros between them heightened the taste of each morsel. When he licked the last of the ruby mustache from his upper lip, Sean looked at Sheerah with one eyebrow up that asked, *Now?* She gave him the sweet nod of agreement, *Now.*

He calls it "Plugging In"—the way he will place himself inside her for a "direct line" to the cosmos. She will reach out with her limbs and bring in the heavens, the full and starry sky with all the constellations; and he in turn will pull up all the earth's secrets, and pour them into her.

Global, Holy Communion. They can stay this way for a long time. And then they switch. He'll be the stars; she'll be the ground. And switch again, passing notes back and forth, many times, never letting go of the "main feed." For hours, they'll become the sustained ecstatic nexus of all the wonder of the Universe.

And then after a timeless forever, a fountain of fluid will go *whoosh* inside her own fluid universe, and the moment will be sealed. Then they'll lie back in the silenced silence. And they did.

Neither one wanted to be the first to break the feeling by uttering a word—but one was trying to escape through Sean, and was having its way… something like the most spacious and fantasmic "Wow," though it came out as "Let's eat!"

They bounced out of bed and went to the fridge. The light was nearly blinding. Grabbing strawberries and sweetened raw cream, they crawled back into bed, circled around each other, and slowly dipped and fed one another the creamy redness. And chocolate. It was dark and rich, and seemed to satisfy every cell.

Finally, it was time to unwrap the gifts from each other, and let the stories unfurl along with them. Sheerah always delighted in his exotic gifts, and was like a child when it came to wrapping and bows. She pulled apart the ribbons with glee, opening up a deep indigo velvet cloth. Inside were a carved phallus and an amazing mushroom.

There was only a faint glow coming from the mushroom's now shriveling body. He showed her photographs of the mushrooms in their full prime, greeny-glow against a pitch-black void. Even their mycelium underneath the soil had phosphorescence to it. Who knows why? They could eat the mushroom and frame the photographs. "It's not psychedelic," he said, "but it definitely has something to say."

She gifted him a special mixture of essential oils that would keep him strong and connected, and also acted as a mosquito repellent.

And so it was they spent their days and nights plugged in, alternately feeding their senses, making love, and resting in beautiful dreams together—breathing in the other's field with every breath, forming a field of their own.

33 | URSULA SAYS YES AND IT DOESN'T GO WELL

"What?" Donny asked, suddenly stopping. "Aren't you enjoying this?"

"Frankly, no." Ursula said. "It's not you."

Donny had been doing his thrusting thing, his G-tickle thing, his circular round the world thing—what he thought of as his best moves. But Ursula, while trying to appear interested, was not getting off, was not changing her color or her breath, or showing any of the other heated physiological changes you see on those science shows on Discovery. Instead, she was memorizing her ceiling—a ceiling she already knew too well.

Somehow Donny, through all his badgering and general pushiness had persuaded her to consent to having sex. He was cute, charming, seductive, playful. His appeal was appealing. She knew she might be falling back into an old pattern, but she thought, this time it could be different. She'd been feeling herself opening to him, feeling more hopeful… but here she was again… looking at that ceiling.

And though it could be said about Donny that what he lacked in sensitivity he made up in technique, a greater man, or lesser one, would have just gone on without her to the finish line. But he was, at heart, a performer; and without an enthusiastic audience, there simply was no show.

"It *is* me," he said, his erection flattening out faster than a fallen soufflé. He thought, *There it is, the "it's not you, it's me"* line employed by him many times as a graceful get-out-as-fast-as-you-can move. And here it was being used on him!

He slid right out of her like an afterbirth, rolled over onto his back, and stared up at the same ceiling. There was an interesting water spot in the shape of Elvis—but now was not the time to bring it up. Damn, he wanted a cigarette!! He didn't have any on him because of her, and now she'd flat out blue-balled him without a decent outlet.

"No, really, it's me. I tried to tell you," Ursula managed, despite her embarrassment. "It's not the first time. I just don't... feel much down there."

"I could do something else. Another way..." he offered.

"Naw," Ursula replied. "At this point it's just annoying. I did try to tell you..." She got up out of the bed and padded off to the bathroom, leaving Donny alone with his aberration of Elvis, his aching balls, and an intense nicotine craving.

That was it? he thought. She didn't even offer him a blow job. She did offer him a greenie-meanie shake to restore his energy, which he quickly declined. If he were going to suffer, he'd rather do it in his own debauching way.

Once inside the bathroom, she sat down on the toilet, her head in both hands. *I knew it, I knew it, I knew it!* She was really starting to like him, he was being so interested and kind and... *It didn't matter one bit, did it? Same outcome as always. What's the use of all this belly dancing? Of making new discoveries, of building new hope when it's always the same? Something's terribly wrong with me, terribly dead.*

Ursula recalled what Sheerah keeps on saying, "Open to yourself first. Cultivate your own sensation. Your orgasm belongs to you." *What orgasm?*

Ursula remained on the toilet. There was no way she was going out there. Not for a long time. She was humiliated enough on her own without hearing whatever angry disappointment he had for her because he didn't get off. She knows from past experience, the right thing to do to would be to make up for her lack, but not now.

It would be wonderful if he were rapping gently on the door inquiring how she was doing. But she heard no such raps.

Meanwhile, he was thinking, *Can't she just come out here and let us try another way? Does it all have to be so serious?* But he saw no such movement.

And this went on for at least half an hour before Donny decided to get dressed and go home by way of the Italian deli.

A friend of Ursula's always says you can cut right to the chase of a long story by asking, "So how did you leave it?"

How did they leave it? Not well.

34 | TRYING TO PITCH A TENT

Paul laid awake that first night, stuffed into a tight mummy bag on the cold ground, inside his pathetic little tent with one side so collapsed it was practically lying on top of him. He'd expected this trip to be rejuvenating and uplifting. What it *was*, was miserable.

Hell, if he was going to be up all night and miserable, he might as well be in his own bed. Here the sky was too vast. He was feeling dwarfed by its enormity and diminished by lights that were too long dead. He resolved to get out more… and understood better why he didn't.

It was the noises that got to him. All the noises in this alleged silence. Crickets, crickets, crickets, and then bullfrogs croaking it up in between the pause in the crickets' pulsing racket. Somebody was banging off shots in the distance. But more alarming, somebody or something large was rustling in the bushes right there between his tent and the shit hole. A snake, a bear? Sasquatch?

He pulled a half empty beer can into his tent in case he had to piss before daylight.

As he lay on the ground, he felt each rock beneath him poking into his back. And the ground sloped. He realized that his head was pointing downward. Of the few things he remembered from Cub Scouts, one was *Never sleep with your head down hill…* or what? All the blood would rush to his head, and it would burst open like an over-ripe melon… that's what. Or if that didn't happen, all the blood would drain out of his feet, and he wouldn't be able to run, should that rustling in the bushes turn out to be a bear. Or if the bear didn't want him, he'd be lying there even longer, draining—and would lose all the circulation in his legs, and they'd be forced to amputate.

So he tried to turn around while remaining in his sleeping bag that he was pretty much wedged into anyway. He flipped around like some fried fish dancing on a hot skillet, knocking into tent poles, knocking over his lantern, and collapsing his tent all around him.

Anyone looking from the outside would have seen a tangled mound of cloth with an occasional blip of light alternating with the sound of the word, "Fuck." "God damn son of a bitch, fuck! fuck! fuck!" were the exact words—and then another blip of light.

Inside, Paul was groping to right the lantern, while cursing "Who the fuck am I fucking kidding? This fucking fuck of a fuck tent. I could be fucking home right now watching Bill Fucking Maher reruns. Fuck!!"

Suddenly, he felt his tent fabric swishing this way and that. The sound of a heavy plastic zipper. *Fuck*, he thought, too scared to call out, *bears can fucking unzip a tent!* Then a bright light blinded his eyes; and instead of a carnivorous growl, he heard a friendly voice. "You all right in there?"

It was Lindey, the girl from Florida. Paul would rather it was the bear, at least then he'd be put out of his mortified misery. Oh, no. She was probably used to these burly, action-figure men who could find their way out of the woods with a single match and a stick of gum—and here he was, swaddled in his own humiliation.

"Wind's kicking up," is all she said. She sounded a whole lot more friendly than when he had met her before. Something about helping other folks brought out the best in her, she would tell him later.

"Need some help?" she asked.

"Shine your flashlight in here, would you, so I can find my lamp," was the only thing he could bring himself to ask for, though he needed much more.

She shined her light around as they ruffled through the tent cloth, found his lamp, and turned it back on. She strapped her flashlight onto the center of her head to free both hands, and started sorting through the mess for the poles and uprooted stakes.

Paul pretended to be doing something valuable that contributed to the re-erecting the tent, but he was at a loss—which is how he'd gotten there in the first place.

Embarrassing as it was, he was glad it was Lindey helping him, and not one of those "big guys" he'd met at dinner. His public shame would certainly have been part of their fee. Lindey was just being, well... she was being capable. She was doing what she knew how to do—and that was all. She had little to prove to anyone, it seemed.

It became obvious to Paul that the best way he could help was to get out of the tent. He found the opening, and crawled out into the night. There it was again. That vast open sky with all those twinkling stars that doesn't exist in LA. The moon had risen overhead and was shining a powerful headlamp on them both. He could see she was wearing clothes. Even nudists, he supposed, don't want to freeze their butts off.

She had found the tent poles, and asked Paul to hold the clips of the tent while she slid the rebuilt poles into place. This kind of teamwork was new to him. *When had he become such an isolated guy?* he asked himself. Truth was, he couldn't remember not being isolated.

The tent was making sense to him now, where it needed to be held up, where it needed to be secured to the ground. How the hell would he know this? He was raised in a high-rise apartment. Lindey hammered in the last peg with a large rock. She pulled on the tent in various places to check its stability. All secure.

They stood on either side of the tent, but the moonlight cast their shadows on the ground as nearly touching.

"I have a little beer in my tent," he fumbled, "if it didn't spill all over."

"No thanks," she said, "I gotta get back to my bunk. I'm on breakfast duty in the morning." Lindey shrugged and walked off.

Paul called after her, "Thanks a lot."

Paul crawled back into his tent, back in his bag, back on his back, and stared up at the tent roof again—only this time he wasn't thinking about the stars. He was thinking that all the world's mysteries are just codes to be broken. Once the pattern is perceived, one can step inside; and the secrets are revealed. The tent was once, only a short time ago, impenetrable to him, and now—he got it. He got the pattern, and now understood all tents everywhere. What could be next?

What *was* next was footsteps, zipper, and a billow of sleeping bag *gooshing* through the doorway, followed by Lindey.

"Changed my mind," she said, as she laid her bag next to his, took off her clothes and her boots, and got in.

As soon as Paul saw her tip of Florida pointing ever so suggestively down, his own tip pointed straight up like a resurrected tent pole.

"You can fuck me if you want," she said. "I know a man needs to be able to say thank you—and words don't always come so easy."

And so it was that Paul had a bunkmate for the rest of his stay at camp—because he couldn't say thank you enough.

35 | HOW LINDEY ENDED UP THERE

Lindey had been on a work-study program at the camp for over six months. She arrived, having hitchhiked with one of the guys who supplied the munitions, and stayed after he moved on. Because she was so competent, and could wield an ax like Paul Bunyan, Papa John created a place for her at the compound. She was one of only three women among the twenty or so men, and the only woman who was not married.

Even though these guys were horny as goats, more so because they were isolated and got so pumped, here a woman could count as a man. Lindey was as good or better than any of them at all these basic survival skills, so she had their respect, and they let her alone. She could run around in the natural (without a damn strangulation bra, thank you very much), and no one dared touch her titties because they knew she'd shoot them right there on the spot.

She could have her pick of any of the men at any time, but it would only create rutting and fighting among the others. She chose Paul because he was an outsider, and he'd be gone soon. Short, full on, and over, that's how she wanted it. The men at the camp didn't get it, they couldn't figure out why she would choose such a scrawny wimp—and she liked that.

She knew the powers women had over men, even when they weren't trying. She despised girlie-girls who insidiously manipulated by playing flirty and silly. The men got what they deserved for falling for such play-acting. Even more, she hated the men who assumed that all women, *and ten-year-old girls,* wanted this kind of attention—even when their actions said no. And their words. And their fists.

A woman had to do everything a man could do, and better, in order to be relieved of their "help." Men were allowed to walk around free. A woman, somehow, always had to be in some sort of relationship to men, or in comparison, or in service to them. If Adam had been made from Eve's rib (which makes more sense biologically), it'd be a whole different story.

She thought about joining a colony of women only—but when they all started cycling together, as women who live together tend to do, jeez! That much out-of-whack emotion was too much for anyone! To be *equal* to a man, in the company of men—much more balanced. And she had to admit that these men, as obsessed and extreme as they might be, had a courage of their convictions that she could align with, and daresay—trust.

Paul had come to survivalist camp motivated by his political beliefs and the acute need to get out of town. He had chosen it because it sounded like a vacation place for misfits. He hadn't reckoned that he'd be a misfit *among* misfits.

And yet, until now, Paul had never met anyone who matched his level of anger and suspicion. These guys were as pissed off as he was. Granted, their complaints about the government went off in the opposite direction of his leftist leanings, and they were horrible racists; but still, they could all be pissed off together in one cabal of "brotherly hate." What a huge relief it was, for once, not to be considered paranoid. In fact, one of them referred to him as a stupid *cocky-optimist!* Him!

But unlike Paul, they didn't just sit around and complain. They were Men of Action. Warriors. Revolutionaries. Paul recognized he had a thing or two he could learn from them, and they were surprisingly open-handed in showing him what he needed to know.

He learned survival skills: fire starting, knot tying, food storage, water filtration, temporary shelter building, generating electricity, and first aid. They were big on seed saving which surprised him. These burly guys came off more as hunters than planters. His favorite activity, besides thanking Lindey, was learning to shoot a gun. They couldn't believe a man could live this long and never have fired a gun, let alone owned one. They gave him a hard time, and a strong rationale to purchase one right there on the spot. Which he did. He bought a pistol and an automatic rifle; and with them, a new sense of himself as a man. Nothing in his misspent youth of video and computer games could hold a candle to the real thing.

Lindey could outshoot him any day. That should go without saying, right? But she had patience, and even compassion, because he was learning something she knew was good for him. Fed by that patience, he grew into a somewhat decent marksman, in every way.

36 | THE 4TH DAY

On the morning of the 4th Day, Sheerah opened the front door, and Sean squinted against the bright sunlight. He was packed, dressed, and all ready to go; but hung back, hesitating…

"My next job doesn't start for two weeks," he said. "We could stay just like this for a while longer."

"We'd burn each other up," Sheerah replied.

"Yeah!" he said with wicked glee. "That could be fun." He was a man who thrived on intensity.

She nudged him playfully out the door.

Turning back to her, he said, "You are my gateway to the wonder."

"You are my spaceship explorer who fuels the mother ship." She smiled. "You've got a mission, Mister."

He leaned down, and there were her lips, ready for his. The two of them entered into the kiss that could last an eternity, but really only lasted five minutes, which is still long by most people's standards. The parting of the kiss was as mutual as the beginning. How do they do that?

She watched him leave, memorizing his gait, feeling the movement of his hips inside her own. He would be back. For now she had plenty to sustain her, and plenty of laundry to do.

37 | WHY MEN LIKE SPORTS

It might look like Donny was staying at his Hollywood-bungalow apartment watching TV sports all day long, sulking, but really he was *remasculating.*

Donny says that men like sports because they have to yell at something…

"NO WAY, you fucking fuck!"

"Are you out of your mind?!?!?!!!"

"Go, go, go! He's safe!"

"Oh, Christ! Kill me now…"

And sports are one of the only places a man's allowed to yell and get away with it. Think about it. In any other situation he'd be considered a raging madman, or a dangerous savage. They'd lock him up. War is another place where men can curse and yell all they want—but the consequences are way too steep.

Television serves many purposes—one is to have something to yell at in your own home… like sports.

What all that yelling does is it clears the mind. *The Masculine Mind.* Donny's theory postulates: if men spend too much time with women and do *not* watch sports, they have no outlet whatsoever for yelling, and it festers in their gonads, and they get so backed up it goes permanent on them. (Or they become abusive, and violent, and wholly unattractive.)

Drinking a heavy volume of alcohol removes the social inhibitions, increases the yelling, and thus amplifies the whole *remasculation* process.

Donny says for a man to *remasculate,* he needs to rid himself of the presence of the female. Get the women out, out, out. Send them to the kitchen, which is where they want to be anyway, out of the line of fire. A man must flush his body with testosterone, without female interference. Yes, that's it.

He sends the testosterone up from the testicles, up through:

The pelvis

The heart (Yes, it's true.)

The chest and lungs

The mind…

In that order.

For some men, it shoots right up to the brain directly, like clanging the bell at the carnival. Those are the guys who get "big ideas" as soon as it clears.

But when men are not cleared, they can become anything from ambivalent to lost. If they're playful, they can get away with "boyish." If they're not, they get labeled "adolescent," and "hopeless." None of which holds much appeal.

Occasionally a man is in the presence of a very sensual female and can *remasculate* through the polarity of her extreme feminine. His then-energized masculine can melt her further into her deep feminine, and so it builds back and forth. But they each have to remain strong in their opposite poles. A collapse in the middle, and they'll tumble into muddle and confusion.

Ursula was not enough of a sensual anything to *remasculate* Donny on her own. Nor did he want her to be. Those kinds of women were really scary to him. They'd work their hoodoo on you, and you'd find yourself doing all sorts of crazy shit like putting her perfume on so you can smell her all day…

And besides, he liked sports too much… in fact, he was going out to meet a few guys at a local sports bar to watch The World Series, as soon as this football game went into halftime.

He had to wonder though, in the time outs, if Ursula's problem was his fault? She said it was *her,* but was it him? Maybe he needed some new moves, some… Bottom line, it was over, so why think about it?

38 | PAUL DRIVES BACK THRU

Paul had stopped here once before, on the way to the survivalist camp. Now, on the way back, he was indeed a different guy. He couldn't quite go so far as to call himself a *man,* and therefore *a different man,* but a different *guy* would do.

After spending two weeks at the camp, chopping his own wood, fetching his own water, what began as aches were actually sprouting into muscles; and there was a certain swagger of confidence he felt walking in his now broken-in boots. He was feeling about as macho as he ever had.

Lindey was sitting beside him in his Volvo station wagon, about as dressed as he'd ever seen her. Her tattoos were peeking out from beneath her midriff tee.

Paul and Lindey pulled up to the gas station. He needed to tank up for the evening drive across the Mojave, and Lindey needed to tap out. She'd been holding it, at Paul's insistence, for the past twenty minutes. Though it did not bode well for his new survivalist persona, he just wasn't ready for public off-road peeing.

"The revolution will not have flush toilets," Lindey sneered at him, truly pissed off. As soon as they stopped, she bolted out of the car and ran for the restroom, spitting over her exit, "Controlling asshole! You still don't know shit about freedom."

"I don't show my freedom by defecating all over the damned place like an animal."

"You're still a wimp."

A wimp? He'd show her who was a wimp! He ran over and blocked the door to the bathroom.

She looked at him scary hard. "You want me to do it right here on your brand new, little REI boots? Get out of my way." And she pushed past him into the bathroom and slammed the door.

"People certainly change out of context," Paul grumbled to himself. He wasn't accustomed to personal arguments because he was never around any people. But he sure didn't like it, and he certainly wasn't going to let this spoil his new heightened sense of self.

He walked back to his car and began self-serving his gas, checking his oil and water—all things he now performed on his own, with confidence. What was she talking about? He *was* a new man. It was great to feel this way. His *fuerte*. His mastery. His sexual power. He glanced across the road to the outlet mall where he'd stopped on the way out here. How different it all seemed now. He saw the little converted Kodak booth and remembered there was free drinking water there.

Patsy had been sitting in that tiny hot box of a drive-thru prayer shack nearly sweating herself back to Jesus since eleven that morning, and it was now a quarter to six. Not a single soul had driven up today, not even for the free bottled water.

She wondered, if this was truly the Lord's calling, why was it so boring? Even her attempts to pray for the water couldn't sustain her interest over these scorching days. Was she the only one who knew the truth, and all those others whose cars whizzed by might as well have kept on driving straight to hell? That's where they were going.

As the newest member of her church youth group to run the prayer booth, she was going to need some serious seniority to get off this shift. She desperately needed to talk with some of those drive-bys to move her up the ladder into the cooler hours of the day.

Without much awareness at all, Paul found himself walking across the hot pavement of the gas station, across the road, right up to that drive-thru prayer booth. He looked inside to see the young woman gazing down in full concentration, doing cat's cradle with a red string. She was near woozy from the heat, and he could see tender beads of perspiration trickle down the fine hairs at her temples.

He stood quietly, watching the patterns she made with the string—her fingers stuck in a web of repetition. She seemed so earnest, and so trapped in that tiny booth, weaving the very net that bound her to its stifling confines. Bound, like he used to be. And maybe still was, but desperately didn't want to be. And could prove he wasn't… and could help *her* not to be.

Patsy was thinking of all the ways she wanted to get out of there, when she felt the presence of somebody. She looked up at the window, and saw this guy she remembered coming through the other week—the one she had been praying for—only now he seemed different. Maybe her prayers had worked after all. Maybe this was a miracle, and she was part of it.

So when Paul held out his hand to her, without a beat, she untangled her string and took his hand—and they both ran giggling back to his Volvo, got in, and drove off into the desert, like outlaws on the run.

They drove, mostly in silence, except for a short giggle or a smile, or the offering of some salty road trip foods like pork rinds and Cheetos, extra spicy, followed by the offering of bottled prayer water. They drove into the night until they could no longer see the road. Then they stopped at a lone motel.

She wanted to save him, he wanted to free her, and they went about trying just that.

As she started to stretch across the queen-size bed, it took only moments for her to realize that she was stretched as far as she'd ever been from her home and everything she knew, and she snapped back. She panicked. She wailed in remorse. She prayed to the Lord for forgiveness. He offered to drive her back.

They drove, again, mostly in silence; only it had a different meaning. Truth is, *he* was the one who wanted to be freed, and *she* was the one who wanted to be saved, and they had it all backwards. They drove past a hitchhiker on the road as they were coming back into town.

He took Patsy right back to the drive-thru prayer booth. She gave him a shy kiss on the cheek, and a short prayer of "God be with you." She reached into the booth, grabbed her colorful string, and kept on walking.

Paul did a U-turn in the parking lot, and headed back out of town.

When he approached the hitchhiker, he slowed to a stop, opened the passenger door, and let Lindey in.

"Asshole," she said.

"I'm sorry."

"Didn't think you had it in you."

"Yeah," he said, kind of amazed he did.

Lindey took a long look at him, cranked up the radio, pulled off her boots, put her bare feet on the dashboard, and away they drove.

39 | THE AWAKENING

Ursula had come to Sheerah's tantric belly dance classes because of the bangles and jingle jangles. At first, she remained in the class because of a certain sense of sisterly belonging she felt with the other dancers. But it didn't take her long to realize she was truly there to listen to Sheerah's wise-woman instruction about the fullness of innate feminine nature. Her innate feminine nature, it was confirmed, was puny, gray, and completely vacant.

Not only did it not go well with Donny, Ursula could see that she wasn't progressing like some of the other members of the class. Their hips were full and fluid. Her hips remained stiff and jerky. The others shimmied with knowing smiles on their faces. Ursula's face knew nothing.

After class, this night, Ursula kept hanging around. Not wanting to leave, but not able to come forward with her question. What was her question anyway? She felt herself flushing red and hot inside, the formation of words stuck like peanut butter in her throat.

She noticed new photographs hanging on the wall. Green glowing mushrooms. Could it be? Other mushrooms that glowed?!

"My sweetie photographed those in Japan," Sheerah told her when she noticed Ursula's fascination. "Amazing, no? Deep in the dark forest, they produce their own light. Why? So the ants can see where they're going? Who knows?"

Ursula wanted to say that she had mushrooms at home that glowed, but instead blurted out, "I want to have an orgasm!"

It surprised the both of them, the velocity of that declaration and the sudden change of subject. Sheerah could see Ursula's embarrassment. Such a thing to be welling up inside, the courage or the sheer impulse it must have taken to bring it forward. She replied with an insider's certainty, "If the mushrooms can be all aglow, why not you?"

Ursula was still roasting in the heat of shame.

"The mushrooms," Sheerah explained compassionately, "recognize that they're an expression of a much larger body of belonging. That, in itself, can make them glow. They know how to feed and be fed—and it gives them great pleasure to do so. What gives you great pleasure, Ursula?"

She had to think about it. "Traveling, and sending others to travel."

"That's great," Sheerah exclaimed. "Think of your orgasm as the expression of your capacity for joy. Open and unstoppable, joyous travel. What blocks it is fear. What are you afraid of?"

"Not having an orgasm," was her immediate reply. Then she considered for a moment. "Being seen," she said. "Being seen... with my face all wrinkled up and my voice too loud and... then this guy... he'll have seen me so... exposed." She couldn't believe she actually said this out loud, but it was the truth.

Sheerah said gently, "Your orgasm is the overflow of your pleasure. The gift of its aliveness belongs to you. If, and when, you want to share it with another, that's also up to you. You may never want to, and that's fine; but at least you can cultivate the sensations for yourself. Right? You're not afraid to be seen by yourself... right?"

Ursula had no response.

"When you unlock your pleasure, you unlock your power. And that can change anything, including the laws of physics, and the world, as we know it. Can we try something?" Sheerah asked, inviting Ursula to make herself comfortable on a huge pile of soft, silk pillows. She encouraged Ursula to place the pillows for support under her head, neck, hips, legs; and then to let all her weight drop and just sink down. Ursula had gotten so tense from her confession, she welcomed the rest.

Sheerah led her into an exercise of gently moving her tongue on the inside of her mouth. At first Ursula felt like she was chewing a wad of gum, but eventually her movement softened; and her tongue relaxed and moved ever so gently, ever so smoothly. Her mouth became wet with saliva. Any surface her tongue touched felt tingly and alive; and that tingly aliveness began to spread throughout her body, and landed right down "there."

She had never felt real satisfaction "there" before—but suddenly she felt as if she had two tongues, one above and one below. The more one licked, the more the other licked. Sweet moisture came into her vagina.

Sheerah could see what was happening to Ursula. She could see the gentle waves that were rippling downward through her torso, like a big neon arrow pointing the way.

She encouraged Ursula to fall back deeper into the plush pillows behind her, to feel their silky textures, their jeweled colors, to feel their invitation through her skin. She told Ursula to let her legs part, feel the silks of her costume drape along the insides of her thighs, and let whatever movements come into her pelvis.

Ursula didn't know whether to allow them to enter, or to shut them out. They were so new. Her mind tangled in a knot of self-conscious confusion.

"Keep sucking your tongue," Sheerah called out like a cheerleader. "The tongue is everything!" Sheerah turned on some World Beat music that had a strong compelling rhythm and a sweet sustaining melody. The music could carry her.

Ursula returned to her tongue sucking. Letting it change shape inside her mouth, she felt her sensations return. Felt a build-up, engorging in her clitoris, and she felt her pelvis move—on its own. She marveled… *on its own!!* Had anything in Ursula's life ever really moved on its own? She pulled herself back.

"Let yourself go into it," Sheerah called sweetly. "Ride the sensation, suck your tongue! Let your hips roll! Unlock your pleasure!"

Once again Ursula dove into herself, licking the roof of her mouth, and felt the licking of her other tongue. The rolling movement was starting to take over again—spine arching, head reaching back. Sheerah was right there. "Stay with it. Be luscious… put your finger in your mouth… suck on that!"

Ursula did, and yet another wave gushed through her. She wanted to ride it, but doubt gripped her. She didn't know if it would come, if it would actually happen, if she could let it. Was she close to the edge? Could she bear to stay with it long enough to actually peak? When? How much more…?

Eyes closed tight, her clitoris began throbbing and gathering, wet and building, up and up—and oh, my God—Sheerah's tongue was on Ursula's pink lady, and she was sucking and slurping and licking with the wild snake that lives inside her mouth. Ursula was climbing and climbing, and she heard moans and screams coming out of her own throat; and she was exploding inside like a fireworks light show, and all the lights were crystallized sugar, melting inside—and she bit the pillow and hammered her hands onto the floor—and Sheerah kept sucking and slurping, and Ursula thought this ride would never end.... and she's afraid it will... and she hopes it won't. And then it does.

And she laughed. A deep laugh from way down in her newly awakened deep.

Sheerah looked up at her through the sheer veils of Ursula's skirt, her lips glistening with Ursula's wet. And she laughed, too.

And they held each other, giggling. Ursula's entire body open and receiving the laugh—the big laugh she had been due all these years.

40 | ATTACK!

Mr. Ed was feeling pretty damned good about himself. For a middle guy, he was at the top of his game.

His statement, "The danger itself is irrelevant. It's the *perception* of danger we're selling," had become an AgriNu catchphrase. Everyone around Corporate was saying it. And he employed it once again in speaking to a roomful of the President's innermost circle. The full desired effect of the ban on spinach wasn't working. Somehow, those slippery liberals had found a way to exempt organic farms that had never grown spinach, from the ban. Organic farms were springing back up like nasty weeds.

The President was happy because spinach was gone for now, and because his stock in AgriNu had gone up 13 points. But none of that put AgriNu any closer to their goal of prying open the damned EU to their seeds, and dominating the world market.

It was clear a next step had to be taken. "Our seeds…" Mr. Ed went on to explain, "have been bred to be resistant to pesticides and herbicides. But that's not all that's needed in these times. At any moment, we could be attacked by some foreign biological agent that could wipe out our food supply altogether. We're lucky it hasn't happened so far. We can't take this kind of risk with the American public. For the safety of our nation, AgriNu has developed seeds that can resist all of the most common biological threats that any terrorist might throw at us. It's the key to our survival. Our farmers must be induced to plant these bio-terrorist resistant seeds right now, before it's too late. Anyone on an AgriNu contract can merely switch over. And as for the organic farms… they *have* to switch over or be shut down."

"But no terrorist has waged an attack on crops…" offered the Secretary of Agriculture.

"Not yet." Mr. Ed smirked, leaning forward, "Wanna see one?"

His comment was met by a mix of sinister smiles and outright incredulity.

"Think of it as insurance against our vulnerability. We need to know so we can be prepared. A contained attack—but enough to demonstrate the need for our seeds, and show why organic farms are simply the worse possible threat to national security."

The Secretary objected. "These farmers already have debt up the yin-yang. They can't afford to convert, any more than they can afford to shut down."

Mr. Ed continued smoothly, "We'll help them. The government will offer subsidies to ease the burden of such a massive outlay of cash. Or AgriNu can buy their land. Many of these farms are in California. Farmers could earn a good price for that expensive real estate out there, even in this low market."

He still felt some resistance in the room. "Gentlemen, and ladies," he deferred, "think of this as a practice drill for what's inevitably to come. It's our responsibility to anticipate the worst, and stay ahead of the game. I'm amazed those crazy ragheads haven't already poisoned our food and water. It's only because they prefer things that go *boom* that they haven't already gotten us where it hurts most. These organics are a chink in our armor, our Achilles' heel. We have to protect ourselves. AgriNu can provide the way."

The President's voice came over the intercom, "I like it." Unbeknownst to the members at the meeting, he was listening in from the other room. "Ed, you make whatever needs to happen, happen, then I'll hold a press conference. They'll need to hear from their President."

Mr. Ed had just knocked it out of the park.

When Mr. Ed went home that night, Bitsy greeted him in nothing but a short, sheer robe, and a g-string. She had given the help the night off after the table had been set with Ed's favorites, chilled lobster with drawn butter, stuffed mushrooms, and a bottle of fine champagne called up from the wine cellar.

It might be mentioned here that Mr. Ed and his wife Bitsy do not have children—hence they did not need to be sent off for the evening, too. She is blonde and beautiful, or was, but she's dry as a twisted piece of driftwood. Just as well she can't bear children—she would have made a terrible mother. Not exactly the nurturing type. She's made up for it by social networking in a way that has greatly benefited those men associated with her, and by bringing lots of aerobic athletics to sex, when she's wanted to. And tonight she wanted to. She was big into punishment *and* reward.

Of course, when Ed married her, he didn't know she couldn't reproduce. He told himself it wouldn't have changed anything—but would it? He was now the last of the Edwards line. He had only sisters. They were all married, and had surrendered their names to their husbands. The Edwards name would come to a grinding halt with him—and it was his own damn fault.

He told himself that his secret desire for an heir had nothing to do with his taking up with Daphne, the blonde in legal. Despite Bitsy's turn of affection, he was tired of her bitching; and after a coup like today, he was entitled to the spoils, was he not?

Turns out that Daphne was recently divorced. Everyone knows divorced women are hot! They haven't had sex in a long time, they're not interested in marriage, and they've got nothing to lose. *Unless they have children...* he thought to himself. Which she did. Then, they want a stable relationship and someone to help raise their kids. He liked kids... At least he knew she could bear offspring.

Whatever Bitsy was offering was too old and too late. He would accept it graciously, tonight, because he was a man of manners. But the way things were going, he would soon be beyond the reach of social convention. He was sitting in circles of power. Men with power did things like have affairs, because... well they could.

Two days later, the big story hit:

> *(AP) A deadly bacterium has been found to have been sprayed over hundreds of acres of crops in Central California.*

Al-Qaeda has already claimed credit for the attack. Farmworkers in the fields are experiencing violent intestinal distress, headaches, and blistering rashes. Temporary emergency centers are being set up in the area…

The spray completely killed the lettuce, tomatoes, cabbage, and corn of the family organic farms that had reopened in the sprayed zone. Their leaves curled brown and shriveled to the ground. The vegetables disintegrated to mush. However, the larger fields—planted with a special, resistant seed—seemed untouched. Scientists were doing analysis right now, and early results showed that not only were these specially protected crops immune to the attack, but a simple washing in AgriNu's *Green Solution* made them perfectly safe for eating.

The President stood in the middle of the undestroyed field, in front of the television cameras, wearing a bio suit. Dramatically, he removed his protective helmet, and gave the all-clear sign.

"I am here to tell the American public that we are safe. Whoever is responsible, rest assured, we will apprehend them, and bring them to justice." He held up a perfect ear of corn. "This ear of corn is our hero, and it's the key to keeping safe food on America's tables. The seed kernels this corn has grown from were especially developed by leading industry scientists to resist such an attack. And they did."

His tone became even graver. "We simply cannot allow our country to go unprotected. A threat to our food supply is a threat to our very existence. We need seeds that grow food that can resist such attacks so this will never happen again. We're calling them *Freedom Seeds,* because the United States will always remain free!"

He went on to say, "After such a shocking and unprovoked attack, we must all be prepared, and… we must all make sacrifices… to make the changes necessary for our safety. Therefore, as of today, any food grown that doesn't originate from terror-resistant Freedom Seeds is hereby outlawed. Any farm that is not planted with Freedom Seeds will be shut down. Any farm that will not spray with approved, anti-terrorist chemicals and treat their soils with approved fertilizers will also be shut down. Any farmers who are unable to comply with the new law can join our land reclamation program and be compensated for the unused portion of their land."

Then, as the camera zoomed in to a close-up of his overly sincere face, he stated, "We are safe, thanks to the scientific advances in our farming industry. Nothing and no one will ever take away our freedom, our democracy, or our food." And he gave a long look into the camera.

"Cut. Great, sir," said the director from beside the camera. The director nodded to Mr. Ed, who nodded to the President, who nodded back.

41 | URSULA HAS AN IDEA

Ursula sat upright in bed that next morning and knew, like she had never known, that she must save our food.

It was as clear to her as the water in Kitty Boy's dish how she would do it.

The party last night had gone late; and Ursula was drinking champagne, of all things, toasting some little secret she was keeping to herself. To her surprise, Donny had showed up, too. Well, it shouldn't have come as too much of a surprise since this was where she'd first met him. She felt awkward seeing him, at first. She felt revealed. This new little secret of hers would remain behind tight lips, that's for sure. But the champagne loosened her conversation with him about other things.

He tried to hold back the surly, sarcastic tone that seemed to always be his fallback with the women he had formerly *known.* It was his best protection against whatever they might throw at him. Instead, he drank a lot, which was no surprise for him, but the surprise was that even with the recent days of renewed food debauchery he had indulged in since he last saw her, all that cleansing had wrecked his capacity for alcohol.

He was higher than a kite, and she was only one more drink away from passing out. Of the two of them, he was used to driving under all kinds of influences, so he drove her home. He offered to stay the night on the couch in the living room and drive her to her car in the morning. Sweet.

"Donny," she whispered as she shook him awake in the early morning. He was still on the couch, burrowed into the fluffy down quilt and pillows she'd laid out for him. "How much money do you have? We have to go to the store."

"I only need coffee," he muttered. He turned with a moan, and buried his head deeper beneath the covers. She saw he was not going anywhere.

"Then give me your keys."

"In my pants," Donny said, starting to come to. "Give me a minute, I'll go with you."

"Never mind." She grabbed his keys from his pocket, threw on a t-shirt and some jeans, tied a scarf in her crazy hair, and slammed the door behind her.

The clerk at the Whole Foods was preparing to open. Ursula pressed her face to the glass door. She pointed at her watch and made a pleading face at the guy. He tried to ignore her. At 8:02 when he finally opened, she hissed, "two minutes late," grabbed a cart, and pushed right past him. This being early fall, she went right to the gardening section where the revolving rack still held packets of vegetable and flower seeds. She took all the ones labeled organic, putting back the brussels sprouts because she didn't really like brussels sprouts—then reconsidered for the sake of others, and took them anyway.

She then went through the produce section and bought anything that was a pod surrounding a pea, or a bean that could be sprouted and planted.

In the parking lot, she opened the trunk and was overcome by the odor of sweaty socks and a half eaten liverwurst sandwich that Donny had hastily tossed in while he was cleaning his car before Ursula rode with him. She put her groceries on the back seat.

That entire morning, Ursula went from health food store to health food store, from hardware store to garden supply shop, buying up all the seeds she could find. She put all the charges on her VISA card.

Here's a question. How do we know when it's time to act? What inner alarm clock goes off inside, and how many times do we press the snooze button and roll over before we actually open our eyes? At least three, that's the average. That's also how many attempts it takes to stop smoking, according to statistics, though in Donny's case, more.

M. Earth has set it so animals get their alarms from the natural world. A change in the weather or the position of the sun tells them it's time to mate, lay eggs, and build nests. The appearance or disappearance of a food source can start the chain reaction to expand or reduce the population.

Perhaps it was the change in the food source that triggered Ursula to finally take action. This was not her first impulse, but it was her first *step* into activism. Perhaps one awakening leads to another and follows its own chain. There ought to be a warning label.

By 10:00 a.m. Donny was curious. By noon he was hungry and getting pissed off. Where was that coffee? By 3:00 he was convinced she had stolen his car and had been planning this for weeks. And by nightfall, when she returned with 1,024 packets of seeds and miscellaneous beans in their shells, Donny was relieved.

She would explain later. Right now she needed his help bringing all the bags inside. Every inch of the car, including the smelly trunk, which she had completely emptied of its previous contents, was filled with bags of seeds.

She planted a big kiss on his lips. It took him by surprise, and he loved surprises. And like that, he was hooked, once again. It's amazing what a man will do for a woman with only the smallest encouragement. And that's good, because the next thing he did for this woman was…

42 | HOW SEEDS SPREAD

How are seeds spread?

According to M. Earth and The Discovery Channel:

> **On the wind:** Seeds are designed with wing-like projections that help them fly, or they are as light as dust, like orchid seeds.
>
> **On the water:** Buoyant seeds ride the currents of rivers or oceans, washing up on shore, where they will open their waterproof shell, and sprout.
>
> **By animals:** Dogs pick up burrs in their fur as they walk around the neighborhood. Birds eat fleshy fruit carrying seeds, fly off and drop them—everyone is surprised that new plants crop up out of nowhere. Squirrels hide nuts for the winter and then forget where they put them.
>
> **In animals:** Elk, high on the slopes of Mount St. Helens, foster vegetation with the seeds contained in their scat. Monkeys, high in the canopy of the rain forest, plant new plants at the base of their living space through their seed-filled droppings.
>
> **Or by people:** Someone like Donny or Ursula…

P.S. Fungi spread their spores in all the same ways.

43 | ROAD TRIP

Not meaning any disrespect to Mother Earth—her wisdom or her rhythms—but if there were any chance Ursula could play some small part in moving things along, well then, she would. Even a speck can plant a few seeds, if they're small enough.

She now had a huge stockpile of organic seeds at home. She could get them started, but… she'd just have to leave it up to the plants to take over from there, and spread themselves. She'd seen it was possible. The occasions when she would pass by her earlier guerilla gardens, haphazardly planted near her office, she took pride in how yet more new plants were growing up among the weeds.

Donny went along with all this. It was a way to make her happy. He saw that by some miracle he, once again, had a foot in the door. Given a second chance, he would not blow it! He decided he'd rather dig dirt than drink the green drinks, but he'd rather make hot monkey love than either of those. Duh. Of course, they were *just friends*. Of course… but that could change.

Ursula knew Donny was fond of road trips, so she let him drive. The two of them headed out each night, in a different direction, from her place in West Hollywood. Sometimes a quick round trip, sometimes they would go so far as to stay overnight in a cheap motel. As friends. Planting by the roadside, or in a park, or in some cases, someone's front yard, these seeds would soon produce chemical free, modification free, wholesome, healthy food.

And by doing this, Donny and Ursula had become rebels.

44 | MR. ED'S SEED

Controlling your seed is not easy business. AgriNu knows this all too well. Even when you've got them controlled all in one place, they are tiny and some of them float out.

When Daphne, the blonde from legal, called to tell Mr. Ed she was pregnant, he laughed out loud at the irony. She did not appreciate it, and hung up on him.

45 | PAUL WILL NOT GO HOME

So Paul, as you recall, went to survivalist camp only to find he'd come away with some new ideas about what it takes to survive. He had learned skills he'd never imagined, experienced humiliations he'd rather forget, and had more sex than he'd had since college. When he left there after two weeks, he was a changed man—more the crowing rooster than Chicken Little. After the argument with Lindey, he picked up that Bible student in the drive-thru prayer booth, dumped Lindey at the bathroom at the Chevron Station, ran off with the prayer girl, returned the prayer girl, and picked up Lindey who had her thumb out looking for a ride.

That is where we left Paul.

Now, Paul and Lindey were traveling west on the 10, blasting country music on the radio. He was not usually fond of country music, but seeing how he'd caused her to spend the night in the restroom, he thought it only fair to let her choose the station. (Little did he know she actually spent the night with the Pakistani gas station owner's family, shared a spicy, delicious meal, and taught his teen-aged daughters how to slip out the bedroom window.)

Paul had apologized—"What was I thinking," and all that. And she had apologized in return. They seemed back on track. The *New Man* he was could let more things roll off his back.

He tuned the music out anyway, preoccupied with his own thoughts about his apartment and the state of putrification he'd left it in. Did he clear the take-out cartons from his desk? Did he empty the trash? Had he even flushed the toilet? He knew the answer was no, because it was always no.

It wasn't just his slovenly bachelor habits that were unacceptable; it was his whole apartment, and really his entire life. No. He simply wasn't going back there. He didn't want Lindey to see the guy he had been. His papers, his reprints, his files, his badly assembled, mismatched Ikea furniture seconds, his unwashed bed. He realized his entire life fell into two categories: obsession and neglect.

Not only did he not want her to see all this about him, he wanted to leave that hermitted, eccentric, lonely, smelly guy behind. He *did* want to get his computer, but he'd sneak back there on his own one day soon.

Maybe now that Donny was spending so much time with Ursula, he would not be using his apartment. Paul could go there with Lindey. He could say it was his place. No. At last check, Donny was a slob, too. Paul surmised the only single guys that were not slobs were overly fastidious gays, or chrome and leather sharks who set out to lure women. Otherwise, men left to themselves were hopelessly detached from decor and hygiene.

They would go to a hotel. Someplace he'd seen before, maybe by the beach. He'd tell her he was sorry for leaving her at the Chevron Station and wanted to make it up to her by taking her someplace nice. Someplace romantic. What woman didn't respond to that?

It would set him back quite a few bucks, but he had no choice. Even though he had the key in his pocket, he no longer had a home he could return to.

So as the radio song crooned about how *He'd treat me better this time*, Paul tried to imagine all the hotels and motels he'd passed endlessly in his travels—though his travels had not been vast.

The seedy prostitute-infested dives near his neighborhood along Sunset Boulevard were all that came to mind, but these were not appropriate. Even he knew that. He needed something more romantic, something with soft sheets. And preferably a low polyester count if that were possible. Plus, this had to be a place he could afford, and pull off both to Lindey and the hotel management that he was the sort of schlub that could pay for such a place.

He remembered he knew a guy who knew a guy who worked the night desk at the Chateau Marmont in the hills above the Sunset Strip. Cool. It was a very secluded, swank retreat frequented by celebrities and rock stars. Tucked away in the trees, the entire city would lie at their feet. This would impress her—though it probably wouldn't take much to impress someone who only owned three t-shirts and a pair of shorts—but he wanted to be sure. Hell, it would impress him!!

He changed freeways to the 101, then headed south over Laurel Canyon to the Hollywood side. The lights were a fantastic, psychedelic play, nearly blinding him after such a minimal sensory ration out there in the desert.

"Where do you live anyway?" she started to ask him as they drove though the wooded canyon.

"Hollywood, but my place is... having the carpets cleaned. And besides, I want to take you someplace special..."

Anyplace would be nicer than where he took her last time.

His eyes grew bigger than saucers when they pulled up to the storybook hotel.

He's thinking... *She's thinking, he can't pitch a tent worth shit, but this guy's smooth in the city.*

She's thinking... *Now, here's a fucking excessive waste of resources, but I could use a bath.*

The valet didn't hide his judgment as he took the filthy, road weary Volvo. Lindey bounded off to the ladies' room. Paul immediately asked for his friend's friend, Jason.

"You are one lucky man," Jason said. "We just had the Rolling Stones and their entire entourage cancel out of the big suites, and we've got all these rooms and their deposits. I can put you in one for free."

Paul had always been a fan of the Stones, so the idea of staying in their room held near-groupie appeal. Paul gave Jason all he had in his pocket, which was a $20, and two crumbled up $1's.

He instructed the front desk to "leave the luggage in the car." Best not to drag the muddy camping gear through the lobby.

The Stones must have pulled out at the very last minute because the room was decked out with all sorts of amenities: liquor, champagne, an enormous fruit basket from the manager, and an array of aromatherapy bath items.

Paul tried not to gawk. He thought if he said nothing he might pull off sophisticated blasé. He had no money to give the bellman, who insisted on coming up with them to show them the room, and insisted on carrying their grubby knapsacks.

Paul said, "I'll take care of you at the end," hoping that would be enough to get rid of him for now. The bellman gave a slight respectful bow. Who knows what he thought he'd be getting by way of a tip.

Lindey immediately took off all her clothes, put on the white bathrobe, and starting jumping on the bed.

Paul opened up the champagne.

"So, how long can we stay here? Paul asked Jason. It was early—6:30 in the morning. Paul was always an early riser, but more than that, Jason was the night clerk, and would be getting off at 7:00. Lindey was sacked out cold in the fluffy feather bed with the eight pillows that Paul had counted, including the little odd shaped ones.

Last night they had devoured the champagne and fruit basket, swum, jacuzzied, drunk everything else in the mini bar, fucked, ate all the candy bars in the mini bar, and zonked out to sleep.

Paul had plans to brew the little individual coffee packets back in the room once he returned, and hoped to hell the stay included a continental breakfast delivered to the door. He wasn't that big on eating, but he did like room service. Pizza delivery was as close as he ever got.

Checkout was at noon, and Paul wanted to know if there was any way they could extend their stay. Jason looked at his computer screen, juggled a few reservations around and said, "Sure, you can stay till Friday. Just keep a low profile. In fact, don't leave the room." That was three more days!

"I owe you, man," Paul said, trying to act cool. "If there's anything I can ever do for you…"

Jason was quick to reply, "Lemme fuck your girlfriend."

Paul's breath caught. He tried to hide his shock.

"Just kiddin' man. Wanted to pull your chain," Jason said, laughing. "Look at you..." He laughed some more, then looked Paul in the eye, "What d'ya say? She's hot." Again, busting up laughing. "Just kiddin'."

Paul smiled uncomfortably, "I can help you hook up free cable sometime..." feeling the need to offer an alternative.

"And don't order room service or use the mini bar," Jason said. "I'll keep the housekeepers away... say that the room is under repair."

Paul felt his throat tighten. Now he'd have to pay for all those exorbitant mini-things they'd eaten the night before. He'd figure it out later, along with the other stuff. Meanwhile Lindey could soon be waking up to the smell of freshly brewed artisan coffee, or she might just sleep in till noon.

Other than his time at survivalist camp, and the subsequent road trip, Paul had never been awake this long without jacking into his computer. He had serious withdrawal symptoms at camp. No computer, no TV, no electronics of any kind—except a demonstration of their high-tracking, solar-powered telecommunications monitoring and emergency warning system. Off the grid did not mean out of touch. These people were wired in to a complex network of other equally "suspicious" people, all out of view.

At camp, the hard labor of daily survival kept Paul more than occupied when his cyber-jones would strike. He was too wiped out at the end of the day to care. But being back in the city, he was feeling the gravitational tug. Once back in the room, he found himself playing with all the remotes—TV, stereo, fake fireplace—just to satisfy his twitching thumbs. He knew they had a business center downstairs.

At some point, he would leave Lindey floating in the oversized bathtub, go back home, reclaim his computer, and bring it back here. A man needed certain essentials; this was part of his survival gear.

46 | FEAR OF FLYING

What Donny did for Ursula was this:

He got on a plane… sober!

Donny never realized he had a fear of flying. The fact that he was partial to taking the red-eye appeared to come from his tendency to be cheap. OK, intermittently employed, and therefore cheap. Or maybe due to the fact that he would rather stay up all night than get up early in the morning. But he always seemed to have two or three drinks before he got on an airplane.

What was not apparent was that if you take the red-eye at 11:00 p.m. or midnight you could already be drinking. You could have three or four glasses of Scotch in you before getting on the plane. Whereas for the breakfast flight, you looked like a loser alcoholic if you were sitting at the bar.

Donny was not a heavy drinker; he was just a guy. Drinking is a guy thing to do—like smoking, or sweating, or farting. Guys need to be somewhat off-putting or the women get in too close and the guy starts getting all fluffy and melty, and in need of urgent *remasculation.* He knows this firsthand.

So what was he doing standing in the security line in the Bradley International Terminal at LAX, at eight fucking o'clock in the fucking morning? She had asked him to do it, and he stepped up, that's what. But now…

He sipped/gulped the coffee he'd brought with him, straight, black, and fast, because of the stupid rule of no liquids through the scanner. He wasn't sure what was rattling his nerves more, his fear of flying, or his fear of being caught and arrested. People could be detained for any sort of suspicious items now, and his could *certainly* be considered suspicious. He felt his heart squeeze down, and his temperature rise. He'd promised not to risk any out of control behavior by drinking, but *jeez…* now he was really at risk of falling out of control. *We have nothing to fear but fear itself,* Donny said to himself over and over, in a voice like Winston Churchill—until he realized it was FDR who had nothing to fear, and switched accents.

What if he couldn't do it? What if he flipped out in the security line, or on the runway, calling undue attention to himself? What if the airline attendants had to restrain him, and felt his soft underbelly? His palms were flowing sweat, and his socks were drenched.

Slowly, surreptitiously, he slipped a pair of Ursula's paisley lace panties from his pocket—he had picked them up off her floor when she wasn't looking—cupped them secretly in his hands, buried his nose there, and sniffed. *Ahhhh, the smell of her.* His brain fluttered a bit and then seemed to right itself, at once reminded of his purpose, the plan, and how much he wanted to please her.

He eyed each of the security check lines that branched off from this endless mother-line he had been standing in for what felt like hours. The TSA people seemed to all be trained at the DMV, which meant they were moving slower than postal workers.

Donny was sussing out which workers seemed to be looking for needles in haystacks, making people go back and back through the metal detector and strip down to the fillings in their teeth. He was also counting who, if any, was being pulled aside for random search, something he was trying to avoid at all cost.

Pretending to retrieve something from his bag, he let two people go in front of him. He'd calculated it would be one of them who would be nabbed. Yep. The punk musician with too many piercings on his face. Donny had called it.

When it came his turn, Donny pulled out three bins and began placing his jacket, cell phone, loose change, watch, and belt inside the first. Inside the second he placed the messenger bag he was carrying with two shirts, a change of underwear and socks, and a paperback novel. He took out his toiletries, in their own Ziploc baggie, and placed them on top. He had been so careful the night before to double check that each of the toothpaste, deodorant, and shaving cream containers were all under the allowable three ounces.

He looked around as he took his shoes off, then placed them in the third bin...

"Shoes go directly on the belt!" a large TSA woman shouted at him.

When he placed them on the moving belt, he observed he was standing in a puddle of water from his own sweat. As he walked towards the body scanner, he dragged a slime trail like a snail. The mother behind him grabbed up her child by the hand and made him walk around it. Others noticed, and were visibly disgusted.

Poker face, poker face... Donny said to himself, as he handed the security screener his boarding pass, and stepped through the scanner. No bells went off. But then, the TSA woman glanced down at the watermark dragged through the screener... "Male check!" she shouted, and indicated for Donny to stand in the glass booth directly behind her.

Shit!!! He was sweating all over, not just his feet. He was panicking. It might be best for him to take his wet socks off entirely, and show he had no bombs between his toes. Donny also had concerns he might be leaking.

"Whoa, keep your clothes on!" the woman barked as she looked at him from the eyes in the back of her head. "Male check, now!"

Donny would explain he had stepped in a big puddle of water before arriving at the airport as a way to avoid...

"I'm going to pat you down, sir," insisted the large black guard.

Donny was fucked. He would be seeing a lot more guys like this in prison.

The guard indicated for Donny to stand with his legs apart as he ran a metal detecting rod along the inside and outside edges of his body. No sounds went off. He ran the rod carefully along Donny's front and backside and saw no unusual bumps. His gaze went downward.

"What is with your feet, man?" he asked.

"Hyperhidosis," Donny flatly replied. "It's a medical condition."

The guard nodded knowingly. "You can go."

Donny left the booth, quickly sat down in a chair, and put on a dry pair of socks. He reattached his belt, put on his jacket, and got the hell out of there. He wanted desperately to go to the bar, but he headed for Starbucks instead.

Donny was a wreck. Of all of Ursula's crazy ideas, this was the craziest. The purpose of taping the mushroom to his abdomen was to place it flat center and not at the sides where they ran their rod and hands. He could also hide it by way of making him look like he had a little belly. Thank God, they didn't touch him there.

The last call for his flight was coming over the loudspeaker. He walked right by the Starbucks and made his way to the gate. His feet were once again sloshing inside his shoes.

He got on that plane and collapsed into his seat. His heart was banging hard against the walls of his constricted chest. He clutched Ursula's panties balled up in his pocket, now moist from his sweaty palms. They could have sprouted seeds right then and there. He let out a huge exhale… He'd made it. Unbelievable!

He fastened his seat belt, and within moments, took off into the blue sky of morning, feeling like some kind of comic book hero whose story was yet to be written.

47 | SHE WAS TOLD

So how is it, you ask, that Donny found himself in this circumstance?

When Ursula went on her seed-shopping spree, she had more in mind than just saving seeds. She had the idea to take these seeds and plant them in as many places as she could.

It wasn't actually her idea. The Kombucha mushrooms in the hallway gave it to her. They spoke to her at length about it. She would never tell anyone this is where the idea came from. Not that she was big on taking credit for another's idea, but she didn't think it would go over well with Donny, and she needed him to carry out the plan.

She heard them while they were glowing. Whether the sound came from outside her ear, or from inside her ear—the message was loud and clear, and something she could not possibly have known otherwise. What the mushrooms said was that they are an ideal planting companion to the seeds, and can help them grow. The mushroom's mycelium breaks down decaying plant life to make for highly enriched soil and draws nutrients to the plants' own roots so the plants can thrive and be abundantly productive. Maybe that's why she had propagated so many. People often don't know why they're doing things, except in hindsight. They don't see the perfection in an action, or its timing, until they look back.

Wow, she thought, *the coupling was brilliant.* Not to mention that now she could have her counter space back.

Without Donny knowing, she'd been slipping in a little bit of the Kombucha mushroom alongside the seeds they were planting in their guerilla outings. The mushrooms seemed happy enough, though she never was able to get back to these planting sites to see what had come of their union.

When it was time to move out, both mother and child offered themselves as a pair for the mission. Like Jihad soldiers. No one left behind to cry for the other.

She did observe that after watering her houseplants with a dilution of one part Kombucha tea in five parts water, their green leaves were full and shiny, and almost seemed to glow.

When the mushrooms said they wanted to go to South America, what could she do? That's what they told her; that's where they wanted to go. They said they would get a boost from that environment, could do their most impressive work. She had free miles.

Donny was much more willing than she ever imagined. She thought she would have to go herself, though there were real drawbacks to that idea. She was known to some of the airlines… but then Donny offered. And then he insisted, in a gallant way. Who was this guy?

The experiment would be this: two mushrooms (mother and child) were packed with their own liquid in a vacuum-sealed bag that was then taped to Donny's abdomen. It was the least likely place he would be searched. The seeds, he would carry in his pocket. The first test would be to see if he could clear security, the second to see what these mushrooms had in mind.

As synchronicities often occur when something is meant to be, Ursula heard from Ernesto the same day the mushrooms told her of their desire to travel to South America. Ernesto, the poet-biologist who was no longer in possession of her pubic hair. Remember him? Was it just coincidence, or had the mushrooms put him up to it?

While she had him on the phone, he told her where some optimal places to plant might be. He suggested his own home country of Ecuador; things grow faster near the equator. He would make the arrangements.

48 | DONNY RISES TO THE OCCASION

Donny was some kind of comic book hero, all right—one whose super powers were about to be revealed. Wasn't it always the way? These men, seemingly mild mannered (or not), who had some secret burning inside them, would meet with a terrible adversity: a spider bite, a nuclear waste spill, a radiant light given off by the impact of a meteor, and literally transform. It might take these fellas a while to figure out their super power, how to use it and handle it—like a young adolescent learns to use his johnson... a lot of misfires.

And then it might take even longer for that fella to learn to use it for good and not evil—seeing that most of them wanted revenge. But by then, his powers would grow, his name would be in all the papers, and he would always be at the right place at the right time.

Above all, this fella had a purpose. It was his strength of purpose that strengthened his convictions, and that strengthened his moral code, and that made his powers effective, and that made his dick hard, and all the women wanted him, and he would fill them with his *superseed,* and they would nearly explode with ecstasy and...

The train of Donny's thoughts had gone way past the station and on to Cincinnati. Sitting there in the aisle seat, row 13, on the Boeing 757 bound for Ecuador by way of Miami, he wondered if indeed this whole *supertizing* process could be happening to him?

What pulled his thoughts back right to the very spot where he was sitting was that this mushroom in its own juices that he had in plastic wrap, taped to his belly, had filled with air, and expanded beneath his shirt. His seat belt was making it pooch out over his pants even further.

As soon as the captain turned off the seat belt sign, Donny got up from his seat and bumped his way down the aisle towards the lavatory looking peculiarly pregnant.

Apologizing all the way, he finally reached the lavatory, went inside, and locked the door behind him. He pushed and pulled at the mushroom planet, trying to let some of the air out by making a tiny puncture hole with his teeth when—*pop* and *whoosh*—his water broke. All over the bathroom floor. Some of the water must have seeped underneath the door because the flight attendant banged politely.

"Are you OK?" she asked.

"Fine, fine," Donny replied. But he was stressing.

In order to save the mushroom and what little juice surrounded it, he had to re-wrap the thing with the tattered plastic wrap, which could only now cover one side. He placed the exposed mushroom up against his belly.

At first it felt awful. Clammy. Clammier than when, as kids, he and little Joey Mattusey would have contests to see who could stand to have the most snails placed on their bellies at once. Clammier, but not dissimilar. And then the God-awful clamminess felt soft and soothing, like it was penetrating his skin and fortifying his abdominals—like (he imagined) if he had Ursula's clam slapped right up against him and her juices were penetrating his skin and abdominals… and that's not all. His "regular guy" was turning into a thunderbolt, supercharged with super powers.

Add *that* to Kombucha's list of health claims!

Great. That's all he needed, a pregnant belly and an erection.

The flight attendant knocked again. "Sir, are you sure you're all right? We have a line waiting."

Donny wasn't sure whether it would be faster to think about his grandmother and her canasta club in their floral housecoats (the mental picture would drain the life out of this wooden soldier) or to whack it off right then and there into the sink. After all, he was soaked from the waist down from his water breaking, and his feet were completely drenched. What could be seen in that mess that could possibly be more embarrassing?

Maybe it was that tantric thing Ursula'd been talking about. Maybe it was, because he wanted to be a concentrated force in her life and give himself only to her. What a strange and new impulse for him. He didn't want to jerk off. Maybe for the first time ever. Was he an idiot? Was all this stress going to his head? And like an answered prayer, his grandmother's friend, Ethel, the one who played with her teeth while she studied her cards, her image came up and was bringing him down. Down, down, all the way down, flat. Thank you, Ethel.

He opened the door, looked the attendant defiantly in the eye, same for each person who growled in line, and returned to his seat. So what that he was wet? People get wet in this life.

49 | MEANWHILE, URSULA...

FYI—Ursula had been doing lots of practicing since her private session with Sheerah. The tongue, she's discovered, IS everything.

She let her tongue play inside her mouth, and let her hips rotate as she traced Donny's route on her globe, trying to feel where exactly on the Earth he was.

50 | A BABY

Donny had never held a baby in his life, nor ever wanted to. He didn't feel drawn to them, was scared of breaking them, and had more tolerance for screaming cats in heat than a baby's cry for milk.

So, what was this feeling that was coming over him as he arrived at his planned meeting place in the village just outside the steaming jungles of Ecuador? Pride? Possessiveness? Protection?

He held a photo in his hand of the man he was to meet, a stranger to him. Ursula had given him a photo of… (he checked the name) who was Señor Marcos Montenegro, anyway? And what could his interest possibly be in the mushroom and seeds he was about to receive? Donny didn't know Señor Montenegro was Ernesto's cousin. Didn't know about Ernesto, and better kept that way.

Donny was seated on a rusted folding chair at a small table outside a tiny—could you even call it a restaurant? It was part store, part eatery, and part beauty salon. Mostly, it was a place you could get ice. He was waiting for Señor Montenegro, acting like he wasn't waiting for Señor Montenegro, drinking a Coke. He wondered if their organic crops might proliferate throughout the world like Coca-Cola had. Some people here didn't have electricity, but they had Coke.

He watched some small children playing with some small dogs, all ribs showing. He realized he'd never been more than a car ride away from a McDonald's, never been further than a lazy man's reluctance from the refrigerator. These creatures were hungry. Could the spreading of this food actually change that?

Señor Montenegro stood politely next to Donny's chair and introduced himself. He showed Donny the photo of Donny he had been given so they would recognize each other.

As instructed, the men exchanged photos, and then Señor Montenegro signaled for Donny to follow him into the back of the store.

The small backroom housed a noisy generator and another rusted folding table and chairs. A photograph of Jesus hung on the wall, next to Pele, and Julio Iglesias.

Donny lifted his shirt and untaped the tattered packaging from his belly. The mushroom had survived the plane ride! He pulled out crumpled napkins and bags full of seeds from his overnight bag. He felt like God Himself as he handed them to this man to be joined together and make life.

They would be welcomed here. Señor Montenegro explained that already around the village, thousands of acres of the jungle were being cut down. One after the other, trees toppled to make grazing land for factory farm cattle. The symbiotic strategy of the rainforest was thoroughly disrupted: animals fled, insects dispersed, and fungi shriveled in the bright sun. Next to the cattle farms, an equal number of acres were razed to plant AgriNu's designer alfalfa and soybeans—grown for feed, guaranteed not to last past this season. The fields were sprayed heavily with herbicide to kill off the weeds. Here, they defined *weeds* as anything that tries to grow that is *not* AgriNu designer alfalfa or soybeans. This is the jungle! Plants grow in a blink of an eye here. But not on AgriNu lands.

The villagers were experiencing all sorts of catastrophic health problems from the spray—chronic diarrhea, a rise in miscarriages, infants born with deformed heads—but having no land of their own, they were forced to work on these farms to earn a wage. They were hoping to earn enough to have some of their own land, where they could plant their own seeds for their own food, and escape these horrid illnesses. This experiment might be an answer for them, before it was too late.

Donny felt odd. What was this flushing, red feeling coming over him? Blushing? Jeez, he must be really tired from his ordeal of the plane ride and this heat and… he was losing it. Tears were coming into his eyes. Oh, great. Fucking great! His hands were sweating, full of mushroom and seeds, so he couldn't even brush away his tears. So here he was standing, hands extended, weeping like a fuckin' wuss… and Señor Montenegro… was crying, too.

They were making a baby. Go figure. The unspoken feeling was that somehow they were making history. They were making creation all over again.

Señor Montenegro accepted the packages of seeds and mushrooms. He treated them tenderly. In a moment he would get in his truck and drive out to the small farm of his brother, and plant the seeds and the mushroom together. And then, like a proud and benevolent parent, sit back and watch them grow.

51 | GOTTA DANCE

Donny, of course, does not dance. Would you expect any different? He's very athletic, very musical, but he's withholding and stubborn as shit. He doesn't even know if he *can* dance because he's never tried. His mother and father, big dancers—oh, how they loved to do the hustle around the apartment when he was growing up. His mother would bite her lower lip and his father's eyes would open wide. His parents even entered a dance contest at the community rec center and won second place.

Donny's never even tried. So why bring this up?

After Donny made his first delivery of the seeds and mushrooms to Señor Montenegro, and those seeds were well planted in the soil of the brother's farm, he was invited to dinner by his host's cousin, the one who owned the restaurant. It was a small gathering of about forty relatives. After dinner, through an interpreter, Donny was asked to dance with his host's cousin's sister, and he knew he must.

He danced like Fred Astaire.

No kidding. This guy who had never even done a two-step was gliding and twirling this cousin's sister around with all the elegance of every 1930s movie he'd ever watched. Like Olympic athletes who run their race in their imagination over and over before they actually compete, I guess you could say Donny had been replaying these steps without moving a foot, until now.

He was pretty pleased, though he kept employing the "clap and wipe" style in between twirls to dry his profusely sweaty palms. Otherwise, he exuded confidence and charm. The clap and wipe only added to his flair.

By the end of the dance, everyone cheered and wanted Donny to marry the sister—an offer he graciously declined by pointing to his empty ring finger. Though they were puzzled since there was nothing there, he did manage to get out quickly, saying he wanted to sleep at the airport to be sure not to miss his flight. He was not about to risk a midnight visit from the sister and be forced into a shotgun wedding.

He slept in a hard and cramped plastic chair at the airport and flew home early the next day—with a few drinks in him this time. He smiled to himself at a job well done.

Donny had been raised by comic book heroes, and now he could be one.

52 | A HERO'S WELCOME

What is it about asparagus that makes your pee smell immediately after you eat it? Ursula wondered to herself. The question was inspired by the smell of her own urination, which she had just completed. *I don't know any other food that does that. Beets will make you pee red, and blueberries will make you poop blue...*

She made a mental note—*Do an experiment with fragrant foods.*

But by the time she stepped out of the bathroom, the thought fell completely from her mind, for there stood Donny in the middle of her living room.

He looked different to her. Like the kind of different when you say to a person, "Did you lose weight?" even though you know they didn't because you just saw them eating four Krispy Kremes the day before. But it's the kind of different that completely changes how they appear and how you receive them.

It wasn't shaving—he hadn't shaved in days. A full beard now filled in that silly Don Johnson stubble left over from some very tired male fantasy that allowed lazy to pass for sexy. No, it wasn't that...

It was... heroism. *He did it! He delivered the seeds and mushrooms!* She could see he must have been successful because, though his eyes were tired, his skin glowed with a light from inside.

Without thinking, she walked over to him (hobbled over, really, for her panties were still down around her ankles) and kissed him deep and hard, right on the lips.

He kissed her back equally deep. Ripe wetness burst from her "down under," and one, two, three, those panties were off from around her ankles, and she took him inside her right there on the living room rug.

Donny hadn't expected this. Or let's say every other time Donny came to Ursula's house he was expecting this with hope and prayer—but today, he came here because he had just been through the biggest triumph of his life, and he was exhausted and thirsty, and there was no other place he could think to go, because this was the only place he *would* go to stay connected with what he had just done.

So that he was now lying on the rug with Ursula's long legs wrapped around his ears like some crazy caduceus seemed a just reward, and just the reward he wanted. *Ahhhhhh.*

And she opened to him. *Ohhhh!*

To say that Ursula had never had an orgasm before that night is now not really the truth. We know that since Sheerah's tongue had played a key role in her awakening, Ursula had been practicing a lot on her own. But she had not ever in all her years of life had an orgasm with a man.

Sheerah made her promise not to have sex with any man until she truly wanted to connect with his entire being. Her desire now pushed ahead of the dread that it might not ever happen.

She was so wet with invitation as he thrust into her again and again, she thought her head would open up and all the joys of her life would explode through. Ursula climaxed, again and again, until the room shook from her screams. The warm nectar of aliveness surged through her from head to toe.

Gotta dance. Gotta dance.

Donny was grateful that he had not yet had to refuse to dance with Ursula. After they made love, he waltzed her around the room like a Viennese Empress. Seamlessly gliding. Her first orgasm—his first waltz. Neither one a virgin, anymore.

53 | SEAN AND SHEERAH LOOK UP TO THE SAME SKY

At that very same moment, Sean and Sheerah each looked up at the very same sky and felt an erotic tingle at the base of their spines. Somewhere, all the Eros in the world gathers together in a common matrix, and they were all tapping into it, right now.

So were the mushrooms, all-aglow, and the tiny sprouts. Elsewhere the cicadas made a shimmy-shimmer, and some people sighed a pleasant little sleepy moan as they rolled over in their beds.

One of them had a craving for spinach—but it soon passed.

54 | SWARMING UP

OK. So now someone's finally getting up in arms. Al-Qaeda bio-bombing our crops with deadly viruses? The general public was running around like headless chickens in a locked coop. Some stopped buying vegetables altogether for fear they might be contaminated. Others overran the grocery stores, hoarding food, buying up canned goods now stamped with the official *Terror-Proof* government seal of approval. AgriNu's *Green Solution* flew off the shelves within the first day.

AgriNu's new slogan: *Freedom Seeds. Leave the Growing to Us.*

The local health food stores, unable to sell healthy food, went out of business. Even the larger health food chains could barely keep their doors open. Farmers' Markets disappeared in one fell swoop. Entire livelihoods and food supplies were destroyed, making food overall, scarce, and more expensive. Neighbors formed Watch Groups, reporting on their very own neighbors' untreated gardens, in exchange for discount coupons on the desperately prized terror-proof food. The National Guard had to be called in when a near-riot broke out at Walmart over the single remaining box of terror-proof instant mashed potatoes.

The World was watching. Phone calls from France, Germany, and other European countries expressed sympathy to our President, secretly glad it happened on someone else's soil.

Environmental groups emailed and twittered their lists like crazy. Already there was talk of a false attack and a conspiracy. Beleaguered farmers formed alliances, protesting the exorbitantly high price of the Freedom Seeds they were now forced to plant. The right wing press was calling for retaliation on al-Qaeda. And finally, people were taking to the streets.

All of them. Like grasshoppers ready to switch.

Except Ursula. She couldn't go out there. Her fear convinced her this was not the way to go, not for her. You speak out, they keep a file, they have your picture; next thing you know, they've killed your cat. She's seen *Silkwood* seven times.

No, Ursula was intent on making her contribution in her own personal way.

55 | PAUL IS A GUN NUT

"Where the fuck have you been?" was Donny's greeting when Paul picked up his cell phone. Donny had been so preoccupied with Ursula and her scheme that he'd entirely forgotten he hadn't talked to Paul in weeks. But Donny missed the goof.

"Man, you wouldn't believe it…" was Paul's whispered reply. He was lying next to Lindey on the fluffy bed, television blaring. Turns out they both liked *Star Trek* reruns.

Paul's old sense of urgency bubbled up as he heard his friend's voice. He told Donny he had some things he really wanted to talk about and could they meet down at The Hide Out, this dive bar Donny liked in Hollywood. Donny was cautious—what rant was he in for now? But hey, it was worth it to see Paul out of his cave.

Paul would also use the time to go back to his place and get his computer. Lindey would be quite content to soak in the jacuzzi. Paul would bring them back some dinner. He didn't want to be gone too long.

"You what?!" Donny exclaimed in outrageous disbelief when he heard Paul had purchased a gun somewhere out in the desert. "Are you going to become an assassin now? You certainly know enough about their M.O."

"Just in case…" Paul replied. "You don't know which way things'll go."

"Yeah, but, like, you can't even make it to the second act of Modern Warfare. You let your ass get blown-up all the time."

"Those are role plays, this is the real thing. Maybe it's because I knew they were a fantasy without any real consequence…"

"I'll tell you where the fantasy is… toting around some semi-automatic rifle…"

"And a 45 pistol..." Paul interrupted.

"And a pistol?! How about a grenade launcher? I'm scared, you running around, male bonding with these hair-trigger nut cases who clearly have father issues..."

"I have father issues..." mused Paul.

"So do I, but I'm not ready to blow his head off! Was anybody wearing a swastika? I hate that shit!"

"They're not that kind of group, though come to think of it, they were all white..."

"Yeah?"

"It's the government they're against—the ones who secretly run the government, and the politicians who front them. They're cool guys really. And not all guys... like Lindey... I told you about her.

"Figures the first lay you've had in a decade is as paranoid as you."

"I learned a lot from these people, how to build shelters, find game, plant seeds... I saw how truly unfit I was to take care of myself in even the most basic situation."

"So now you're going to go hunt your own food in the park?"

"No, I'm gonna riot in the market over Eggos and terrorist-approved Cocoa Puffs," Paul snapped. "What if I had to sleep outdoors—like after an earthquake?"

"But you're staying in a hotel..."

Paul ignored that. "I saw how dependent I am on 'them,' any 'them,' for my own existence, and if 'they' decide to pull the strings and cut it off—food, water, oil, freedom—I'd be inept, and grubbing for whatever they wanted to give me in exchange for whatever they wanted from me. They got us by the balls, the stomachs, the minds... and the more we pretend it's not true, the more they've got us..."

"And I used to think you were no fun at all..." replied Donny.

"I mean if they start telling you you can't shit and flush your toilet except when they say—or like when they make you pay to use the men's room at the subway—and if you can't pay, you have to pee on the wall; and if they catch you peeing on the wall, they arrest you. There'll be no place we can shit or pee and that is societal control! You're gonna need a gun for when they tell you you can't shit!"

"Is this something they told you or did you read about it?"

"Everything I've read has scared the shit out of me, and my proving it right just made it worse! I kept thinking the more I know, the more I can stay ahead of their game—but I never thought I could do something about it, except watch out. Never thought I could do something about my fears... but now I can."

Donny had heard Paul rant many times. Once he got going, he could talk himself into a trance and become irretrievable, but something about what he was saying this time must have made some kind of screwy sense to Donny, because he was still there listening, and the rant was pretty thick. But a gun? In this mutt's hands? Didn't seem healthy for anyone.

Paul asked Donny for $100.

"More ammo?"

"I gotta bring some food back for Lindey..."

Oh, yeah, he's got a woman. This was so amusing to Donny that he gave him an extra $20. "What's she like?" he asked.

"Blonde." Then he added, "Tough. And she's got a tattoo in the shape of Florida."

"Sweet," Donny said as he left to go back to his own sweet thing.

Paul used the extra $20 to get his car washed, and then headed for his apartment. He barely recognized it from the outside. This was not just because he was rarely outside; it was that everything about him had changed, and it seemed, so had his surroundings.

He stopped the car. He could feel the intense gravitational pull of his computer, literally drawing him forward in his seat. But all around that computer was the life and its fossilized artifacts that he had no interest in rejoining. Paul turned on the ignition and drove away.

He stopped at the Falafel Place and bought pita and the works. Lindey was a vegetarian for the most part. Rule of law for survivalists—unless you kill it, you don't eat it. Seeing as there was no wild deer to shoot down on Santa Monica Boulevard, falafel seemed more exotic than pizza.

56 | PAUL RETURNS TO THE HOTEL

Paul felt a little better giving the valet his beat up Volvo now that it was clean. As he walked through the lobby, Jason called him over to the front desk. “I had to change your room,” he confided, “but you can stay all week. You’re now in 205.” He tossed Paul the key.

Paul winked at him, gave him a $20 like a big spender. He went up the elevator, excited by the extended stay.

When he entered, Lindey was settled in to the new bed, wearing the white robe from this room.

“Whatcha been doing?” he asked in his cheeriest tone.

“Nothing much. Jason came by. He told me we were going to have to leave… so I fucked him. Now we can stay another week. I made him throw in the mini bar.”

Paul’s stomach curdled.

“But I’ve got to do him every night,” she said, flatly.

That little snake! Paul was ready to reach for his gun.

“It’s not a big deal. He comes really fast.”

Lindey acted like she didn’t care, but of course she did. The hotel was nice, but what kind of bullshit was this? She decided she was going to leave Paul once they got kicked out of the hotel.

Paul needed desperately to make it up to her. A bag of falafel and fixings was not going to do it. But at the moment, it was all he had.

57 | HITTING THEIR STRIDE

Now that Ursula's "doorbell" was working, Donny was pressing it all the time. Like any new explorer, she was thrilled at her new discovery. Sometimes it worked better than others, but she wanted to know the world through her vagina, and he was more than happy to be her tour operator.

And now that the transport mission to plant the coupled seeds and mushrooms near the equator was a success, the two of them continued their guerilla gardening forays with elevated confidence, feeling part of A Greater Plan.

Organic seeds were nearly impossible to find. No seeds were available in the stores or through seed catalogs. Online sources read, *Unavailable.* Community seed exchange libraries were confiscated. Flurries of protester blogs popped up for concerned gardeners to tap into underground sources, but many of those sites met with "technical difficulties" and were suddenly blocked from their servers.

Donny and Ursula continued to plant what they had, which was still quite a bit, accompanied by the mushrooms, of course.

They had hit their stride. Not just in the teamwork of planting, but as a couple, they had found their dance.

It's this way in all relationships—you're either the lover or the beloved. Even if it doesn't appear to start out that way, all things being equal, it's already been determined which one is which. Slowly over time, the cloud of mutual infatuation drifts by the moon, and you see just who loves a little more, and who is loved.

Donny always wanted to see himself as the "bed'um and leave'um" type, like all the smooth James Bond secret agent characters he grew up watching. He wanted to see himself that way, though he looked and acted nothing like them—except maybe he could open a car door without a key, but he learned that from his hoodlum friends in Queens, not from Her Majesty's Secret Service.

When it came to Ursula, he was clearly the lover and she, the beloved. Why? Because… he just couldn't get enough of her. She was so quirky and impossible to win over at first, and then later the pleasure she took from the simple blush of her skin in her newly discovered ecstasy—well it made him feel so valued, and accomplished, and useful that it made him love her all the more. It also made him feel scared, naked, and over the edge, which was part of love's cost.

In order for this configuration to work, the beloved must truly enjoy receiving, and the lover cannot be stingy or withholding. Donny had spent his whole life withholding. Whatever it was he knew you wanted, whatever might make him more successful or attractive, he held it back. So, on the surface, he was not a good candidate for the lover. And Ursula was only just learning how to receive herself, let alone receive another.

All he knew was that he wanted to be around her all the time, and show and share, and to be in service to her. It caused feelings he didn't recognize. He'd never derived such pleasure before from pleasing a woman.

As the beloved, she would accept his offerings—his bouquets of flowers, his magazine subscriptions, his prized Sandy Koufax card embedded in Lucite—with demure pleasure; although sometimes, she had to stretch to share the same value he placed on such things.

All of this is not to say that love is not mutual, and that lovers are not caught with the same fever that infects them both. It's just that one leans slightly forward and the other, slightly back. That's how you dance. That's how you glide across the floor like Fred Astaire and Ginger Rogers.

Donny, who was always a playful sort, thought the intensity of this *dance of relationship,* and all this planning and planting, was getting to be a little much. Couldn't they possibly do something normal like maybe normal people do? Like go away for the weekend? Donny's friend, Gabe, had a mountain cabin in Big Bear they could use for free. Donny was never one to turn down such a thing—so off they went to the woods to have a relaxing getaway vacation. Ursula brought some seeds and mushrooms, just in case.

They arrived there by noon and immediately walked down to the lake and untied the aluminum rowboat from the dock where his friend said it would be. Donny liked to row. He grabbed the oars, and pumped them out to the middle of the lake in no time. Ursula had brought along sandwiches, which meant some shredded vegetables wrapped in some other vegetables. Donny didn't care. It was a beautiful day. He let go of the oars and let the boat float. What was more restful than drifting where the current takes you, not caring at all where you go?

M. Earth wonders *How long before one of them gets the urge towards self-direction, sticks the oar in the water, and pushes the boat towards a particular destination?*

The truth is, Donny and Ursula have always been floating on M. Earth's current—carried towards her particular destination, despite their self-determined flailing about. They each have a particular role to fill in this story, despite what they continue to tell themselves. It's the truth, and they are the first not to know it.

Think again about the 13-year cicadas, who are nothing if not fulfillers of their own mysterious destiny, which seems to be to reproduce and perpetuate… their mysterious destiny. Each cicada is but a small part of a larger wave. Together, they must crack out of their shells, take to the trees, mate, die, and leave their eggs behind. Even if they were to stop for a cigarette, they inevitably would end up in the same place—as an ancestor, who just set up the next generation.

Donny and Ursula don't think of themselves as cicadas. They think of themselves as rugged individuals, who despite being the product of their respective upbringings, are shaping their own lives, thank you very much. Why else would Ursula be so bent on self-improvement if she didn't believe it were up to her, and therefore possible? And why would Donny be able to change despite his best efforts not to?

Could it be that the needs of the mushrooms have orchestrated this romance? That the erotic reproductive urges of the spores themselves have created this whole harebrained scheme in order to get themselves moved around the world?

M. Earth knows it's a bit cruel to let D and U think they have such importance, that these ideas are their own, that they not only will *change* the world, but may *save* the world… when really, they might just be laying eggs in a twig that is meant to fall back into the earth and ensure the repeating of this nonsensical cycle. Or not.

58 | CHANGE OF CARS

Donny had not been back to his apartment in days. His mailbox was stuffed and overflowing. He added this mail to an already calcifying pile of unopened letters that covered his desk. Something at the bottom, though, caught his attention. An official looking envelope from the City of West Hollywood. He opened it and found several photographs printed onto a single page.

This first one was of his car outside the intersection of Fairfax and Fountain, with a clock in the upper right corner of the frame; then one of his car inside the intersection, a second clock in the frame. The next was a close-up of his license plate; then a close-up of him behind the wheel, gesturing largely—with Ursula in the passenger seat! It was clearly her, even though they had blacked out her face.

"What?!" he screamed looking down at the page. How could this have happened? Though Donny made a habit of charging through questionably yellow traffic lights, he had developed a sixth sense about police presence, probably left over from his stoner days. His stomach clenched as he saw the garden tools thrown in the back seat behind them, and recognized this as one of their night planting missions. He must've been too preoccupied with their conversation to notice the flash of one of those secret cameras set up at the intersection as he whizzed through the light. *Shit! Now those bastards have our picture and my license plate! I'm in their system.*

Who's to say "they" couldn't manipulate the image, put his picture in someone else's car? Or put someone else's license plate on his car? Or fake the intersection? "They" could fabricate anything with digital photography and computer imaging. His mind was racing.

He would not tell Ursula. She was so proud of him now; and he, oh, so enjoyed reaping the rewards. He was not about to do anything to curb her expression... which is why he traded in his car that very morning at the Toyota dealer in North Hollywood, and drove up to her house in a completely new set of wheels. His only explanation to her, “I needed a bigger trunk.”

59 | URSULA MUST SPEAK

As we've said before, Ursula tried as long as she could to be anonymous. She lived this way even before she knew it was necessary in order to pull off her plan—even before there was a plan. Because of her anonymity, she was able to act under the radar. There was nothing obvious about buying up all the organic seeds in Los Angeles and sprinkling them about—nothing apparent about raising an overrun colony of mushrooms in her darkened home. It just seemed eccentric. No one thought twice about her studying world maps and climate regions, or tracking flight schedules from her computer at the travel agency where she worked.

But there comes a time when everyone must speak up. Even her. Once the words arrive, they can't be stopped.

Let's walk it back.

Ursula hadn't come here with the idea of standing up—in fact she hadn't come with the idea of coming at all. She had merely been swept up in a frenzied sisterhood of belly dancing that ended in sweaty, breast-heaving, spent-it-all kind of exhaustion. Her classmates said they were all joining some other friends to heckle the President from inside a fundraiser dinner where he would be speaking. She should come.

She would've much rather they'd all gone to the raw juice bar like they did last week, but now they were piled into Lorena's Prius and heading for a fancy hotel in Beverly Hills.

Tickets to the event were courtesy of one of the gals' high-contributing parents who were thrilled to see she'd "finally come around." They all tucked their long skirts up under their coats and left the bangly belts and bras in the car so as to blend in (which, of course, they couldn't, but at least they were covered up).

Behind the closed doors of the Grand Ballroom, drunken $25,000-a-plate supporters chatted while waiting to shake the President's hand. Ursula and her friends made their way to the table where the friends from FemForce were already seated. They were even less likely to blend into this mostly gray crowd, but had made an effort to cover up their tattoos and coif their close-cropped hair. They were pleased at how near to the stage the table was. This girl's parents must have been BIG supporters.

The President made his way to the podium, and after a few jokes, went into full swing. He was for the workingman, for NAFTA, the WTO, the Man in the Moon. He was opposed to abortion; illegal terrorist-liberals; oil-hating, shrimp-hugging environmental-pacifists; or anyone else who did not love this country. He was all for the right to carry firearms and the requirement to carry a government-issued ID. Preaching to the choir, he got them all singing the same tune. Then he opened the floor for a few questions.

A long uncomfortable silence in the audience, then… "Mr. President, sir… I have a question." Ursula looked around and couldn't believe this sound came from her, or that she was actually standing up, addressing this man. But she was.

The President chuckled a little and nodded in her direction.

All eyes went to her as an assistant gave her the microphone. Every fear she had tried to give it back. She felt dizzy; her mouth went dry. Here she had the power to register her complaint and have her questions answered, but in the very same moment she would be exposed, recorded, and remembered. What was she going to do? Panic? Pander? Become the idiot girl he was signaling her to be?

Her heart pounded in her throat. "What about the seeds?" she asked.

The President pretended not to understand the question.

"Why are innocent farmers being forced to rip out their fields and turn over their seeds?"

The President responded in an over-serious tone, "These unprotected seeds are a threat to our nation. You saw what happened? And that was on a small scale. We can't risk another bio-terrorist attack, or something worse, that could wipe us all out. Every seed has to be a Freedom Seed, resistant to our enemies' determined plots to destroy us. We're at war, but this war won't come onto our soil. Not on my watch. Now why don't you go finish your dinner? Guaranteed grown with Freedom Seeds."

The crowd laughed, glad to break the tension. Ursula stood firm.

"Does anyone else know of the rest of your plans?" she asked, looking at him directly.

His face washed blank for just a fraction of an instant. He put his hand to his ear. Frantic voices were shouting in there, "What does she know?!!?? Stop talking to her! Now!!"

For just a split second, the President lost his bearings. His Secret Service instantly surrounded him and started pushing him towards the exit. Receiving instructions to make an excuse for a hasty retreat, he just smiled and said, "I'm being called away. Thank you all for coming."

The FemForce gals took this as their moment. Stepping up to the stage, they unfurled their giant banner, which read, WE NEED ABORTION, BECAUSE WE'RE BEING FUCKED! The President turned to avoid them, tripped and fell, tangling up in the banner.

The Secret Service grabbed the President. Several others grabbed the FemForce gals; and two agents ran over and grabbed Ursula, even though she was nowhere near the banner incident. Taking one look at her skirt, one agent yelled, "Holy crap, check her for explosives!" And rushed her out to God knows where.

60 | JUST THE DAY BEFORE

What Ursula didn't know, and what they thought she did, is that just that day the ever-grateful President had signed secret orders to allow AgriNu to take things a step further. AgriNu was getting sick and tired of dealing with these bullheaded, unswayable world leaders who would not come around to the logic of an open and free market, and even more sick of public opinion that clearly didn't understand the deeper issues at hand.

Having firmly established that the blame would all go to al-Qaeda, AgriNu, through its growing global organization, would be authorized to stage more bio-attacks in "problem spots" of the world—those "problem spots" being the uncooperative countries that still were in opposition to accepting their seeds. Let's say it out loud… the European Union. Something had to convince them.

At this point, people were so afraid of their food, even these stubborn-ass governments couldn't take a chance. Times were different now. It didn't take nearly as long to create a panic. With people so on guard and on edge, the slightest thing could trigger fear. Look at the avian flu epidemic. Look at the alleged shortage of iPads last Christmas.

Bomb them, and the EU would be clamoring for Freedom Seeds—whose price just went up again. And AgriNu would be happy to deliver.

61 | DONNY IS NOT ONE TO CALL

On the night Ursula disappeared into the system, Donny freaked. He was waiting for her in bed at her house. He kept listening for the turn of the key. He watched too much late night TV.

But no Ursula.

He called Sheerah. She was already asleep and not pleased about being awakened. She said Ursula and some of the girls had gone to see the President…

"Who did she go with?" he asked anxiously.

"Minnie, Micki, Daisy…"

He blew up at her. "Oh, come on… cooperate here."

"That's their names!" She matched his volume. "You can see why I'm suggesting they take spiritual ones…"

"Can you give me their phone numbers?"

"Why is it men have such a hard time when their women want to have their own fun?"

"I just want to make sure she's OK."

"She's probably curled up in conversation at one of their houses…"

"I just want to know…"

Sheerah gave him Minnie's and Daisy's phone numbers and told him to take a few breaths before calling.

Donny called Minnie. No answer. Left a message.

He called Daisy, same thing.

He paced the floor, and started eating energy bars from Ursula's emergency supplies.

Then the phone rang. It was Daisy. She said Ursula had been arrested… for doing nothing, really… for exercising her free speech. No one had seen her since. And there were others. She'd called a friend who was a lawyer who called her friend at the ACLU, but no one had been able to see her.

"Why didn't you call *me?*" Donny asked.

"We didn't know you were someone to call."

That stung. Donny was practically living with Ursula… well… he was staying with her an awful lot. He kept his apartment to use as an office where a guy goes when he needs to fart up the place, but still… Ursula hadn't told her friends about him in such a way that they would know to call him if she got fucking arrested??

He thanked Daisy obligatorily, caught up in his own concerns. He called Paul. No answer. That guy had completely disappeared, too.

Donny called every agency, government office, Internet connection, free speech defender he could find. Of course they were all closed at 2:00 a.m.—but he started again at 7:00.

Donny was grateful for one thing. He had Cheetos in his car—the red spicy kind, in large supply. His heartburn would get him through the day.

62 | FLAT AS A PANCAKE

Flat as a pancake. This was the phrase Ursula used to describe the landscape of the plains of Oklahoma she grew up on, the dimensions of her chest until age seventeen, and the way she tried to feel right now. Flat. Not registering upset or elation. No affect at all, just frozen, numb, and flat. That's what she wanted, but it took great effort to bring herself to this place. She, who had once been so muted, was now at risk of feeling too much.

She tried to remember this phrase, *flat as a pancake,* and the sensation that went along with it as she sat in the tiny cell. She had been separated from the other women who had all been arrested earlier that night for allegedly attacking the President with an offensive banner. She was all alone in the jail cell, not knowing why.

Ursula never admitted this, but she was claustrophobic. She panicked in tight, airless spaces, and this would definitely qualify as one. There were only a plastic mattress on the floor and a toilet in this cramped room where there was no way to see out, and only a small slot in the door to see in. No doubt there was a video camera watching her every move. They never turned off the lights.

"Flat as a pancake," she spoke to coach herself to calm. "Meditate, center, keep it flat." She'd managed for a moment to find her breath again, but then a thought dashed across the flattened plains—*What are they going to do to me?* And the elevator of fear went right back up to her throat.

Flat as a pancake. Does anyone even know I'm here?

Ursula pictured herself as a young girl riding in the back of her uncle's pickup truck, driving across his fields of soy. The road went on and on, cutting a swath through the green. She pictured herself now, going out towards the sun, driving and driving, and never catching the horizon—the edge of the world mercifully extending to keep her from falling off and dropping all the way to China…

Suddenly, the door flung open. "Time for a little chat," said the female security guard as she clamped restraints on Ursula's ankles and wrists, and guided her out the door.

Ursula was placed in an interrogation room and shown to sit down at the table. The fear was salivating again in her throat so much she thought she'd throw up. Two very butch women, with closely cropped hair, came in and sat down on the other side of the table.

Ursula had to admit they bore an ironic resemblance to the women from FemForce in a parallel universe—which led her to wonder what had happened to those women. She wanted to ask, but had enough sense to know this was not a time to speak.

The butch interrogators asked Ursula what her interest was in the seeds. Ursula was careful. She simply said, "I eat organic, and know a lot of people who are concerned about their health and style of eating."

She launched into a lecture about the benefits of organic food. Butch 1 stopped her right there. Butch 2 asked her if that was all. Ursula repeated herself, word for word. She'd seen enough war movies to know that interrogators are looking for some hole in the prisoner's story through which to enter. She gave them none. She had no idea what they wanted of her, but Ursula would not be cracked.

What they wanted was to find out just how much she knew about the permission the government had just given to AgriNu. How did she know the US had just authorized AgriNu to tamper with the food supply of our "allies" and enemies? Since that was just about everyone else who wasn't us—it was a substantial campaign. The President, despite his skyrocketing approval poll numbers since the attack, still needed more leverage, more money, and a re-election—all of which AgriNu could help deliver. Not to mention, Mr. Ed and these guys who had gotten rid of spinach were his heroes of the moment and could do no wrong.

Was it a mere coincidence that this young woman should be asking about this on the very day after the secret agreement had been signed?

Highly unlikely. And with her Middle Eastern affiliations… the Butches' questions were getting nowhere. They attempted to confuse, to imply, to threaten. They told her if she spoke up, they could protect her—and a pretty girl like her was going to need protection in a place like this—where, frankly, she could get lost for a very long time.

"The dykes in here will have you for lunch… and breakfast, and dinner." Butch 1 licked her lips. Both Butches laughed hard. Then they left the room, and someone else came in.

When Ursula woke up she was no longer where she thought she had been, but lying down flat on the lumpy mattress. She was back in her cell. Her lungs felt heavy. Her eyelids felt heavier. Her upper arm throbbed but she couldn't see anything other than the tiny incision where her time-release birth control was inserted.

She wanted to be alert for every moment, but it was too much to stay awake. She fell back to sleep, falling into the back of the pickup truck, chasing the edge of the world.

"OK, let's go. You're being released," said a voice from out of nowhere. The cell door opened. Ursula focused her eyes. Standing next to the guard were the FemForce lawyer, the ACLU lawyer, the public defender, and a representative from some civil rights watchdog group.

"Are you alright?" FemForce asked. "Did they hurt you in any way? Intimidate you? Threaten you?"

Ursula said, "No. They asked me some questions." But she knew they had changed her. She just didn't know how.

63 | URSULA COMES BACK

Ursula stepped out into the mid-morning sunlight. So bright, it hurt her skin.

She was once again in her jingle-jangle skirt and midriff top, covered by her beige trench coat. She was so rumpled that to look at her you'd think she'd slept in those clothes. But we know she'd been wearing some hideous, baggy, orange ensemble.

She held her shoes in one hand and walked barefoot into the day. The lawyers insisted on giving her a ride, but she wanted to walk. She wanted to know the ground through her feet: stone, pebble, mud, and the sweet soft grass in all its textures. She wanted to contact the earth once again.

Wherever she had been, locked in that cold, hard cell, she had been in suspension. The concrete and steel blocked out the receiving of any sort of life signal, isolating her from any bio-feed at all.

In suspension, also, because they had given her drugs—and because she didn't know what the outcome of all this would be.

Ursula's fear had always been that she would get arrested. And she did. Her fear now was that when she was in jail, they had implanted some kind of tracking, electronic frequency, hormone-regulating, brain-altering microchip under her skin. They might have removed her time-release birth control insert, and replaced it with a chip.

When Ursula spent time in jail, they did not rape her. You don't need to destroy a person if you can control them. She was afraid that right now, they were either monitoring her thoughts and actions, or causing them.

Some line in her has now been crossed. She knows it's all different now. She can no longer close her eyes to the truth, or hide out for fear of its consequences. Or be lulled into complacency with a happy meal and a toy, or be hypnotized into obsessing about her weight as a distraction to keep from seeing what is really wrong in this world.

There is mourning at the dawn of awareness. And now she can locate it on the map as to where and when it first occurred.

Ursula looked up at the sky. According to the sun, it was ten o'clock on a Tuesday morning. She checked the newspaper front page at the newsstand at the corner. Wednesday. *I probably should go to work,* she thought, and she headed in that direction.

64 | URSULA RETURNS TO WORK

They were fairly easy going at the travel agency when she returned. Trusted employees get to work somewhat independently, and she always did her job well. But in order to serve the clients, no matter what time of day, you needed to be available by phone, text, and email. If someone in Europe didn't like their cabin on the QE2, or if someone had an emergency at home and had to rebook their flight, you had to be on it.

The travel agency business was near extinction, and the only way to hang on was to provide clients, usually high end, with impeccable service. Ursula didn't like cell phones, or crackberries, or most electronic devices—though she did like her computer, and she's had a few interesting nights with a vibrator while Donny was away. She hated how some people couldn't go ten minutes without talking to someone, anyone—the dry cleaners, even telemarketers—just to stay connected. She didn't want to be like them, wired for sound.

But Ursula was convinced she was. Her arm felt so strange. She could kind of taste it in her mouth. She had heard somewhere that our ears actually make a sound of their own. If you put a very sensitive microphone right up to the ear, it makes its own high-pitched squeak. That being so, a listening device would also produce its own sound, even a concealed one that had no business giving itself away.

When Ursula finally walked into work, Sid asked her where she'd been. He said to her, all pissy, "You were not on your cell, and the Fletchers got rained out at St. Bart's and wanted to switch somewhere else, dry. I sent them to a dude ranch in Montana. And apparently Mr. Fletcher is allergic to hay." Suddenly noticing her pale color, he added, "You look awful. Maybe you should go home."

"No, I need to catch up on my work," she said, and headed for her desk.

She turned on her computer and her phone. Message after message from Donny was waiting for her. Cute, then impatient, then frantic—*Where are you?!*

She called him. He stopped what he was doing and rushed right over.

As soon as he saw her, he grabbed her up in his arms and kissed her and kissed her, and stroked her hair. He asked her over and over again, "Are you OK?"

She was relieved to be in his arms, but surprised by how little she wanted to say. He asked if they could go to lunch. Sid rolled his eyes, but said yes.

They went to this little place around the corner. Ursula ordered French fries and a bagel with cream cheese. She was, she realized, famished and in need of comfort food. She couldn't remember, but she'd hardly eaten anything in that jail. Who can eat when they're terrified? And jails care nothing about nutrition. Neither did she in this moment.

"I want to hear all about it. Were you scared? Did they hurt you? Are you all right?"

"I don't really want to talk about it," she said, crossing her arms, placing her hand over the sore spot. "Not really anything to say… I'm fine."

Donny looked puzzled.

Ursula took a pen from his pocket and wrote on the napkin, *I'm being bugged.*

Donny looked around. Anyone, he guessed, even in that hippie cafe could be a surveillance guy.

She pointed to her arm. He didn't get it.

I'll explain later, she wrote. They sat in very potent silence. Donny became more and more uncomfortable.

"Ursula, we have to talk…" he said, almost blurting. He couldn't believe *he* was in the "we have to talk" position. It was so unnerving. "I have to ask you…"

Can we do this later? I'm really tired, she wrote, taking her last bite of bagel.

What?! He allowed himself to be in the "we have to talk" position, and she, a woman, was not going to talk? He bit down on his jaw against all the words that wanted to come spilling out. *Why am I not somebody your friends know to contact if you are... say, arrested? Why don't you want your friends to know about me? Don't we have this wild and crazy sex life? Don't you think you can rely on me? Don't I mean something to you?* But instead, he only said... "Let's be each other's emergency contact number."

This was his first concession towards commitment.

65 | URSULA TAKES TO BED

Ursula went home, crawled into bed, pulled the comforter up to her chin, and fell asleep.

66 | PAUL CAN'T GO HOME

Paul was really mixed up. He kept asking himself, *What kind of guy am I that would let my girlfriend fuck another guy just so I can prove that I'm some other kind of guy than who I really am? Which was a schmoe... and now I'm a schmuck.* He keeps telling himself he's changed. He's not that cloistered, overly mental, crusty booger of a mole anymore, he's become something else, something more. No... he's still a coward, just a different kind.

Lindey says not to worry about it. He should think of it as her way of paying half the bill.

She was still going to leave him at the end of the week. But this was just part of the reason. Ultimately, she only wanted to be with people who could survive on their own. And Paul was neither strong, nor skilled, nor clever. He did know a lot of unnecessary information that, he pointed out, could prove useful someday—but so far, it hadn't.

She had slept with him to allow him to say thank you. And then it was kind of fun to have a fuck buddy who was so new to everything, so harmless and so eager. But, enough of that. Paul had a need, and she was tired of serving it. At least with this Jason, it was a direct exchange of services, and that economy made more sense to her.

The question that was even more present for Paul was, *What should I do with myself while Lindey is paying the bill?* He started out at the bar. Agitated and easily bored with that, he moved to the business center. At least they had CNN in there and not sports.

The top story was how European farmers were responding to the recent al-Qaeda bio-attacks by testing the crops in each farm, isolating and destroying the affected areas of contamination, but no more. Despite the public panic, their governments were still saying "No thank you" to our government's offer of Freedom Seeds. That started a whole new round of resolve and protest from the organic movement here.

"Hah," Paul uttered smugly to himself. These events had AgriNu written all over them. He checked his blog, which he hadn't posted on since before he left for the camp. In his absence, one of his followers had side tracked the conversations to a review of the latest *Twilight* movie, and had gained sixty new followers. He wasn't about to let his site be hijacked. He began writing:

> **The characters in Twilight are DEAD. Their supernatural pwers** (delete) **powr** (backspace) **powers are an escape. Our ONLY REAL ESCAPE is to get off the fcking** (delete) **fucking guck** (delete) **grid. I now know 1st hand that it's possilbe** (delete) **posd** (backspace) **possible...**

The keyboard was impossibly old and frustratingly slow. It made him jones for his computer back home. He had turned away from going back once before, but now he was filled with enough alcohol and melancholy to do self-destructive things—to embrace them, in fact. So he went out to the valet and got his car.

He was justifiably apprehensive when he turned the key to his front door. The possibilities that the place had been taken over by bacteria, mold or other life forms were extremely high. He had learned how to hold his breath for at least a minute—the time it takes to put on your gas mask in an attack. He might need one once inside the door. He took a deep breath and entered.

He scanned the room... and saw it. Or didn't see it. His computer. It was gone! His files, his papers, all ransacked. Who was it? FBI? CIA? They had finally caught on to him and confiscated his research. His breath expelled with a startle—which turned out not to be such a good idea. The stink in the place was horrid. He quickly went through the files to see what was missing. All his primary research on JFK was still there. *Curious,* he thought. Then again, they took his computer, and it contained everything. Even the FBI has gone paperless. If it wasn't that, then what were they looking for?

He wasn't going to stick around to find out.

He went into his bedroom (another mistake), grabbed up his soft pillow, threw a few more clothes into a broken suitcase, and left in great haste, locking the door behind him.

It turns out Donny's place was also ransacked and raided, but he couldn't tell the difference.

67 | URSULA SLEEPS

The first three days, Ursula slept for hours at a time. She would awaken, only to fall back to sleep again. Donny, who did not consider himself a hoverer, hovered over her. He sat in a chair by the bed, then moved to the other room to watch TV, then back. When she did awaken, she would ask for water, but by the time he brought it to her, she'd be asleep again. It was like attending someone in a coma.

It was making Donny a little crazy, this bouncing between acute worry over her condition and pissed-off fury that she didn't consider him, not even *the* one but *some* one who needed to be called when she was in jail. Instead, he had been left to play out all sorts of horrible scenarios in his imagination. When she snapped out of this, they were going to have to talk. Some things just had to be made clear, that's all. *Jesus, he was starting to sound like a girl.*

As for Ursula, her bed was everything her cell was not. It felt fluffy and soft, warm, and yet lightweight. Crawling down between the white sheets and down comforter was like being inside a puffy cave with filtered white light. She would sink way down, spread, and practically dissolve into the surrounding softness. Each time she woke, she'd flip or roll, or shift, and sink and spread again.

Sometimes the sinking and the flipping got pretty violent—more like thrashing and lashing. In her dreams, she felt like she was looking hard for something that had been taken, and she was looking to take it back.

Day 4, she got a fever and got very still. Donny called the doctor and hovered even closer. The doctor even made a house call. Said she was burning through something, and as long as she stayed hydrated, there was no need to move her.

Donny, not being a religious guy of any sort, knew he was beyond his league and asked Sheerah and a few of her belly dancing friends to come over and do something… say some prayers, or whatever they do.

They arrived with candles and incense, and held chanting vigils that made Donny so agitated he left the house, only to walk around the block, return, and ask them to leave.

Sheerah remained. She told him that she had the ability to track where Ursula was, and could actually see her dreams. She sipped some tea made from the mushroom Sean brought her to heighten the connection. She placed her hand on Ursula's sleeping body, closed her eyes, and joined her in a matrix of unspoken, vivid connection.

In that fever dream, Ursula felt a battle within her, like a foreign object inside her arm was trying to take hold, and her body was working its hardest to resist and reject its reach. She could feel herself struggling for ownership. Then suddenly it was like all the parts of her vaporized into thin air. She could not move, or feel her own edges, and yet she felt profound waves rippling through what she knew of as her body. Like she was being rewired…

At the end of that evening, Sheerah removed her hand, and asked Donny to call her once Ursula had come back. Donny wanted to know more. Sheerah just told him to call.

On Day 5, nothing changed. Ursula was traveling far.

On Day 6, he only realized another day had passed after nightfall.

On Day 7, Ursula popped awake. She took in her surroundings. She stretched, yawned, and rolled over to see his face—right above hers.

"Hello," he said, gratefully.

She gave a little smile.

"Are you OK?"

"Um hmm," she murmured

"Can we talk?"

She held up a finger and pointed to the bathroom.

He helped her to the bathroom, then waited for her in the bed she had occupied for so long.

When she returned, Donny threw the covers over the both of them and held her tight. When she was unconscious, drifting, hibernating, whatever she was doing, he was afraid to touch her—she seemed so tenuous he thought he might break her. But now that her eyes were open, and she even walked to the bathroom and back by herself—all he could do was hold her tight.

She was not sure where she had traveled, down tunnels and spirals both dark and full of color. Montages of unconnected images took her this way and that. Voices and snippets of sound filtered through. Her location was always suspended, and who knows how long all that went on for. But now she was located, right here. Her bed. Her room. This man. She felt safe. Donny's chest hairs tickled her nose as it flattened against his chest from him holding her too tight. His wet palms slid across her back. It was a welcome comfort.

Donny felt her closeness. He felt his heart racing. For a guy to whom words came so flippantly easy, he found himself rehearsing a line over and over again, as if it had to be just right in order to be brought out before company. The more he rehearsed it, the tighter the gates of his mouth clenched. What was the line? *Ursula, I have something to say...* which is so not a line he would say—because it says nothing! It's saying you have something to say which is pretty obvious. So, why not just say what you actually want to say?

Each time he did try to bring this now inane line out of his mouth, he lost the gushy, rushy feeling that was surging in his blood, that feeling that he had to pull Ursula tighter and tighter to him or he would explode. He liked that feeling, and he was losing it because his words were so bound up in his nervousness. So nervous it made him laugh out loud.

His laughter broke the spell of the idiot loop inside his brain.

"I've been so scared. I want to know what happened to you in that prison. I want to know what happened to you while you've been lying here in bed all week. I want to know why your friends did *not* think I was someone who needed to be called when you were locked up and disappeared from sight. Why they wouldn't know that I was the one waiting for you to come home. I want to know who I am to you!" He found himself shouting.

"Shhhhhhh," Ursula said softly nuzzling inside the crook of his arm. And with this she fell silent. These were the last words she spoke.

For the next two hours, they made love in a sweet and gentle way, as an antidote to all that had happened. Then they ate some miso soup and dehydrated kale chips. Then he called Sheerah.

68 | RESEARCHING THE FIELD

Sheerah had already been talking with Sean. She told him that when she tapped into Ursula's dreams, she could sense that something very large was afoot. She couldn't see the images that Ursula was dancing with, but she had a strong feeling there were big changes to come.

Sean had lots of experience with Shamans and plant medicine-keepers, both indigenous and entrepreneurial, from his photographic journeys all over the world. People who had visions and could read symbols for their meaning.

When Sheerah said she saw a glowing network, Sean said, "Ahhh." When she told him she saw mushrooms, he said, "Ohhhh." When she suggested they have an emergency meeting to find out more, he said, "You betcha!" And was on the next plane and in her bed within twenty-four hours.

They plugged in, this time not for their own sheer pleasure, but for the discovery and understanding of what Ursula had tapped. Which is not to say they didn't enjoy it. They were both avid researchers and thoroughly delighted in their study time together.

69 | URSULA GOES SILENT

It seemed like the only thing to do. Stop talking so there'd be nothing to hear, nothing to spy on and report back to whomever they were reporting to for whatever it was they wanted. Anything could be bugged, and she was convinced everything probably was. She was sure she noticed a picture hanging crooked on the wall, pillows on the couch out of place that she knew she had not rearranged.

She would have to stop the gardening expeditions, lest someone was following her. And she would not go to belly dancing class, lest it be considered some sort of sleeper cell. Anything out of the ordinary could be deemed suspicious behavior and risk her getting jailed again. Ursula still had no idea why they had detained her at all.

Likewise, the ACLU lawyers told Ursula to report to them anything out of the ordinary. They would be looking out for her. They had made *that* clear to those who had held her without cause. But it would be best if she kept her life small and very normal.

70 | ... AND DONNY MOVES IN

Once Ursula had gone silent, it became more and more difficult to have a phone conversation with her. She would lift up the receiver and then not speak…

"Ursula, it's Donny."

Silence.

"How are you?"

Silence.

"Can I come over? One tap for yes"

Tap.

"What time?"

Silence.

"I'll be there at seven." Click.

Which is why Donny moved in. He did it to spare himself these endless, inane phone conversations. And the worst of it? Ursula was a talker; she didn't like to hang up. Now Donny, he was a talker, too. For a woman this is not so unusual, but for a guy it is. So when Donny said that Ursula was a talker, he knew what he was talking about.

Instead of talking, she was now mouthing rapidly or constantly tapping the whiteboard she carried everywhere, scribbling things like, *There's a yellow butterfly out the window,* which he might have noticed if his attention weren't on the whiteboard instead of the window. He might even have seen the butterfly if the whiteboard tapping hadn't frightened the thing into flittering off. (Besides, who gives a shit about butterflies?)

And she wouldn't text. Fucking everybody texts, but now she wouldn't do it because "they" were keeping track of everything. She had no proof of this; and to his mind, her imagination was taking her way overboard. There were real criminals, terrorists, and opposition party leaders to listen in on. Who was going to waste their time on a kooky flower child? He indulged her, but her fears were unfounded.

Now if you want to talk about real fear…

Donny had never lived with a woman before. There were several almosts. The *I've got most of my best stuff at her place* and *we'll get a place together after we get married* almosts… but he always found himself back at his Hollywood-bungalow apartment, alone.

This is what was really mystifying to him: he, who could be such a dog when it came to women, was not moving in because of the mind-blowing sex (even though there'd been plenty since Ursula had become orgasmic); it was because Ursula had stopped talking, and he had to be near her to know what she was saying.

Who knew it would be communication—his brain and not his dick—that would make a cohabitor out of this slovenly bachelor? Who knew?

He kept his place as an office. (He's thinking of writing a sitcom about a guy who moves in with a woman for the first time…) Plus, he needed somewhere to store his comic book collection. Ursula said it took up too much space. In carefully selecting what to bring over—her sheets were cleaner, her plates were nicer—he decided to bring over a number of books. He needed *some* of his stuff to feel he was there, and books could cover a wide area. The mushrooms on every surface presented a bit of an obstacle, but Donny would work around them.

What he didn't realize was that even before he'd moved in, he was already making a home for himself inside her. By offering her his favorite books to read, and taking her to all the weird places he liked to go, he had been digging a den within her and filling it with his own familiar stuff—what might be the equivalent of his La-Z-Boy, his wash-worn Giants jersey, and a cold Sam Adams—so he might recognize himself in there when he came to rest inside of her. Otherwise, it'd just be too foreign.

Donny was far from the silent type. This could be inferred from his every action. It was so damned quiet in the house that sometimes, Donny's own busy, lumbering sounds clamored through the rooms. Perhaps it was a good thing, making up for her silence should anyone be listening in.

71 | MESSAGE FROM THE WALL

When Ursula returned to work after her long absence, she wrote out for Sid that, due to her silence, she could not use the telephone. She would only be available for work on the computer and for interoffice communication via the small whiteboard. She could also text—but only about matters pertaining to work in the work setting.

She requested that he take care of all calls, and she could be the back up. Sid was not crazy about this idea. He himself was not the most social of characters, and agreed only with the qualification that "This had better be just a passing phase."

Ursula begged him not to tell the boss, who was never there anyway, but who she was sure would not be keen on her not speaking to the clients.

It was harder coming back to work than she thought it would be. Her senses were easily overwhelmed, and her eyes were still sensitive to light. She had received many images during the time she was traveling in her dreams. Pictures she saw that she didn't understand. Clearly there was a message there, but what? Right now, the rims of her eyes were burning from staring at the computer screen for some flight changes. She stared off into space to rest them, moving them about the room.

Her eyes landed on her Wall of Strangers. She always took comfort there. Each stranger smiling back at her, some anxious, some posed, some goofing off—each one on as much of an adventure as they would allow. The first part of that adventure was allowing themselves to be photographed with a total stranger for the benefit of yet another person unknown to them.

If she'd ever wondered how people face the unknown, well, here were all the ways right in front of her—random and varied.

She continued to stare at the photos of friendly strangers with her lids half closed. Her vision blurred as she scanned the rows, then took in the canvas as a whole… and she noticed a pattern. There were those strangers smiling with closed lips, those with parted lips, and those with full teeth showing. When she softened her focus, she could see an intersecting matrix, a constellation of smiling strangers in the shape of… Whoa.

Ursula had written each stranger's address on the back of their photo before pinning them up. She hastily marked their hometowns on the globe in her office—and curiously enough, the lines connecting them formed the indisputable shape of a… mushroom. Once she saw it like this, she couldn't see it any other way.

Like Cheesus. She'd seen pictures on YouTube of Jesus appearing as a Cheeto, right out of the bag. Since then, she looked for him in every single package Donny still sneaked home. Or like when she was a kid, when The Lord's shadow had appeared on her neighbor's refrigerator door—that Kenmore could never be seen as anything but a sacred receiving station.

Her wall had become a receiving station for the message from the mushrooms, and she knew exactly what to do.

Her plan would be this: she would send the seeds with the growing medium of her mushrooms to each of the people in each of these places, for planting. The mushrooms were asking for this, to be received by smiling strangers for the sake of the seeds. If mushrooms were connected with each other through an underground mycelial network in the soil—why not in an above ground network as well? The message here was clear.

As for the snack formations of Jesus or the shadow of Elvis that Donny had seen on the ceiling that night of the coital mishap, who's to say that their spirits are not spreading their own messages throughout the world? Who's to say they're not the ones telling us what songs to sing in the shower?

What is their message?

Love Me Tender?

What is the message of the mushrooms?

I Will Survive.

When she ran this idea by Sean and Sheerah, they said it made sense to them. It was obvious from their mutual glow that they'd been deep in research since Sheerah had entered Ursula's dreams. They were picking up some sort of mushroom thing, too—a huge expansive network below, directly reflecting the cosmos above. Very cool.

Sean turned down an assignment in Bhutan to continue their "studies" together.

72 | PAUL AND LINDEY RETURN

"VERY few people get this far," Papa John said in a menacing tone, as he looked straight at Paul. "It's only because of Lindey that you're here."

Paul started coughing. It was dusty in the underground shelter. The air was close, and these men did not believe in bathing.

Where they were was called The Pass Through. It was the waiting station at the entry to The Entire System. Paul had no real clue what The Entire System was, or how far it extended, but these guys spoke of it so ominously, he knew it must be something like the time/space continuum on the other side of a wormhole. He imagined it was a catacomb network of underground tunnels, connecting to other sites where other survivalists were posted. For exactly what purpose, he didn't know. This place, where he and Lindey were sitting with Papa John and three other "survivors," seemed more like Purgatory.

One of the survivors turned to Lindey. "You're still with this loser?"

"The outside world sucks. I needed a ride back," she replied matter-of-factly, showing no loyalty whatsoever to Paul. He knew he deserved it. He couldn't even keep her in a nice hotel without her having to finance their stay.

This was already Day 4 for Paul and Lindey in The Pass Through. Papa John wanted to make sure no one was on their trail. Paul's Volvo was being driven across the Mexican border and broken down into parts. When you disappear off the grid, you leave no traces.

Paul thought this disappearing was the safest way, not only for him but for Lindey, who by mere association could be in deep doo-doo with the government, as well.

How they got there?

After Paul saw that his apartment had been raided, he returned immediately to the hotel. He burst into the room just as Jason was zipping up his fly. He fought back the urge to pull out his gun and blow this guy's head off, the urge to slice off his balls with his four-in-one hunting blade, the urge to pull out the weasel's vocal chords with his bare hands. Instead, Paul stood there, silent, holding the door open for Jason to leave.

"Thanks," Jason said in a smug winner's tone.

Paul burned inside, saying nothing. He had larger urgencies to attend to, and when necessary, he had razor focus.

As soon as the door closed, he pulled out his backpack and threw his few things in there. He said to Lindey, "We're checking out."

She was sarcastic. "I've already paid for the night."

That stung, but Paul would not be deterred.

"Pack your things right now. My place has been raided. They've confiscated my computer… we've got to get out of here, fast. I'm afraid you could be in danger, too."

"Who are you?" She was suddenly getting interested in him again.

"Just somebody who knows a lot of shit. Let's go."

He opened the mini bar and emptied its content into a plastic laundry bag—as much for spite as for road food.

They snuck out through the garden, so as not to go through the lobby. He might never get the satisfaction of punching Jason out, but that was one of the things he was going to have to live with.

Lindey was planning to leave Paul once the hotel stay had ended, but now they were in different circumstances. What could a wimp like this possibly have done to have the government after him? And what kind of shit did he know? If they were really in danger, the only place she wanted to be was with Papa John. Paul, at least, owed her that.

73 | A SON

When Daphne called Mr. Ed saying she wanted to see him right away, he canceled his afternoon and practically flew over to her apartment. She had not returned his calls in over two weeks—only texted lame excuses that she was very busy with an overburdened court case.

Even without much contact, Edwin was all puffed up with pride at the possibility of a son—a drive that far outweighed his panic over the effect this would have on his marriage.

But hell! He was becoming a man of power. Isn't this what happens for them? Increased sexual opportunity with better and better females? More offspring as a demonstration of their virility? Doesn't this mean he's really made the big time?

Daphne was carrying his child. Bitsy would just have to bite it. She'd put him through all kinds of personal humiliation with her affairs, the worst by far being cuckolded by his boss, who was now his pal; but still, it lingered, unspoken, in the atmosphere between them. No. She would have to find a way to live with this. He would not rub it in her face. He was that much of a gentleman.

Or maybe Mr. Ed would leave Bitsy, marry Daphne and create a new family. He was one of only a few of his friends who were still on their first wives. New life. New flow. Something growing. Something flourishing. And if it were a son, Mr. Ed would be in the fine position to bring Edwin, Jr. into a world where an Edwards could take a seat at the big table—which, he was finding, was the only place to be.

In fact, the more he thought about it, the more he realized that for his son to have his proper seat at the table, he had to be a full-blooded, fully embraced, fully elevated Edwards, not some bastard boy—which is why when Bitsy came home and asked Mr. Ed where he was going, Mr. Ed replied, "I'm leaving you," smiled, and walked out the door.

When Daphne sat him down and told him, "I've had an abortion," all the lifeblood of possibility drained from him and pooled at his feet. He couldn't move. His throat closed, and his eyes burned. She said it was just too complicated. Her not-yet-ex was vindictive, and her divorce was not yet final. She couldn't risk losing custody of her own children, let alone afford to raise another.

"But I want to marry you… adopt all your children," he said, practically begging.

She took a long airless pause. "It's best if we stop seeing each other."

That was the sucker punch to his already pummeled dreams.

"Why?" he pleaded.

"It's done." She got up off the couch and showed him out.

After the door closed behind him, Mr. Ed realized that now that his life had been full of such new possibility, he had already grown into it. Even if he could return to Bitsy and the way things were, it all felt pale and void. No. Worse. Like a knife had eviscerated his entire existence, and all its entrails had spilled out.

The next day, Mr. Ed called a meeting with the President again.

The result being… as of Monday, every seed saving son-of-a-bitch in the USA would be treated as a terrorist conspirator. Farmers, gardeners, people who kept their trash too long, anyone who saved a seed would be a criminal.

Leave the Growing to Us. *Because we're the only ones allowed.*

The conversion to Freedom Seeds hadn't been happening fast enough to satisfy AgriNu. So, if the EU didn't want to make more of this contamination panic, AgriNu and the US government certainly would. Fuck the EU! They'd stage more attacks here. Escalate the message—*Danger, danger, danger. No seeds but ours are safe. Extreme times require extreme measures. It's not just a matter of National Security; it's a matter of survival!*

From now on, the only seeds to be planted anywhere in the US will be AgriNu's government approved Freedom Seeds, and anyone in possession of any heirloom, native, or "unprotected" seeds can and will be arrested.

If Mr. Ed's seeds weren't being saved, no one's would.

And as quickly as that, Donny and Ursula were no longer rebels, they were outlaws.

74 | WORKING THE PLAN

If Paul were not in hiding, he'd be blogging like crazy right now. If the mainstream Press weren't in the corporations' pockets, they'd be reporting this all over the front page. If the city folks who'd never seen a carrot growing gave a rat's ass about a farm… or if concern-minded people weren't in such shocked disbelief, they would act. If the Internet providers weren't shutting down the lines of communication between the activists, at least *they* would be swarming up in huge numbers. And if those who *were* swarming weren't being pepper-sprayed by the police, there might be more of them. If fear didn't stop everything in its tracks… something would be done…

Though both only specks, Ursula and Donny were doing something. They were spending long nights laying out a grid on a map of the world. When Ursula drew out the constellation she had seen in the smiling faces of the perfect strangers, they all seemed to congregate in the Equatorial region where plants are abundant and grow extremely fast. South America, Central America, Western Africa, all over Indonesia… if only the world were still Pangaea, it would be so much easier to get from place to place.

The two of them made larger maps of each area and located the addresses of each stranger. She then drew lines from each to the other, and from here to there. The grid was elaborate, for sure. The design was so clear; she knew she was on the right track. And since this new and frightening law regarding seed saving, her urgency was on red alert.

She had Sid fax, e-mail, or write each of the individuals in the chosen photos and ask if they would be willing to meet another stranger. Most people were responding well to her odd request.

Meanwhile, Ursula's crop of Kombucha friends had now reached 541. They were multiplying exponentially, and at greater speed, it seemed to her. She continued to hear their instruction, sometimes amplified so loudly she had to plug up her ears. Not that it helped. They were all excited for their mission, which only increased their glow. Since no one else could see or hear this—Ursula kept this part to herself.

Despite Donny's habitual skepticism, he wanted to be supportive. He enjoyed spending time with her like this, drawing up a secret plan. It appealed to his spy/hero fantasies, and it only added to her allure. For, in addition to the obvious reasons for attraction, she was a good strategist; so was he, from all the games he'd played. She was surprisingly cool under pressure. Whatever her eccentricities about this whole thing, a new resolve had come to her since her arrest.

Donny had been told, "Whoever says it first loses all power in the relationship." It was the advice he offered to friends. It was the strict policy he lived by—never ever be the one to say it first. There were far too many ways to lose the delicate power play between the sexes without throwing in the one that was sure to sink a man's ship all the way to the ocean's deep. He was amazed, really, that he had managed to move in with Ursula without saying *the words.*

Yet tonight, as he looked over the table at her, her little pink tongue poking out of the corner of her mouth in deep concentration while she carefully measured lines from Cusco to Cameroon… he heard himself say in a clear and audible tone, "I love you." It just slipped out.

She hadn't even asked him a question he had to maneuver around. She wasn't even talking at all… and he said it first! What the hell was he doing?

He felt naked. He hoped maybe she'd make an exception, open her mouth and meet his courting call with the words, "I love you, too," but she just stared at him, smiling inquisitively.

What? She didn't hear? She doesn't understand? I'm going to have to say it again?! Maybe she's fucking with me.

Warning, warning, warning, went off in his head. He felt so hot he wanted to jump out of his skin. Leave, flee, run right now.

But she pointed to her ear, and gave him that big-eyed questioning look of innocence he'd come to know.

She didn't hear him after all. He was saved. So he said, instead, "It's late," and took her by the hand and led her to the bedroom.

As they undressed, he sat her down and took her face in his hands and kissed her lips. She kissed him back, luscious and full. Spontaneously, she climbed on top of his lap. He could feel himself drawing up towards her… and before he knew it, it happened again.

"I love you," he repeated. *Damn!*

This time she heard him. She took his words in on her next inhale and let them fill her, holding the sensation within her body as long as she could before snuggling in to his chest and exhaling a long sigh.

Donny listened nervously for her response. *Why did she bury herself? Maybe she couldn't face him because she didn't feel it back?*

He felt a tiny drop of wet on his chest where his shirt was open. He recognized her tear rolling down and coming to rest in the cave of his sternum. She lifted her head, looked back up into his face, and he knew.

And, as if he was going to burst and had to keep himself from flying apart, he wrapped himself all around her, and instead of climaxing, melted with her, and… relaxed. For once maybe in ever, he relaxed… and fell asleep with a smile all over his body.

As they sleep, bodies entwined, they are growing, together.

Donny and Ursula have planted seeds in each other and are growing into the lovers they need to be. They are growing each other in order to truly meet somewhere in the unique blending of who they are; and through this, each of them is growing into the hero she or he needs to become.

When they unite in coital bliss, it feels like coming home; because he's built a house in her, and she's lit a hearth in him. The particular way they each lean in towards the sun of their own co-joining is shaped and directed by the ways the other now moves inside them.

This is more than sex. It's more like destiny—and who they each must become in order to fulfill their own destiny rests in the other lover as well.

M. Earth carefully tends the gardens inside lovers, laying the fertile ground, watering, pinching back the dead leaves. The shimmer of Eros awakens the growth spurt. Love breaks up the crusted dirt so the new sprouts can surface. Sometimes there are huge clumps to be cleared. It takes time. And it takes the time it takes.

Donny and Ursula sleep together in a nice hum. That's because they are planted inside each other and growing towards a mutual sun. No wonder.

75 | SWIMMING UPSTREAM

As the plan was perfected, it became clear that they needed to do another "test drive" through the airport with the mushrooms and seeds. The packaging for the mushrooms' transport needed to be improved. Donny, for one, did not want to *give birth* like he did the last time. And now that there were grave consequences for being in possession of contraband seed, they had to be extremely cautious.

Ursula had been in touch with Sean and Sheerah, who thought it was a brilliant idea; and Sheerah gave them a mixture of essential oils that would bring out courage and calm—because that's what was needed.

Based on what Ursula had observed before at the airport, she wanted to see if it was possible to bypass security altogether by going up through baggage claim. They would need to have a pre-printed boarding pass and only one piece of carry on luggage. They would also need a boarding pass from a flight that just landed—each pass stamped with the suitable security seal.

The plan was to go in through the opened doors at baggage claim when passengers with claimed baggage were going out. Once inside they would go upstream to the elevators that would take them up to the level of the arrival gates. If questioned, they would make a panicked fuss about having left their glasses on the plane… and, if need be, show the boarding pass for that flight.

Their first attempt at "swimming against the current" had to be without mushrooms and especially without seeds. Since the bio-attacks, airport security was tighter than ever. If apprehended, they'd better be clean!

Donny would be the first to try, since he'd already had some experience in what not to do. But he needed Paul. Paul could call up the blueprints to the airport terminals on his computer and hack into the TSA rotation schedule. He could do that shit. And more than that, Donny could trust him.

He called Paul. No answer. He called a half hour later. Still no answer. What was with this disappearing act Paul was playing out?

Donny knew he had to go to Paul's apartment to find him—not something he wanted to do. He had a key, given to him in case Paul should die and needed someone to come open the door and identify the body. The overpowering smell in the apartment could easily have been a rotting corpse, as Donny opened the door and nearly passed out from the putrid odor rushing toward the open air. It took a moment to focus.

The first thing he noticed when he regained equilibrium was that Paul's computer was gone. Then he noticed his bed sheets and pillow were gone. What the hell?!

Donny called the Chateau Marmont to see when Paul had checked out. They said they had no such guest registered—which is what they always say about their guests, but this time it was true.

Donny couldn't imagine where Paul had gone.

Lying on Paul's desk, where his computer used to be, Donny found a folded up *Survival* magazine opened to the ad for the survivalist's camp, minus the discount coupon. He picked up the phone and called their 1-800 number.

76 | PAUL AND LINDEY GET SENT UNDERGROUND

After what seemed like an eternity in purgatory, Paul and Lindey were allowed to pass through. *Shupe!* Sucked up like the egg in the bottle. They traveled along the hidden tunnels and transports of the survivalist network and disappeared from sight.

77 | URSULA DOES ALL SORTS OF THINGS TO HER BUGGING DEVICE

Donny wanted to spend the night at his place, to *remasculate* for his mission. That it happened the Yankees were playing the Red Sox was perhaps no small coincidence. Ursula didn't have a TV. That goes without saying.

Usually, Ursula didn't mind a night off. Donny was always such a large presence. She liked her privacy and the new quiet that went along with her own silence. But her suspicion that she was being monitored was making her fearful and putting her on edge. She knew that Donny didn't really believe her. She herself couldn't be sure… but she was sure. It made her scared, and it made her mad; and as the night went on, it bothered her more and more.

She felt literally pulled, in a tug of war between the mission of the mushrooms and the voice of her fears.

"Take us, we're ready to go."

Don't go ANYWHERE, "they" are watching your every move!

What if the plan doesn't work? What if Donny gets picked up? What if "they" know everything?

She couldn't stand it anymore. She got angry! She got vengeful! She got out of control!!

Things Ursula did to her bugging device that night (in case there were such a thing):

> Blasted the radio right into her arm.
>
> Stood near microwave ovens, wifi modems, and large magnets.
>
> Covered the incision site with a band-aid.

> Made poultices from the Kombucha mushroom to see if it could penetrate and mess things up.

There were times where she'd swear she could hear it squeal.

She got more and more angry. She thrashed about, spinning around endlessly in circles, to throw those fuckers off. Turning and turning—and with each turn, building up a fire within that was burning through her fears…

Did we mention that since Donny had moved in, and moved inside her, her hips had become a whole lot more free? Once she sweated some of the heated frustration out of her system, her pelvis began moving around in various configurations, drawing out the alphabet and the shape of infinity. Was this the kind of power unlocking that Sheerah was talking about? Ursula had no idea where this was going, but she was very curious indeed.

78 | A VISIT

The next morning… the knock on the door wasn't the same. It had a different tone, a disguised casualness. Three even beats—each one crisp and sharp.

Ursula knew it wasn't Donny. He had a key and his own idiosyncratic way of unlocking and turning the doorknob. When the knocking yielded no answer, whoever it was began ringing the bell in a more pressing fashion.

Ursula made herself very still, tiny silent breaths in the nostrils like a frozen deer. She stilled her heart, she stilled her sound, everything to make herself undetectable and make them go away.

Bam-Bam-Bam. She became more still yet—she didn't want her own sound waves to bounce back to theirs. Then she heard a quick *jiggle, jiggle, click, click, click* and the door was open.

Two men stepped into the room. They were wearing suits and ties, pretty much advertising who they were. Ursula just stood there in the center, so still as to be wearing a cloak of invisibility. But they saw her anyway.

"Excuse me, Ma'am," one said, startled but smooth. "We didn't know anyone was here."

Then, why the hell did you come in?! she wanted to scream. But she only nodded.

"We're from the office of Homeland Agricultural Security Terrorist Seed Sector," he stated. "We wanted to have a word with you."

"We're still interested in your interest in the seeds," said the other.

Ursula stared at them for a moment, then scribbled on her board, *I can't speak.*

They looked at each other strangely. They hadn't read this in her file. One of them asked for the board, and wrote back, *What is your interest in the seeds?*

"She can hear," the first agent said impatiently. "Mind if we look around?"

Of course she minded. She wanted to say, *Go to Hell, you fucking fucks. Get out of my house and take your Nazi needle-dicks with you…* but they didn't wait for an answer. She was sweating hard as they moved about the house in search of…

"Holy Mother of Christ!" she heard one scream from the other room. She knew exactly what they had come upon.

Since Donny had moved in, Ursula had gathered all the mushrooms from the hallways and moved them in to the dining room area. She had placed them on floor to ceiling shelf racks, and had set two air filters in there to dissipate the smell. She wasn't sure if this inevitably had more or less impact on these Homeland spooks, having them all in one place. Whatever it was, it was a hell of a shock. One agent ran out to the backyard, his handkerchief over his nose. Ursula tried not to smile.

The serious one got more serious. He was not going to lose his cool to this weirdo. He pulled Ursula into the dining room. "What are they?" he insisted.

Kombucha mushrooms. I bottle their juice as a digestive aid.

"Is this a business? Do you have a license?"

Personal use. I have stomach problems. Is there some law against it?

"No," he said, looking straight at her, "but there *is* a law against saving seeds.

He proceeded to the kitchen, pulled open the cabinets, opening bottles, and emptying spice jars.

He would find nothing there. She was always careful to hide away any signs of the preparation for their mission. Still the heat of panic was rising in her chest.

He searched the refrigerator, the freezer…

"Hey look at this," the other agent chuckled, as he came back in holding up two tomato plants ripped out from her vegetable garden. "Bingo." Ursula felt like they had ripped something out from her own body.

Those are Freedom tomatoes, she was about to write—

"And these," he said, producing a watertight box of seeds Ursula had buried in her backyard. He was still brushing off some large larvae that clung stubbornly to the box. "And there's tons more," he said. "A real treasure hunt."

Ursula wanted to scream out in horror.

"We won't take you in… not yet," the agent said, pulling out a small device from his pocket. "Section 275.3 of the New Anti-Terrorism Seed Act states that all violators of the law will be branded so other citizens can identify you as a danger to your country." They quickly grabbed her, pulled back her sleeve, and rendered a jolt to her arm that left an indelible mark. It burned like crazy. Ursula's whole body went into shock.

"We're going to watch you. Closely. And… if you do anything to keep us from watching you, we'll be back here again, just like today."

Ursula wanted to yell and scream and spit and rage, but it was all she could do to raise her arm and point to the door.

The agents opened the door. One went back to the dining room and snatched up a mushroom in its glass bowl. "We'll be back for the rest of this shit, as soon as we figure out what it is," he said. They left, taking her precious seeds, not even closing the door behind them.

Ursula grabbed a pillow off the couch, and holding it tightly to her face, opened her mouth and screamed at the top of her voice into the silencing fibers of the Dacron filling.

79 | QUAKING BELIEFS

Even though she had suspected they'd been tracking her and watching everything around her, she wasn't 100% sure. Now she was. Her silence hadn't really covered the truth. Nor had her uncertainty or denial.

Ursula had always been good at suspending her belief by pretending or looking the other way. She could look at a thing by kind of blurring her eyes so that what she was seeing got all watery and swimmy-like, and didn't hold its shape… like how she discovered the message from The Wall of Strangers.

The 1994 Northridge Earthquake shook her family's apartment, shook her belongings, and shook her to the core. In the waves of the aftershocks, while unearthing shards of kitchen debris, she felt like an archaeologist of her own life. There was history in that rubble pile that hadn't been history until those things had been crashed into past tense. And being in past tense, were of no practical use to her anymore. They became the fractal vessels of her collected story—each small piece carried the imprint of the whole, and now the whole lot of it could be scooped up by the bucketful and dumped into the trash.

She could not assume that a spoon would remain a spoon; or a bowl remain a bowl; or that the earth would ever stop shaking; or that gravity would remain constant, and working, and a friend.

She would not ride in elevators, or stop for a red light beneath a freeway overpass. She would not stand too close to a heavy-laden bookcase, or go inside any skyscraper. The illusion that "the world's movement is constant, but imperceptible" had been dissolved.

M. Earth says the tectonic plates shift and drift at the rate of toenail growth, but we don't feel that either. There's a lot we don't feel, until we do.

Over time, the necessity to function just couldn't keep Ursula out of every elevator, or keep her off the road. Ecologically, she didn't feel right about eating off of paper plates forever. So the frames of her slowed down movie began to move through the camera faster and faster, the dots became connected again, and life went back to "normal."

Then those planes hit the Twin Towers on 9/11 and Ursula's film snapped again. *Anything could happen anywhere, at any time*—and neither she nor the rest of her country could pretend it was any different.

And now this. *Anything could happen at any time…* because it had.

Her life had splayed apart and it was not coming back together. And now with every step, she could feel her toenails grow, and the earth move.

80 | THEY ALSO CAME FOR DONNY

Donny's plane wasn't leaving until that afternoon, so he had time to run out for a bagel before getting ready to go.

When he arrived back at his apartment/now office, the same two Terrorist Seed Sector agents were inside, thumbing through Donny's prized comic collection, all pulled out of their protective jackets. Donny felt the acid from his stomach rise up into his throat. *Who were they? What were they doing there? How greasy were their hands?* They had clearly been through his desk. His hidden pack of cigarettes and lighter lay out on the top.

One of the agents asked if he could bum a cigarette. "Nice collection," he said. "Aren't you concerned about a fire, old building like this?" He lit the lighter, and threw it down on top of the Superman #1 comic book—in good condition. (The rarest one Donny owned.)

Donny's gaze followed that lighter so deliberately tossed right on top of Superman's chest. Their threat was not lost on him. These guys are very good at finding out what you value most and messing with it.

"What do you know about the seeds?" the other agent asked.

"What seeds?" Donny said innocently, but his mind was starting to race.

"We know the company you keep." The agent tossed down the photo from the red light, with Ursula in the passenger seat, not blacked out this time.

Donny nearly shit his pants.

"Don't let her drag you down. Seed saving is treason. Think about it." The agent ground out his cigarette right on top of Superman's S.

After the agents left, Donny phoned Ursula. She didn't want to pick up, so he left a message that something had come up and he needed to postpone his trip for a day or two.

He then spent the rest of the day moving his comic book collection to a temperature-controlled storage unit in Lancaster. He left his car in front of his house, and got his neighbor to rent a truck and drive it, to throw the goons off his trail.

81 | URSULA GETS A CALL

Ursula sat frozen in the living room for a long time after those agents left. When she heard Donny's message about postponing the trip, she was both relieved and angry. Relieved, obviously, for his safety. If these people were watching her, they were probably watching him as well. And angry because... well because what could be more important than this mission?

She received a second call not long after Donny's... this time from Ernesto in Ecuador. As soon as he started to speak, she picked up the receiver and started tapping into it, and hung up. This happened several times before she texted him that she had lost her voice. She asked him to call anyway, and say whatever it was he had to say as a poem, in flowery verse, to entertain her—as if he were reading it to somebody else. Since he was a poet-biologist, she figured he could couch what he had to say in metaphor.

Well, let's just say he was handsome, but not the poet he purported to be. His was some of the worst she had come across. But the gist of his message was devastating—the mushrooms and the seeds were not growing. They began well enough, but then the shoots withered in the fields. Nothing from what Señor Montenegro had planted lived. Nothing.

How could this be? Had the plants not been treated with enough care? Had they been thwarted by hungry insects?

Ursula went down. Her heart, her hopes, her confidence, all the way down. Her body went cold and numb in dreadful disappointment.

82 | TOO MUCH TENSION

When Donny came home to Ursula's that night he was shaken, but he didn't want to tell her. He didn't want to frighten her or compound her fears. As well, Ursula did not tell Donny. Not yet. She was carrying two sets of horrible news—the seeds had failed to grow in South America, and Homeland Security had taken all the others.

Even through his own wet-palmed angst, Donny could sense she was upset. She twirled the hair on the left side of her head over and over—something he hadn't seen her do in a long time. He sat down next to her on the couch and began stroking her hair in a comforting gesture. He kissed her face, sweetly.

Some people can't possibly have sex when they're upset; others use sex as the very way to let off steam. All this was so new to Ursula that she didn't know which type she was—whereas Donny always welcomed the chance to straighten out his GPS. It had been a very stressful day. But he wouldn't push it. Just see where things went.

His kissing her was welcome. The moment she felt a tingling "down there," her worries and sadness receded to the background. She was relieved to know she could feel something other than pure anguish. She swiftly pulled up her full skirt and dropped her panties. She had to know if there was anything else she could feel in this haze.

Wow. Seeing she was all business made him sit up straight. He went to enter her right away. She stopped his hand and shook her head, no. Instead, she directed his hand to her on-button, and indicated for him to gently flick the switch. He did this in a special circular motion, looking directly at her face. Nothing. He tried a rubbing technique. Nothing. He used his tongue and entire mouth. Not even a buzz. She knew it.

Completely embarrassed, she pushed down her skirt, curled tight on the couch, and sobbed. Donny put his arms around her, not knowing what the hell was going on.

He lifted up her face to his. She managed to look up, but couldn't look directly into his face, instead, stared across his shoulder out the window. Through teary eyes she saw it… the trunk of his car was billowing smoke. She turned him around and pointed out the window in alarm.

Donny leaped from his seat. He ran for the front door, then had to run back for his pants, then back to the door, shouting, "Shit, Shit. Shit," the whole time.

He ran outside and over to his car. Like an idiot, he unlocked the trunk with the key and flung it open. Immediately, flames burst up from the enclosure. "Shit!" he exclaimed. He could see that his gym shorts were on fire—and in a few seconds, so were the entire contents of his trunk.

Ursula ran out there, too, throwing whatever baking soda she had from the kitchen. It had no effect.

"Fire Extinguisher!" Donny shouted. Ursula remembered she had one under the kitchen sink.

It was expired, but Donny tried it anyway. The foam oozed out as a liquid.

Ursula came back out with heavy blankets, and the two of them beat at the gym shorts, the melting basketball, and… the remainder of the seeds from their expeditions—the seeds that were now covered with the expired retardant formula.

Ursula felt sick to her stomach. Donny felt sick to his stomach for other reasons.

Once they were back inside the house, Ursula sat on the couch and wrote: *Those were our last seeds. I didn't tell you yet. Mine were confiscated by homeland security today. I'm so sorry. I think they did that to your car.* She quickly erased it.

Donny looked around the room and experienced a heat wave of nausea. He had to fight back the urge to throw up.

They're not going to leave me alone… she wrote.

He opened his mouth to speak, but his throat was completely dry. He moved some saliva around his tongue and tried to speak again, barely getting the words out. "I think it was my cigarette."

Ursula looked right at him. "What?!" she mouthed in shock.

"I was leaning over the trunk, and an ash must've fallen in. I must not have noticed… and closed the trunk. I think that's what happened…"

A volcano erupted inside Ursula. Her anger seemed to explode out the top of her head. She scribbled madly on the board: *You're smoking?!?!* Erase.

"I got scared. I always smoke when I'm nervous," Donny replied.

Scared? I got arrested and inserted and broken into, and you're scared?

"Yes, I am."

Smoking? Really? How can I trust you? She held the board right to his face.

"I could have lied to you just now. Isn't that something to trust?"

Silence.

"You're not the only one with a lot going on… they came to my house, too. They threatened my comic books."

I just got branded. She thrust her arm forward.

"Well they've got our picture!"

She brought her finger up to her lips to shush him. She buried her arm in the couch pillow, then flashed him an angry, questioning look.

Leaning close, he hissed in a whisper, "We need to stop this. It started out as an interesting idea, but now we're into some serious shit! And these mushrooms creep me out!"

You're afraid of the wrong things.

Whatever Ursula had meant when she'd written that, it stung like nothing had. So of course, Donny countered.

"You just want to control me. Like all women."

No. I want you to be free to act, and you can't be if you have to feed a habit.

"Says you."

Says the mushrooms. And they can't trust you either.

That was it. He landed his blow.

"These are not real mushrooms!"

She wrote furiously, *Shhh. Don't let them hear you.*

"They're just slime."

She stopped, faltering—then scribbled, defensively, *Don't you think I know that?*

But really, she didn't.

"I don't care," Donny snarled. "I don't care about your fucking mushrooms or your ridiculous cause. And you... are out of your mind!"

And with this he stormed out the door.

Once he was outside, he realized that he didn't have a functioning car. But he'd already made his grand exit so there was no going back. He'd walk toward the boulevard and get a cab.

As he walked, his anger kept repeating, *What's the big fucking deal? So I smoked a few cigarettes? It's not the end of the world.* By the time he arrived at the major street, he'd convinced himself this was just as well. Better to find out now this girl was a total nutcase, controlling bitch. *Better to be done with her and out of danger. It's better.*

83 | GONE

What Donny said hurt, but it was true. These were not the right mushrooms, and in fact, they were not real mushrooms at all. Turns out her mushrooms were merely bacteria floating on fermented tea. Real mushrooms are something else altogether. They have tiny mycelium. They have spores. They have more integrity. (Note from M. Earth: *People should get their terms straight before they go passing off something as a mushroom that isn't.*)

What had been some sort of gifted inspiration to plant the seeds alongside the mushrooms as a growing medium had felt so right. It somehow seemed like there was a divine purpose for her being stuck with the last Kombucha in all of LA.

But bacteria posing as mushrooms? Honestly, how could they have lied to her? She knew too well that traveling to foreign places had great appeal. In the bio-world, each species has its own opportunistic agenda for survival and perpetuation. So Kombucha were no different than anyone else. They knew what they needed to survive, and they were willing to manipulate her to get there.

Ursula felt betrayed by everyone. Donny, these bacteria, even Sid. Why did he choose now to prove to her that the spiraling of water in the opposite direction below the equator was strictly urban myth??? He was still mad at her for making him talk to clients.

But worst of all… her orgasm was gone. She knew this for a fact. Lost was the happy hum that connected her with the world—although it was that hum that connected her with these lying slime, and she wasn't sorry about that! Still… she fell into despair.

She went on a fast, called in sick to work, and would not "speak" with anyone.

She plummeted into Donny's "why bother" attitude, and realized it had resided in her all along. And with nothing of real pleasure to distract or amuse her, she was once again flat as a pancake with no expectation of ever rising up.

84 | DONNY HAS HEARTBURN ALL THE TIME

Donny stayed drunk and had heartburn all the time. He watched an awful lot of sports, but to no avail. He was still heartsick. Sweat poured from his palms day and night. He stayed up till the wee hours of the morning trying to be productive, at least, and turn his breakup into his next screenplay; but nothing came.

Who says cigarettes, bologna sandwiches, Internet games, and a stack of used books don't comprise a life? Didn't he have a playoff game to watch later that evening? Wasn't he invited over to some friend's house to watch it? Well, an acquaintance actually. But he had places to go.

Fuck her.

85 | URSULA CLEANS HOUSE

Ursula didn't care how quiet the house got; she simply would not listen to those Kombuchas anymore, no matter what they told her. Even if they were trying to apologize, she wasn't going to hear it. Lalalalalala.

She couldn't toss them because they were living creatures. But she was now only half-hearted in their care, and she could barely look at them while she was tending.

The house was quiet, mostly because Donny wasn't there—though his stuff remained in every room. That man sure spread out quickly.

She pulled out his clothes, threw them in large green garbage bags, and stashed them at the back of the hall closet. She hung scarves and fabric pieces on the bookshelves in front of his books. She gathered up his shampoo and soap from the bathroom, and threw them in the trash.

A few of his comics were sitting on the back of the toilet. She was about to throw those away, too. She knew they couldn't be valuable since they weren't hermetically sealed in those stupid plastic sheaths. *What a thing for a man to spend his time and money on,* she thought. But then she had to smile. His boyishness was one of the things she liked most about him. She had come to rely on it to lift her when she could get so serious—like now.

She picked one up and thumbed through it. She'd never paid much attention to comics. Though she'd read her share of Betty and Veronica and Richie Rich when she was young, she glossed over the whole superhero genre. All that violence and mayhem. But now she got it, these heroes *had* to have superhuman advantage to battle the kind of Evil on these pages. Their violence was justified. Look what they were up against.

She put down the toilet seat, sat down on the john and read through them all.

She understood those impulses, now. Vengeance was a fiery and necessary cleanser. Oh, yeah. By the time she'd turned the last pages on a reinvented Batman, she was ready to get tough! She was going to get even! She was going to destroy those lying fuckers!! Every last one of those Kombucha imposters!

She started scooping up all the bowls. She didn't care that she was treating them roughly. She was getting them out…

She didn't want to throw them all together in one garbage bag, lest they form into a Super Blob, combine with some funky stuff at the dump, and start eating human flesh. She should cook them! That would serve them right. But then they'd start screaming…

She decided she would go out to the park and spread them on the ground among stands of trees where dried summer leaves were just beginning to fall. They might become part of the scene somehow. Alive or dead, it didn't really matter to her. Maybe real mushrooms might reclaim them back into the soil, if they were the forgiving sorts.

Surely it would be deemed suspicious behavior. If the Anti-Seed Terrorist spooks were following her, fine. While it could be considered littering, it had nothing to do with a single seed. If they questioned her, she would tell them she was cleaning house.

She pulled out several large Tupperware bins…

86 | NO ANSWER

Donny has called Ursula several times now, and she's refused to pick up. He's calling her, why? *To get his things back*, he's told himself. How dare she keep his stuff! Doesn't she know he needs it?

Ursula has been trying to call up her missing O. But there's no answer there either.

87 | SPREADING THEM AROUND

It's exactly what she thought. When she dumped those fuckers onto the ground and mixed them in with piles of fallen leaves, they screamed and complained and begged her not to leave them. And despite her attempted disguise in a red wig, somebody was watching her. A man in a running suit, walking a dog, who was a bit too over-trained to be just a house pet. A drug dog, perhaps, now trained as a seed-sniffer?

But ya know what? Even with her heart racing, she left those Kombuchas, right there in the leaves, and walked past the man and said, "Hello."

When she got far enough away, she turned and watched as the man took his dog over to the leaf pile and rummaged through it. Even at a distance, she could see him recoil at the globby mess all over his hands. The dog rolled in it, getting it all over himself, while the man yanked and yanked at his harness. She had to laugh.

Anger makes one less afraid. So does laughter. Both contain the shimmer of Eros that loosens up the tight tie of fear.

88 | DONNY NEEDS HIS TRIMMER

Since he's been back at his own place, Donny's been pleasantly reminded just how much can be accomplished while never leaving the couch.

He has his computer, phone, and all the remotes within arms reach. With just one call, the world's cuisines are available for delivery right to his doorstep. And he's saving water, electricity, and laundry soap by remaining in the same clothes for days.

He tells himself he's content in the return to his "normal" life, except that he wants to find Paul. He no longer wants to recruit him for that crazy bitch's scheme, but just to find out where the fuck he is. Donny tells himself it's out of boredom, but really, he misses him.

Donny had already called that survivalist camp where Paul had "trained" several times now. Each time, the survivalist on the other end was ruder than the last. Suspicious, condescending, and brash—how on earth did they expect to get people to come to their stupid camp when they talked to them that way?

Calling that place was getting him nowhere. He had a new rental while the smoke damage in his own car was being repaired. He could use a road trip. He needed to get the stink off him.

If he were going on a road trip, he needed his beard trimmer. Of course, right? Who doesn't need his beard trimmer on such a trip? It was still at Ursula's. He'd have to go by. And he could tell her he'd be out of town... in case she'd want to know. Naw, that was just habit. He was done with her. Except, he couldn't stop thinking about her.

On the way over, he listed 10 Reasons Why She is Nuts:

Talking to mushrooms (slime)
Listening to mushrooms (slime)
Seeing mushrooms glow in the dark (ridiculous)

Drinking grass
Eating dirt
Won't talk
Unreasonably rigid and manipulative
Doesn't like sports
Has no TV
Frigid

The more he thought about his reasons, the more they fueled his fire. There was no way they should be together. If she went ballistic over a cigarette, just wait a few years down the road; she'd be blowing up at him all the time for all sort of nonsense. She'd capture his freedom for sure. Not to mention the kind of danger she'd put him in because of something some floating *ooze* told her. How could she? How dare she! At least he'd get through this scene quickly, since there'd be no chance for a lingering conversation. He'd get his trimmer and get out.

He parked and walked purposefully to her front door. He hesitated in his choice of knocks. Should he use the familiar? Would she even answer if she knew it were him? Not taking a chance, he banged twice, *boom, boom,* then followed with another. *Boom.*

He waited for some long, uncomfortable moments. One more reason he didn't belong with her and all her bullshit. She took her time with everything. He'd already wasted too much…

The door opened. Ursula looked straight at him. Then down to her blank board, picking up her pen. He stopped her.

"Please Ursula," he pleaded. "I'm sorry."

She scribbled, *I hate you.*

He scribbled back, *I know. Come to bed with me.*

No! she scribbled, hard.

"I am terribly flawed. Come to bed with me. I want to show you can trust me."

She backed away, eyebrows pinched fiercely.

She disappeared into the house, came back dragging several heavy green trash bags. She lifted one up and threw it at him like a medicine ball—then the next, then the next…

"Ah Jeez, all right," Donny said in between catches. "So you're not coming to bed with me. Can I have my beard trimmer, please?"

She disappeared again, returned with the white board.

Haven't seen it.

"This IS where I left it."

She shrugged and shook her head, no.

"You're going to keep my beard trimmer? What, out of spite?"

Take your books and your other shit.

"I will, but right now I need my beard trimmer." It suddenly became very important.

She shrugged.

"May I come in and look for it?

No reaction.

"That's all I'm going to do. Go in the bathroom and look for it."

She rolled her eyes, and then reluctantly stepped aside for him to enter, eyeing his every move. He passed her, nodding a sarcastic thank you.

He went directly to the bathroom, noticing along the way the absence of the mushrooms and their accompanying aroma. He looked around. No trace of him or his stuff on any surface in there. She smirked at him.

But that's not where his beard trimmer was. He'd remembered that it had fallen behind the opened-backed shelf and he'd left it there. That way he'd always know where to find it. He pulled the shelf away from the wall and brought up the trimmer, covered with hairballs and dust bunnies.

"There," he said, proving his point.

She watched him meticulously pick off the crap from the trimmer as if it was his most prized (neglected) possession. He was, in that moment, perfectly imperfect; and instead of being annoyed, she found him dear.

He hadn't really lied to her, hadn't really done something so terribly wrong. He had been on his way, after all, to perform their mission. Everyone gets scared. Wasn't she scared? It was a far-out scheme; she could see that even more now that those imposters weren't pestering her… Smoking was a disgusting habit, but so was farting, which she was prone to do on her raw binges…

He saw her expression toward him change, as she stepped towards him, took him by the hand and led him to the bedroom. He put down the trimmer and followed her, flushed with not knowing.

She kept hold of his hand as they entered the bedroom and she brought him to sit on the bed next to her. She placed her other hand on his cheek. They began to touch each other, slowly, in a remembering way. Each movement, for her, created a tiny opening to let him in; and he stayed right at the edge of her allowing, until she allowed a little more. As she opened, he moved himself slightly further and deeper inside her. She was trusting him and that's all that mattered.

It was a very slow and deliberate entry. They could feel themselves at each moment, all along the way. Ursula felt her resistance, and let that dissolve; and then felt new resistance, and then found more dissolve. Donny was patient, accepting of each plateau.

Slowly, this built. It built a steady rise in temperature. It built and built until they no longer recognized whose parts belonged to whom. This is what the volcano feels like when she's getting ready to blow…

One ignited fireball blazing together, they climaxed at the same instant. And did she scream??? Yes, she did—despite her vow of silence. She let out a clear open throated animal call—and he matched hers in simultaneous response. And they felt the elixir of life wash over them—bathing them in the radioactive love juice that activated their super powers. Pow! Zots! Zamm!!

In their imagination that's how it went… but it didn't. Ursula didn't Pow or Zot. He Zammed, and she remained flat. She was glad he Zammed, but then she cried. He stroked her skin. She was so sad; his heart went out to her.

He sang to her in his best Frank:

"The best is yet to come, and babe, won't it be fine…"

It made her laugh. He loves when he can make her laugh. It makes his soul soar. And while he had her laughing, he determined then and there his purpose… **to retrieve Ursula's orgasm and return it to her.**

It also meant finding some seeds…

It is said we each know three hundred people. Among those people there is at least one nature photographer, one tantric belly dance teacher, one poet-biologist, one paranoid researcher, and at least a few criminals and potheads… of which Donny knows more than his share. He also knows of these crazy survivalists…

The next morning, he woke beside the rise and fall of Ursula's sweet sleeping. He got dressed very quietly, and sat down next to her on the bed. He sang softly to her, a song about lovers and rebels and sweet things to come. And with that, he kissed her gently on the cheek and went off to do what he had to do.

It's so breathtaking.

Of all the danger in this story, the most dangerous thing is to let these rebels bring out the fire in each other.

When the rebel in her touched the rebel in him, and the rebel in him touched the rebel in her, their fears incinerated. When his rebel sperm penetrated her rebel egg, that mysterious shimmer burst forth a blinding light, and a calcium wave signaled the information everywhere it could go. It has turned her into a visionary and turned him into a warrior—on a mission for M. Earth, in the name of Love.

89 | WHAT MUST BE DONE

Donny went to the long-term car rental place and traded in his Ford Focus for a small truck, short term. He drove out to the storage unit in Lancaster and loaded up all his comic books, including his rare favorites.

He took all of them to Comix and Cards in Hollywood—a store that was somewhat of a second home to him—and sold them to Jake, the owner, for one lump sum. Donny knew his collection, but he didn't have time to haggle one by one. And he figured even if Jake ended up on the better end of the deal, it was far more important that Donny have the cash in his pocket—he was going to need it.

He held back his original Mickey Mantle card embedded in Lucite, even though he knew Jake would be out of his mind to have his hands on such a thing. Jake was getting a steal already.

90 | URSULA NEEDS ANOTHER KIND OF MUSHROOM

When Ursula awoke, the first thing she felt was that her heart had blossomed. So curious how all the stored energy that might have been released in her orgasm had somehow exploded into her heart, instead, and pushed it wide open. She could still feel the rippling. It gave her strength and courage, and it lifted her to consider new possibilities, once again.

She knew Donny had gone, and she might not see him for a while. She noticed that he had, indeed, taken his beard trimmer, which made her a bit more secure in his sincerity. And she felt much better, knowing that the two of them were back in this together.

Even though those Kombuchas had lied to her about being real mushrooms, she still instinctively felt that what they had said about mushrooms being a helpful partner for the seeds was right. This was part of what she had seen in her dream. She just needed to find the right mushroom.

Sean had sent her some books on mushrooms through Amazon.com, but frankly they were all too confusing—each looking equally strange and otherworldly. There were hundreds of varieties, all seemingly vying for her attention. Some had vibrant colors, some had incredible medicinal properties, some could rebuild the soil, while others were delicious to eat. One of the mushrooms in the photo winked at her. She would not fall for anyone's self interest again.

Those watching her were no doubt watching those around her. Who could she consult without endangering them? She didn't dare get back in touch with Sean, who she had heard was still in "deep research" over at Sheerah's. She wanted to get in touch with Ernesto, see if he was a better biologist than a poet. She wanted to go to the library or search the Internet, but she couldn't reach out or Homeland Seed Sector would capture her plan and anyone associated with it.

She found herself mindlessly spinning her globe, as was her habit when she wanted to let her thoughts wander. She found that as she was spinning the globe, her hips were making gentle circles, mirroring its orbit. She could feel the synchronicity of timing, globe and belly circling together. And that circle became a spiral, pleasurably working its way up her spine—clockwise, of course. She felt in connection with the globe, with The Earth it represented, and with herself. Not an orgasm, but something very magnetic and vibrant.

Then the idea hit her—just like the guerilla gardening, she would scatter *all types* of fungi and see what took hold. Variety, diversity—that's what was needed!! Had to be. Not just one. Different fungi for different plants; different fungi for different regions. It wasn't really up to her to choose… it was up to them. Of course!

She was so excited she jumped up and down. Then she halted. Which one of these species of fungi was giving her the idea? And what agenda were they promoting? Or was it all some sort of Master Mushroom Mind that had come together, speaking in one voice? How would she know what to trust?

She recognized that when she stopped circling her hips, the voice that had given her the idea stopped speaking to her—if "speaking" was the accurate word. If she resumed rotating her hips, the flow of ideas returned. Hmmmm. So, were these directions coming from "down there" somehow, or through "there" somehow…? (And how much can you trust that?)

Spiraling below her own equator, her hips had become a receiving station for something other than mere pleasure… stranger things have happened… and well… OK, it wasn't a half-bad idea she had received.

Go figure. Life is amazing.

She went into work. She was going to "talk" with Sid, in private.

91 | DONNY GOES TO SURVIVAL CAMP

When Donny stopped at the guard booth in front of the survivalist camp, it was exactly as he'd expected. The big guy who immediately stepped out to block Donny's way was perfectly cast—all the way down to his exposed weapon.

When Donny showed him the ad, and explained that he was there for the training camp, the guard grunted, "Classes are full. Should've called first."

Donny wasn't going to go into how he had called several times and been treated badly, even by *his* standards. That sort of thing wouldn't have mattered to a guy like this.

"Damn," Donny feigned upset. "I've driven all this way."

"Like I said, should've called first."

"Can I at least have some water… it's really hot here."

"Back towards town, there's a booth…"

Donny sat back in his car, wondering what to do.

From down the trail past the guard booth, two young men walked towards them, with haste in their step. They each carried heavy backpacks and all the latest high tech gear. They spoke in excited voices.

"I didn't know it was this kind of place. I thought we'd get some outback skills…"

"Yeah, like sheep fucking. Taught by that guy back there with the big hard on all the time. Crazy shit."

"I just want to go to the Sierras and forget this place…"

They went perfectly quiet when they walked past the guard booth, eyeing the guard who eyed them back.

"Pansies," grumbled the guard to Donny.

"Were they in the class?" Donny inquired.

"Yeah. But they don't get their money back," he called in a voice loud enough for the young men to hear.

"I suppose there's room now?"

The guard didn't like to have to agree. He was the kind of man who, once he said something, stood by it, regardless of how things changed.

"Could you check?"

The guard reluctantly pulled out his cell phone, and walked out of voice range.

When he returned, he told Donny, "OK, you can go in. But you're out of uniform." He chuckled to himself. Donny noted that those guys who just left weren't in any uniform.

"I'll get it inside?"

"Sure," the guard replied, and then went to remove the coiled barbed wire barrier that lay across the road. He was thinking, *another pansy,* as Donny drove through.

Oh, now I get the joke. "Asshole," Donny said out loud, as he looked out over the camp and saw a sea of naked men, all hairy asses and knuckles. Not all of them. Some of them were pale and hairless, obviously the newbies. This was clearly not a place where he would need his beard trimmer. Donny was, by far, not a modest man, but there were places for nakedness, and roughing it in the outdoors didn't seem like one of them—too much exposure to sun, insects, and thorns.

But he knew he couldn't stay in the car forever. He was thinking about turning back when he saw a large man approach, and he figured he'd better get out. He didn't want to be trapped into a full frontal view framed in his car window.

Donny hopped out of his car with his hand extended.

"Donny Cucciari."

"They call me Papa John."

Donny shook his hand. He tried not to look down, but it was obvious this man was top rank.

"I've come to learn a few things. It's getting pretty hairy" (that was a slip) "out there."

"How'd you hear about us?"

"Your ad. And my friend… Paul Blake, he was through here not too long ago…"

Papa John registered no reaction at all.

"You can start by dropping your pants, picking up that shovel down there, and digging a pit. That pit might become the place to bury all your valuables, your shit, or your family, if things get really rough. We'll all meet up at 16:00."

Papa John started to walk off.

"Do you have any sun block?" Donny called after him, but not very loud.

Donny was loath to admit it, but he felt a certain tribal belonging with these men. He had enough hair on his body to qualify as kin. Digging in the dirt, alongside other hairy men digging in the dirt—that was a bonding that went beyond words. He was curious as hell what brought each of his other tribesmen here. Bet there was some crazy-shit paranoia running in these streams. Maybe he didn't want to know.

He liberally sprinkled Paul's name into much of his conversation (which consisted of concise, one line sentences, each required to contain at least one curse word) in case anyone knew him. If they did, no one was saying.

At 16:00 he met back up with Papa John. Unlike Paul, Donny was built for physical work, and apparently his digging met with Papa John's approval.

He only knew this because he was not pathetically ridiculed, and was told to "walk with me."

Papa John took Donny on a short tour of the area. He pointed out the various things he would learn over his time there, "compost toilet, temporary shelter, storing water, storing food, growing food..."

"So let me ask you..." Donny interrupted. "You've got seeds here, right?"

"How else we gonna eat?"

In a whispered tone, "You save them yourselves?"

"That anti-terrorist seed shit's a bunch of bull, they've got mind control drugs in them," Papa John claimed, defiantly.

"What about this new law..."

"Guess that makes us a bunch of outlaws." He cracked up at his own joke.

Donny nodded and took note.

"Now it's my turn to ask questions. Why is Homeland Security after you?"

This threw Donny. How did he know that?

"We do checks," Papa John said, stating the obvious.

"Something to do with the friends I keep."

"Then I don't want you as my friend. You've got to go."

"Take me to Paul. I need his help."

"I don't know where your friend is."

"That's bullshit."

"No, I really don't. It's better for everyone."

"Then disappear me, too," Donny said impulsively. He wasn't sure where it came from, but it was a good idea. "I've got nothing but trouble waiting for me at home."

Papa John looked at him closely. "That's a serious request."

“I’ve got to find Paul,” Donny said. “He’s my best friend in the world, and a person can’t survive without his good buddy.”

Papa John considered for a while. “I want you to send him a message. Don’t sign it. If he knows it’s from you, then you can go to him.”

Donny knew exactly what to write. He scribbled something down on a piece of paper and handed it to Papa John.

I’ve got Cheetos in the car.

“That’s it? That’s your message?”

“That’s it,” Donny replied smugly. “And his note back to me will say, *Flaming Hots? You suck!* or something like that.”

Papa John called over one of the senior and seriously hairy guys and gave him the note and instructions. “Meanwhile,” he said to Donny, “go over there and build yourself a crapper.” And he left.

92 | CHANGE OF COURSE

When Ursula got home, she stepped into the living room, only to find the two Terrorist Seed Sector agents sitting on her couch. She gasped.

"We let ourselves in, since we know how," one agent said. "Come join us." He indicated for her to sit in the chair. She knew she had to.

"What *was* that horrible crap you were spreading around in the park the other day? Our agent's got hair all over his hands, and his dog's gone bald. Is it some new bio-weapon you're trying out?"

Despite her fear, Ursula had to stifle a laugh.

They waited for an answer. She pointed to her throat.

"Oh, yeah, you don't speak…" he said. "No worries… you don't have to say anything. We brought something for you."

And with that, the other agent grabbed her leg and clamped a big metal tracking device on her ankle.

"We should've taken you in when we found your seeds. But now you're going to stay right here. If you go out your door, you're going to get a *big* shock you're not going to like. Might not even be able to make a second attempt. Your muscles go to jelly. Can't walk, can't stand. You'll regret it if you don't believe me. But if somehow you do make it out of the house, this thing will tell us exactly where you are; and we'll come back and turn up the volume."

He took a moment to register her expression of shock.

"If you're asking… why me? You're not alone. We've got these things on all you hippie seed-savers…"

The agents weren't making that up. The government was experimenting with creating camps on retired military bases to house the arrested seed-savers. Tent cities passed off as a generous government handout to the rapidly increasing homeless population. Only *these* campers would be strictly guarded "for their own protection."

But having all those revolutionaries in one place posed a major problem. Their minds could all start working together, making their plans... the grandmas and the Garden Society ladies were especially dangerous...

Better to put all violators under house arrest. Separate them, and watch them. All offenders would be strapped with tracking anklets that could deliver such a strong shock it would fry their nervous systems if they stepped through their doorways. Mr. Ed's brother-in-law happened to own an empire of electronics plants that were easily converted to make those tracking anklets. Once again Mr. Ed was pronounced a hero for coming up with the right solution at the right time.

Congress praised the President for creating a whole new job sector of Seed Protection Security to monitor these branded traitors. Between this and the TSA, nearly everyone was working for the government now.

93 | DONNY AT THE PASS THROUGH

When the note came back, *They'd better be flaming hots, you fuckwit,* Papa John deemed it was close enough, and let Donny pass through. What followed were endless days on the move. Donny crawled through underground tunnels, went from car to truck to helicopter, walked miles along railway tracks. He hardly slept at all.

Donny was a good tracker, but even he had no clue where they were taking him. He wished they'd get there already. Traveling up a dried and parched ravine on an ATV four-wheeler, he had to admit, all these vehicles and road dust made him feel… *rugged.* Being an urban guy, rugged wasn't something he'd ever come in contact with. *There might be something to this survival shit after all. The whole gun thing. The whole your-own-free-man thing. This was the real way to remasculate.* He felt keen and alive, and surging with testosterone. He felt strong and invincible, and very cool. He wanted to kick this ATV into gear and take it up the hill… *Focus,* he told himself. *Find Paul. Find seeds.* What he wouldn't give for a liter of Coke.

94 | SID DOES RESEARCH

Sid had been more than a little pissed off when all his hard work finding the nearest capital city to each of the Strangers, plus creating all the elaborate flight schedules, had been put on hold.

Now, with Ursula's new request, he felt downright put upon. Why should her problems become his burden? Was he the only guy with a computer in all of LA? She had to promise to take care of his slobber dog the next six times he went out of town.

Grumbling as he went on to various websites that were selling mushroom growing kits, much to his surprise, he became fascinated. These things just sprouted out of small logs and bags of sawdust? They could be cultivated again outdoors in old logs and the right soil? He ordered as many as the websites could supply. He found mycorrhizal soil additives that enhanced plant growth through mycelium. He ordered pounds of that.

Ursula wanted him to find some morels and stinkhorns to add to the mix, because of their absolute phallic resemblance. The thought amused her, an "up yours" to AgriNu and a "come to papa" to whoever was near. There was that stinkhorn that Sean and Sheerah had told her about in Hawaii that could bring a woman to orgasm just from its scent. If Sid could find them, Sheerah wanted to spread lots of those around.

Sid's eyes were tired and burning. He'd been on the computer so long, he'd almost skipped his Skype date with Janeene. But this particular activity could revive him. He'd located those Hawaiian stinkhorns and had already FedExed one to her and wanted to watch what happened...

95 | DONNY FINDS PAUL

After another hot and dusty day of adventure on the ATVs, Donny's convoy dropped him off at a settlement up in the red rocks of Arizona, with a flat field extending behind the camp for maneuver practice. At least here, the survivalists got to wear clothes. Perhaps it was protection against the desert sun. Perhaps it was that man was truly meant to wear clothes, and left to his own, he will.

It didn't take long for Donny to spot Paul working in deep concentration, a pile of odd electronics parts strewn about his feet. Donny was so happy to see him, he practically ran.

"Great to see you, man," Donny said to Paul. He would've hugged Paul if it hadn't been for the surrounding debris separating them.

"My Cheetos?" Paul replied, not looking up.

Donny produced the small bag he had carried all this way—now completely crushed. Paul opened the bag and poured the crumbs down his throat like a man dying of thirst. He was happier to see Donny than he would let on.

"You've got to come back," Donny told him.

"Can't. They're looking for me. They took all my research on JFK."

"Thank God. But I don't think that's what they were after. What they're after has to do with seeds and Ursula and anyone associated with her. Bastards got her under surveillance; they've been messing with my place..."

Paul looked around carefully and whispered, "I'm not sure these guys'll let me go."

Donny took in the scene in detail for the first time. There were five guys. Seems the deeper underground you go, the more hairy the guys get. The women, it appeared, had left a long time ago, burdened or bored, or both.

"They've got me building this shit out of old parts." Paul held up some tangle of wires and rusted circuit boards. "Does this look like a power generator to you? Survival means using what you've got, but this is ridiculous."

Donny kept his mouth shut.

"Lindey's over there, if you want to meet her. But don't say you're my friend. She'd probably haul off and slug you."

Donny looked over. Indeed there was a woman, her tool belt hanging just below Tampa as she whacked nails into what looked like a table. "Nice," is all he said.

"Yeah. She's done with me."

"Then there's no reason to stay. You've got to get out of here."

Paul put his work down. "And go where?"

"With me. Ursula's got this plan… and I've got to help her. And I need you to help me… You think you're actually safe here? Look at these guys."

Paul had to admit he'd been enormously uncomfortable since he first arrived. Slight and hairless, he was by far the smallest and least fit of the group, least able to fend for himself or to fend off others. He could tell by the way these guys horsed around that as soon as they really got it that Lindey was not going to be anyone's plaything, they might come after him. He'd be made someone's bitch for sure—made worse by Lindey looking on and laughing her head off. Donny was thinking the same thing.

"We gotta get out of here," he said.

"But how? These guys are trained killers," replied Paul.

"I'll think of something… What are they like?"

"They're die-hard zealots who make jerky out of anything that moves…"

"What else?"

"… they play a lot of touch football."

"Any good?"

"They're good at everything. They're like the bad guys and the good guys, rolled into one."

Donny's mind started turning. It took exactly twenty-three seconds. "Got it," he said to Paul. "Watch this." Then he stood up and called out to the men, "Who here likes comic books?"

They looked around at each other, and all said, "Hell, yeah!"

"Who here likes Batman, Spider-Man, Iron Man?" Donny was pumping it up.

"I like The Hulk," said one.

"Hey, me, too!" said another.

"So, here it is," Donny said. "It's a game. Everyone here is a superhero with their own special powers. We make two teams like the Justice League vs. The Fantastic Four, and we battle it out." Donny had them by their boyhood wonder. "Winning team makes slaves out of the losers."

"How 'bout we make slaves out of you now...?" the hairiest one laughed.

Nobody else responded. Paul was afraid he'd scream.

Donny teased, "Too easy. I'd think you guys would be up for some sports. A real contest, with real stakes."

Still no response.

"Isn't the waiting killing ya? Another day gone by and the world still hasn't come to an end. You're already prepared. I'd think by now you'd be looking for something else to do."

They did have to agree they were tired of digging, and rigging, and preparing for the day that didn't come. Frankly, they had to get themselves all worked up each morning with renewed fervor to keep the end of the world scenario from falling into tedium.

"And if we win," Donny explained, "our prize is to leave. As our slaves, you not only let us, but you carry out our things."

"And as our slaves..." One of them broke out into cruel laughter. Paul shuddered. "We'll just leave that to your imagination."

“What’s the game?” another chimed in.

Donny hadn’t gotten that far in his thinking…

“Sudden Ultimate Death Xingo!”

He went on to explain, making up the rules as he went. “Each team has a ‘thing’, a big totem or an item the other has to capture. It’ll be well guarded. And you can move it all around.”

“Sounds like Capture the Flag…”

“But each player gets to use their super powers against the enemy…”

They liked that.

Donny continued, “If you get taken prisoner, you can try to fight your way out. And if you do, you go up a level, and you are even more powerful… and you can blow things up. You guys have shit that blows things up, right?”

They certainly did. All the guys, other than Donny and Paul, went into a huddle.

“Are you out of your mind?” Paul hissed right in Donny’s face. “We can’t go up against those guys.”

“What’s the choice? They’re not going to let us go otherwise.”

“They’ll kill us… or worse, we’ll be their slaves!”

“We would anyway if we stick around. Come on, it’s a game. You and I know games up and down. At least this way we’ll have a chance. Just make sure your hero’s got the right powers, OK?!”

Lindey tried to join in the huddle. The men told her, “No women.” No offense to her, but even with super powers she’d just slow them down.

Well, this was not the woman to tell that sort of thing to. All her feminist ire came shooting out like a launched missile. Lightning fast, she hauled off and punched one of them right in the stomach, leaving him keeled over in surprise. She stormed off, all hot headed and defiant, to join Paul and Donny’s team, temporarily blinded from seeing just who she’d aligned with.

The others broke their huddle. They all wanted to be on the same team. "That's not going to work," Donny told them. At least one of them had to come over to his, Paul, and Lindey's team. No one made a move.

Exasperated, Lindey offered a blow job to whoever came over.

These guys may not have wanted the dead weight of a girl on their team, but they were more than willing to have her lift a little weight off their dumbbell. Yeah. Everyone but the guy still holding his gut raised his hand to volunteer. Not one of these guys had been with a woman in quite some time, and really, who needed an excuse?

Lindey, amused, chose the big guy, the one who'd killed the mountain lion last week with the machete he made out of a saguaro cactus. He seemed very capable of guarding their "flag." And, he was the cutest of the bunch.

Paul had nothing to say in the matter. Lindey had cut off all sex with him once they left the hotel. He understood that. He had under-performed in so many ways. But he knew, even though he had gone from boyfriend to ride, that with the exception of that one little error back there at the gas station, he'd shown more respect for her than any of these Neanderthals had. Given the chance he would show her. She may have been his ticket in, but he was going to be her ticket out. If he survived, he wanted to be her hero.

Roger, the big guy, could feel Paul's eyes burning a hole right between his own. He told Lindey he could collect later, wanted to save himself for the game. He didn't want to be sabotaged by his own teammates out of jealousy. And a blow job was a great motivating prize.

There must have been an express lane to this place, because Papa John arrived the next morning, saying he wouldn't miss this for the world. He'd always idolized the heroes, tried to live his life by their codes of justice and revenge. He brought with him enough long john sets and fabric to equip everyone with something that resembled a tight fitting super suit. Headgear, they fashioned themselves from the plant life and animal bones around the area.

Papa John named himself as the referee, so Donny had to explain all the rules to him, still making them up in the telling. Papa John nodded, sometimes frowned, in confusion, and more than once insisted on changing them. In most cases, Donny yielded.

> Each team can place, guard, and move their flag however they want.
>
> Each player will choose a superhero persona and a *super power* to go with it, realized as best they can.
>
> No hand to hand combat, no shooting, stabbing, or bombing of any of the players.
>
> You can take prisoners, but not torture them.
>
> There are no safe zones.
>
> The game is over once a flag is recovered and brought to Papa John.

The teams lined up, opposing each other on the field in what was every six-year-old boy's dream come true:

> CAPTAIN MARVEL faced DAREDEVIL.
>
> WONDER WOMAN faced off SPIDER-MAN.
>
> FLASH squared off against IRON MAN.
>
> THE HUMAN TORCH burned a fiery look right though THOR.

Each team was determined to win. For Donny, as Captain Marvel, it was to champion his woman and carry out her plan. For Paul, as Flash, it was the best chance he had to escape this hellhole and redeem himself in Lindey's eyes. For Wonder Woman, although she didn't really want to leave the camp, she would love to have these guys as *her* slaves for a change. And for Thor, Roger the defector from the other side, a victory might award him a more extensive sensuous celebration than just a blow job, and even without it, he welcomed any opportunity to blow things up!

The other team—Daredevil, Spider-Man, Iron Man and The Human Torch—were calling themselves The Mother Fuckin' Fantastic Four. Unbeknownst to Donny and Paul, all but Spider-Man had served in Special Forces in Desert Storm and who knows where else... When it came to maneuvers, they were overqualified.

Papa John, who was given his first choice of superheroes, chose Superman—a giant S painted directly on his sculpted chest. He fired a gunshot into the air and commenced the game.

96 | CREATING THE KITS

Even though it seemed that Sid might have gone overboard, 50 pounds of spores and various cultivation kits were just the beginning, and had arrived at a mailbox center in Hollywood. Ursula's belly dance classmates each ordered the same. They said they'd be happy to assemble her kits, since Ursula could do nothing in or out of her house. Spores are not seeds, and no one in the government really gave a damn about mushrooms, so this was not an official act of terrorism—just leading to one.

Sheerah offered her studio for the gathering. Six women shook their hips in time to the music, while they made up packets of spores as instructed. They assembled over 500 kits.

Ursula could feel it all the way over at her house, her hips gyrating in time with theirs. She'd stop and think about Donny, appreciating that he was doing something important but wondering where he was.

Hopefully he was getting his hands on some seeds.

97 | BACK AT CAMP

The Xingo game went on all day. If it weren't so menacing, it would be the goofiest show of leaping underwear that anyone had ever seen.

Before the start, each team hid their flag to deter its capture. Donny's team, the Justice League, found a fierce-looking mountain lion's jaw, with sharp teeth still intact. They rigged it like a spring trap, the jaws set to chomp closed if someone touched the flag inside. The other team defended their flag with three agitated rattlesnakes in a makeshift cage, with a precarious latch. Donny's League climbed up a cliff to hide their flag in a crevice in the rock face. The Mother Fuckin' Fantastics hid theirs in a cave, with one team member stationed to guard the opening at all times. The rest of the team members were free to run about, reeking havoc and general mayhem, in search of the other team's spoils.

Each player chose one super power he or she could approximate under these earthbound circumstances.

Captain Marvel relied only on his pure will, courage, and strategic leadership. Donny knew he could never out-strength the opposing team, but he could out-smart them. And he did. Always claiming the higher ground, not only did the League keep relocating their flag to keep it near to them as they moved, but they managed to anticipate the moves of the other team and stay one step ahead.

Paul, as Flash, possessed invisibility. The real Flash could vibrate his molecules so he could barely be seen and could phase through solid objects. This was in addition to being the fastest man alive—which Paul wasn't, so he opted for invisibility as his power. He could sneak around wherever he wanted and the other team was not allowed to notice him, even if they saw him. Very cool.

Wonder Woman had limitless strength and recuperative abilities. She could fly and move fast, thanks to her special sandals. She also possessed the Lasso of Truth, which compels anyone to a full confession. Lindey opted for that power, using her bullwhip, with which she was quite skilled, as a stand-in.

The League's other teammate, Thor, the finest physical specimen of all the Asgardian gods, possessed a magic hammer named Mjolnir. When he hurls Mjolnir, thunder, lightning, and all sorts of catastrophic disruptions occur. Roger had his saguaro machete, remember? And strong arms… and a few strategically placed explosives here and there—not to hurt anyone, just as a deterrent…

But these super power advantages seemed to really slow things down. Like when The Human Torch used a real flame-thrower to block Wonder Woman's passage and set half the brush on fire. She tripped him with her whip as payback, he fell forward, and his clothing burst into flames. They had to stop the game to extinguish the brush fire, and him.

Or when Spider-Man rigged a web-like rope swing across the gorge… It was a good thing he landed on some thick vegetation. Despite his supersuit, he was pretty cut up from the thorns.

No one was allowed to actually fight; they couldn't lay their hands on each other, or use any kind of actual weapons, but that didn't stop them from creating booby traps and ambushes all along the way.

Iron Man and Daredevil did their fair share of mischief, cheating constantly when no one was looking. They "liberated" an ATV from the base camp and used it to climb up the slippery shale rock hill Captain Marvel and Thor had built at the foot of the path up to the ridge, only to have it blasted out from beneath them.

Superman managed to show up everywhere, perhaps the biggest mystery in this whole play. It seemed like every time he did, the rules changed in favor of the other team—like giving Daredevil X-ray vision in the form of a long distance scope, because he was blind.

It was only because our heroes had been so good at hiding their flag that The Justice League survived as long as they did. Donny felt justified for all the hours he'd *misspent* in front of the Xbox screen. Games are games, no matter what the stakes.

At one point everyone had been captured, so Superman called a restart.

On the second go round, tempers, tactics, and testosterone levels ratcheted way up. Starting over had given the Mother Fuckin' Fantastic Four the chance to come together and strategize. This time, no messing around. They were pissed and ready to make some slaves.

Captain Marvel and Thor moved their flag to the top of a different ridge, where Thor would remain posted to guard it with his life.

The Fantastic Four decided to spread out and attack from all sides. First they would take the others all prisoners; and then, unimpeded, easily take their flag.

Daredevil spotted Wonder Woman leaning against a tree, her back towards him. He dropped down and crawled on his belly, stealthily moving in on her. Flash saw him and started kicking dirt up all around him, blinding his eyes. Daredevil stumbled around, covering his face, and got snapped up into a rope trap that hung him upside down from the tree. Wonder Woman took great pleasure in seeing him dangle there. She only had to *threaten* to use her bullwhip for him to tell the truth about where their flag was, and Flash ran to go get it—in plain sight—since no one was allowed to see him.

Yes. No one was allowed to see him or approach him—but it didn't mean they hadn't anticipated him—or another of his team. The Human Torch was setting a trap, and Paul was running right into it.

Donny was still on the ridge with their flag. He figured he had the best vantage point from up there. He fished out Daredevil's scope, which he had pocketed at the base camp during their restart, and went out to the edge of the cliff to take a look around. Down below, across the narrow gorge, he could see enemy activity surrounding a cave. Must be where the other team was now hiding their flag, the one guarded by the rattlers. He had a real problem with snakes, but if he could get down there somehow… he could have their flag, he could have their seeds…

He'd have to climb all the way down off the ridge and scramble over these big rocks to get to the cave. Could take him a good half hour…

He watched as The Human Torch finished hiding a wire that ran from the entrance to something like a gas tank and some explosives. The trip wire would ignite a ring of fire once someone entered, trapping them in the flames. *Clever,* he thought, *but I am more clever.* Then he saw Paul running towards the cave…

This was no longer a game.

Donny had to do something. It was at least 30 feet across the gorge, and down. If he jumped, he'd break all his bones. He'd seen Spider-Man attempt it with the rope, seen him swing out over the gorge. The rope broke, and he fell into that spiky thicket of bushes over there—the only thing that saved him.

Maybe if Donny jumped far enough he could reach the bushes. Maybe they would break his fall. What choice did he have? Paul was about to run into that cave and become toast.

Donny had to act, and it had to be NOW. But nothing moved. His feet stood heavy, like frozen lead. His heart sped. His mind raced. *Paul was down there. Ursula was counting on him…*

Suddenly, he felt his *masculinization* surge up, galvanizing a fire in his heart.

He knew exactly what to do. It was a move he'd practiced over and over again in the comic book of his childhood imagination…

Eyes focused on Paul and that bramble patch; he took aim. He took a running start. He called upon what he knew—what it felt like to connect with a baseball through the bat, how the energy of his intention lined up and carried all the way to the stands. He became the bat, became the ball, became the momentum itself…

"Shazam!" he cried, shouting the incantation that gave Captain Marvel his magical powers. He pushed off… he leaped… the wind caught his cape and he sailed through the air as if his heart burst golden wings out the back. And for that one moment he could fly. Suspended in both speed and slow motion—he soared over the gorge. No thought, all action. Just movement.

Paul was running fast toward the cave, and the prize. Speeding towards him, Donny screamed, "No!" loud enough to get his attention. Paul looked up. The sight of Donny flying through the air was enough to stop him in his tracks—and then get the hell out of the way. Flying just above the ground, Donny broke off a large stick, and flew into the cave. He fought off the snakes, tossing them behind him, one by one, to smash on the rocks in the deeper recesses. Then he grabbed the flag and the cage, and flew out of there, careful not to trip the wire.

Donny was the guy afraid of flying… now look at him.

Astonished, Paul said "What the fuck?"

And Donny said, "I know," and no sooner than that, he crashed right into the cliff wall and fell to the ground, his makeshift cape tangling all around him. "Fuck!"

But damn, he was triumphant!

And even though it hurt like hell, Donny ran that cage down the field and placed it at Superman's feet. They won. Damn.

As soon as Donny presented the other team's flag to Superman, Papa John distanced himself from the losing team who were now fated to be slaves. He reminded them all he was impartial, and therefore not part of the deal.

The Four refused to be slaves. No surprise there. But Thor, being a real life demolition expert, had already rigged their tents with explosives that he could set off from his wristwatch—in case things turned out just this way.

Cursing and fuming, the Fantastic Four hurled threats and flying objects at our heroes. Donny, now filled with super-courage, held up his hand to settle them, "It's not going to be that bad…"

They looked up, quieting down for just a moment.

"Number one, you let us go," he said.

They were imagining far worse.

"Number two… I need a team of skilled, fearless, gun-toting crazy people like yourselves to carry out a plan." They perked up. "You'll fly around the world transporting some very precious cargo on your persons, and hand it off to other equally skilled and crazy people like yourselves."

"I thought you were going to fuck us in the ass!" Spider-Man laughed, nervously.

"Yeah, you wish," chortled Thor.

"What's the precious cargo?" Superman demanded.

"Oh, yeah, number three… give us your seeds." Donny always had good comic timing.

"What?!!" Superman was furious. "The seeds are not the property of these slaves."

"Since they're my slaves, I could order them to steal the seeds, tie you up and pull every hair off your body, one by one, and then…

"Charlie Foxtrot!" Papa John tore off his cape and threw it to the ground. "Whadya want with them?"

"Plant them."

"Where?"

"Not sure yet."

"You're not giving them to those ragheads!"

"No, probably not. More likely wetbacks, jungle boogies, swamis, and gooks. Problem there?"

"Yeah." He looked Donny straight in the eye.

"I could tell you how important this is, not just for your little band of survivo-nuts here, but for everyone on the planet, and about all the karma points you'll get in heaven for your good deeds, but… you don't have a choice," Donny said pointing to Thor's watch. Thor nodded.

"We get to use our guns?" Iron Man asked.

"Actually not. We have to pass through airport security. But we'll make sure guns are waiting on the other end. Maybe we can capture a few seed banks!" That seemed to satisfy.

And so it was that all the superheroes formed a league of their own they called, ASSS—Army of Seed-Saving-Sons-of-a-bitch. They added BAD to the name. It suited them better. So the BAD ASSS piled into two Hummers and a pickup truck, with over one hundred small containers of seeds hidden beneath the floor mats, and headed for the Tucson airport to await instructions. They each had a fake ID and a small overnight bag filled with enough survival gear to handle any climate.

But first, Donny made them all shave their bellies.

98 | SPREADING THE SEEDS

Getting word back to Ursula was no easy feat. Everything about her person and environ was being monitored. And the BAD ASSS were not a bunch you wanted to bring home to dinner, even when the government wasn't watching.

So Papa John provided Donny with a secret way to get word to Sheerah, and Donny had the money from the sale of his comic collection transferred to her account via some tricky bank routing. She and the other belly-gals packed up each of the fungi kits in its own plastic bag. Daisy paid Ursula a visit with the excuse of bringing her groceries and new music—which they played very loud. Minnie went to see Sid, receiving from him all the travel arrangements necessary for the mission—now all rerouted to originate out of TUS. We don't know how he did it—how he put the travel charges through other clients' accounts and reimbursed them from Sheerah's money. It sounds quite illegal, and there's enough of that going on already.

The Men and Woman of BAD ASSS slept in several different hotels near the airport. As rough as these guys were, they went nuts sleeping on the big cozy beds. And apparently they liked room service, too!

Paul shared a room with Donny, since he no longer had sleeping rights with Lindey, who now insisted upon being called Wonder Woman all the time.

Thor didn't press his advantage, nor did he ever try to collect his victor's reward from her. As horny as he was, she had been an excellent teammate, and he wanted to honor her as the warrior goddess she was.

Paul was having serious reservations about going on this mission. He was a guy who didn't go out much, and never on planes. He'd never even heard of this plan before Donny laid it out. Knowing Donny, he probably made it up then and there. And now Paul was considered a champion of the plan by association. In a time when people can get arrested for just possessing seeds, here they were deliberately transporting them... He wondered if they served Cheetos in jail.

But if he didn't go, he would disappoint his best friend, who had come all the way out to that godforsaken nowhere, and risked his life to rescue him. Also he would forever be like a larva to Lindey—something pale, weak, and as yet unformed.

He tossed and turned all night. Donny, on the other hand, slept like a bear in winter. He had thoroughly enjoyed every bit of that game—especially the part where he made slaves of those hairy He-men—even more than the flying. Which was still a miracle and a mystery, one he may never come to understand or repeat.

He was proud his comic book money could finance this whole endeavor. He was finally cashing in his boyhood to become a man. (Some would say "it's about time!" but those people are not in this chapter.) Ursula may have started this wacky plan, but Donny was the one who figured out how to make it happen. He felt *masculated* in a way he'd never experienced before.

But that money only went so far. When he realized that all the BAD ASSS boys and girl were going to need to clean up their appearance, get some less conspicuous clothing and have some spending money for when they reached their locations... he had no choice but to max out his credit card and take the cash advance at something like 29%.

The next day, Donny went to the bank, and the BAD ASSS all went shopping.

On the 3rd day, they all went to the airport and sat in the bar drinking coffee. Gone were the camo and flack jackets in favor of preppy polo shirts and pressed chinos. All the metal belt buckles, zipper clips, and things that beep had been trashed. To look at them you'd think they were off to a golf resort.

When these women-starved men saw the colorful belly-gals coming right over to them, hips swaying in unison as they glided through the airport—they thought they had died and gone to heaven. And as long as these guys kept their sun-baked, crackpot mouths shut, the women found them refreshingly manly and attractive, and were settling into their laps before even saying hello. The belly-gals had been told by Sheerah that they might have to inspire the men. All of them being single, they didn't mind. After all, they were supporting the troops—not the same at all as throwing yourself away. Turns out, these guys didn't mind being slaves at all.

Daisy was especially drawn to Thor's big arms, and he was drawn to her dark beauty. Any prejudice he might have had about women of color incinerated in the electricity of his attraction. The rest of the women chose randomly for the fun of it.

In somebody's fantasy, right there in public, each of these women wrapped herself around one of the ASSS guys, spreading her big skirt over their lap so no one could see Army thrust his steel hard joy-stick up inside and throttle her to blast off. No one would even see her rock and ride him to an almighty power surge, because no one was looking. In all their fantasies, there wasn't a condom in sight. Full and direct, skin to skin contact.

That wasn't Donny's fantasy, he was thinking about Ursula.

Paul was thinking about Lindey, and she was thinking about having another cappuccino.

What *did* happen is that each of them received many small plastic bags containing seeds, mushrooms, and mycorrhizal fungi. They were instructed to go to the bathroom and tape them to their freshly shaved bellies.

These were guys who knew how to hide things, so even with their packets, their simple t-shirts seemed to lie flat across muscular frames. Paul couldn't bring himself to tape on a packet. He wasn't afraid of the tape pulling his chest hair; he had none. He desperately didn't want to get caught!

He stared himself down in the mirror in the men's room, long and hard. What kind of larval existence had he been living all this time, and what creature was he hatching to be? Was he forever going to be researching life instead of living it? If he didn't go now, he'd never know…

Paul nearly burst out of the men's room, walking proud. Because he stood concave in the chest, he also had no problem hiding the seed packets without a bulge. He'd put on two t-shirts, a short sleeve over a long sleeve, just in case.

Lindey placed hers right over Central Florida. She was so excited about all of this; she nearly bounced. She leaned over and enthusiastically kissed Paul on the cheek. He asked if he could sit next to her on the plane.

The women handed out the airline tickets and itineraries. Each member of the ASSS would be heading out in a different direction, making different connections as they traveled the globe—all within 20 degrees of the equator. They would each be met at their destination by a perfect stranger. Ursula had wanted them to make a picture with the stranger for her, but that was from another time. Each of the BAD ASSS would spend a few days to rest and re-supply, then get on another plane and meet another stranger. And so it would go until all their seeds were spent.

Daredevil went through the islands of Indonesia and up into Thailand and Cambodia. The Human Torch went to Nigeria, then through the Congo and into Zaire. Thor went to the Samoas and throughout the Archipelago. Spider-Man went to Romania because one of the mushrooms had a cousin there... Flash and Wonder Woman decided to travel together to Sri Lanka and India, but it was strictly hands off. Donny liked the feel of Central and Southern America and took the routes there.

The mushrooms were excited about the trip. It wasn't every day they got to move so quickly.

99 | URSULA'S HIPS

Meanwhile, Ursula felt like a mother whose kids were off at school. She wondered what lessons they were learning. Who were they eating lunch with? It's hard to be the one left at home to imagine. But she had managed to lie low beneath the attention of Homeland Security, and she wasn't about to blow it.

She didn't dare make contact with Sheerah or Sid during this time. Donny was completely out of the question, though she beamed him loving thoughts every hour. She had taken to twirling her hair again, but that's understandable. She would just have to trust.

She passed the time by studying her globe, slowly spinning it around, trying to feel where each member was. As she followed the movement with her eyes, her whole body went with the circling, around and around. She remembered from before, she liked this feeling. It was both comforting and sensual. The forces of gravity settled in her pelvis, and she felt the earth inside her, like a multi-directional gyroscope turning round on its axis. A golden ball with a magnetic pull.

This amused her no end, so she practiced circling some more. With each pass through, she felt more power building inside her bowl; the movement got slower, stronger and harder to pull against.

Suddenly her car keys scooted along the counter and dropped to the floor near her feet. Paper clips jumped across the desk towards her. The coins on her skirt shimmered with an electrical charge, becoming tiny magnets, themselves sounding like groves of climaxing cicadas.

Another surprising event in a story of surprising events… this was fun.

She threw open the front door to get access to the front yard. This new discovery was so compelling that she rushed outside, forgetting about her anklet… Zitz! The shock went right to her bone. Her leg buckled in intense pain. Not nearly as crippling as the agents had described, but enough to make her go back inside, immediately.

After some rest, she tried her experiment again, this time, standing just inside the open doorway in order to zero in on objects outside.

She tried it out with bicycles and passing cars. She found she had to rotate much harder, but she could feel the current of connection between them. The bike riders and car drivers looked totally perplexed and panicked at their lack of control. Sheerah had told her that by unlocking her Eros she could defy the laws of physics, but Ursula thought that was just a metaphor.

She spotted an airplane flying overhead—aimed her right hip, and with slow undulating circles she felt a lock onto the plane, felt its pull, and she pulled back. Even at such a distance it was too powerful for her. Well of course… it's a plane! But still. Maybe she could fly the planes from down here if she got good enough.

She could hold this tantric, magnetic tango for a long time, playing with the build in current, pulling it back just before it spilled over the edge endangering the plane to come crashing down. Or so she could imagine.

She was both energized and exhausted by the gyrations. Going back inside the living room, she stood still and took a few deep breaths. Her coins immediately calmed and laid flat against the fabric. When she sat on the couch, she felt the spiraling fumes of all that had gone on, still residing there inside her bowl. She swore she could hear it humming. She couldn't help herself, she decided to hum along.

Hmmmmm, hmmmmm, hmmmmmmmm.

On a short list of really cool things, this was way up there. Needless to say, despite the shock she had received earlier, Ursula was feeling quite good "down there."

What she didn't know was that this magnetic play was sending a little shimmer up M. Earth's spine, triggering an imperceptible tremor in The Earth—causing M. Earth to wish she'd knock it off.

And another thing she didn't notice was that all this magnetic activity was jamming her tracking devices.

The next day, Homeland Security paid Ursula a visit to "turn up the shock volume" on her anklet. They also waved a frequency wand over the outside of her body. Though they wouldn't let on, she knew they were checking her implant. They couldn't locate the interference. It seemed to be working fine right now.

As they turned up the setting, they let her know if she went out again, this time the shock from her anklet would kill her.

100 | IT WAS ALMOST DONE

Even though Daphne from legal had transferred weeks ago, Mr. Ed could not stop thinking about her. Her sudden transfer to their offices in West Sussex came as a blow to him—he had hoped to win her back after things settled down a bit. She didn't say as much, but she couldn't leave town fast enough. Between Mr. Ed's constant calling, and her soon-to-be-ex practically stalking her, she needed to take her children and go far away. Someone was challenging the legality of the contents of the seed bank there…

Mr. Ed felt empty. His days were filled with the absolute triumph of his program. He had received two promotions since this story began—now he was simply, "Head of Special Projects." Seems the more important one becomes, the simpler their title. And big bonuses. Yes, yes, but at night… empty.

He didn't understand it, really. Why should he be unhappy? The seed banks around the world were full—full of Freedom Seeds from AgriNu, and strains of *pure* banked seeds were in laboratories right now awaiting modification and new patents. Not only were these seeds the *master parents* from which all other seeds would be produced, but the literal library of available plants and food on earth was now being made stronger than ever, and totally within their control.

But he missed his son. The one he'd thought he was going to have. Mr. Ed had already formed a picture, and what he recognized now as a relationship… with something that would never be. The question that he couldn't shake was, *What was the point of all this if he had no one to pass it on to?*

And while our superheroes were flying around spreading seeds across the globe, and AgriNu was spreading their seeds in the final phase of their master plan in all of North America, Central America, South America, Africa, the Middle East, Central Asia, Asia, Indonesia, and most of the islands of the Pacific with just a few exceptions that weren't worth the trouble… Mr. Ed's seed was going nowhere.

As for the EU, Mr. Ed had tried to handle the changeover to AgriNu seed publicly. It's always better if you win over the public perception—even by fanning fear. But in truth—and you promise not to tell—what became know as Freedom Seeds and their precursors had "accidentally" slipped into the EU seed supply many years back. The same was true in Mexico, South America, the Middle East, and Asia. No one could tell the difference; they all look the same from the outside… And the panic over the lack of productivity in their crops after a season only sent the farmers running to a more productive solution—AgriNu, and the magic of chemicals. Or it would… soon enough.

Mr. Ed was trying to pry open the European markets in public. But this had already been going on in *private* for some time now. AgriNu inspectors would soon identify the presence of AgriNu seeds in all growers' *supposedly* pure Euro crops, and they'd not only have to pay, they'd be sued.

It was almost done.

Soon, there won't be a country in the world that doesn't have to buy their seed from AgriNu. Mr. Ed is claiming they own *growth* itself.

Why are they doing this? Because they can.

But there's still that thing he can't…

Mr. Ed got on a plane to England. He was going to try and see Daphne. Maybe she would have a change of heart.

101 | THEY COME HOME

Donny was the first one to come in. He stayed at a friend's house, pretending he'd been on a giant binge and couldn't go home. Thor came in next and immediately went to see Daisy. She invited him in and shut the door behind them for several days.

The Human Torch, Daredevil, and Spider-Man each decided to stay on in their last destination and create new survival colonies of their own. Iron Man just flat out disappeared.

Paul and Lindey had separated by necessity a few countries back, because their itineraries dictated. But when she returned to LAX Sunday morning, he was waiting for her by the curb. Boy was he glad he'd decided to be a BAD ASSS, after all. He carried her bags to his rental car and held the door open for her. As he started the ignition, he wondered where he would take her. Certainly not the Chateau Marmont.

Everyone could breathe a collective sigh at a job well done. The rest was up to M. Earth and her strategists, the mushrooms.

Donny had secretly been circling Ursula's block, passing by her house to see if it was under surveillance. He was surprised to see it wasn't. He was dying to tell her every single inch of his adventure and to show her the *fuerte* of courage that had come to him, through her love. But there was still one more thing he had to do…

102 | THEY CAN'T STAY

Donny spent the day in a flurry of errands, burying his essential tasks among more mundane activities, should anyone be watching. He had the airline tickets in his pocket and a small packed duffel in his trunk. He could see by the long food ration lines at the grocery stores he passed that it was only a matter of time before all hell broke loose here. He, Ursula and their friends were all targets. Even his masterful denial mechanism couldn't talk him out of this one. It was time to go.

For Donny, the only person it was hard to say goodbye to was Mickey Mantle. A 1952 Topps in mint condition... do you know what kind of bidding war he could have started on eBay? But having no time, he sold it for cash to that thief, Jake, for a third of what it was worth—and a new set of forged IDs for himself and Ursula. Jake had all sorts of dubious connections and came by the name "thief" honestly.

Ursula heard that familiar knock at the door. At first she feared it was Homeland Seed Security coming for her, but when she cautiously opened it, there was Donny standing in front of her. Looking into each other's faces, they could see how they'd each been changed by all that had happened. They immediately fell into an urgent kiss.

Donny had to break the moment. "We've got to go..." Ursula pushed her hands over his mouth to keep him from saying more. He indicated for her to give him her whiteboard, then wrote, *Now. Pack a bag. Daisy and Thor are in the car keeping a watch. Paul and Lindey will meet us at the airport.*

She wrote, *I can't.*

Only now did he notice the electronic anklet beneath her full skirt. His heart filled with horror.

It's to keep me from leaving.

"How bad is it?" he mouthed.

They tell me the shock will kill me.

Donny hadn't counted on this. "We'll figure something out," he mouthed, "go," and pushed her towards her bedroom.

Ursula rushed off to pack. Donny paced the room, trying to think.

She emerged moments later, suitcase in hand. But Donny hadn't thought of a thing. Nothing that wouldn't put her life at risk, and he wouldn't do that. He now knew the difference between games and real life. He mouthed to her, "I'm not going without you."

She wrote, *I can't let you stay.*

She knew any day, any minute, they could all be locked away forever. She was the one who'd gotten them into this trouble, and she wouldn't let it happen to him. She could tell by the response from the Homeland Seed Monkeys that her hip gyrations had made some effect on all their surveillance devices, because they kept coming back to check. But she couldn't be sure how much effect it had, or if it jammed the shock anklet. Which it probably did, because the agents spent an awful lot of time checking the anklet when they'd come.

So, let's say it did. And let's say she could keep her hips going enough to get out the door. Then Donny would be safe. And if it didn't work, then at least he'd be free to escape without her. She wished she'd had more time to try it out.

She wrote, *I've been playing around with jamming the electronic signals. It seems to work.*

He looked at her, hopeful.

She nodded yes. *I do it with my hips.*

His hopes sank. *No, not another crazy idea,* he thought.

She looked at him and nodded in earnest.

He took the board from her. *You've tried this before? You know it works?*

She bluffed. *Yes.*

He hesitated, then wrote, *No. This is not a good idea.*

I want to try.

She picked up her suitcase and stood by the door. Donny came to meet her, or block her; he wasn't sure which. He couldn't let her do it. No. This crazy idea could kill her, and he couldn't bear the thought. Ursula slipped back into doubt. Her hips were not always something she could rely on, and now their lives depended on them…

They heard the car horn honking, urgently, from outside.

She mouthed to him, "I can do this. Trust me."

But could he? Let her fly in the face of trust? And then he remembered the curious circumstances of his own flight. "Stranger things have happened," he marveled, and offered his hand to her. "You ready?"

She took a deep breath. She placed her hand in his, squeezed hard.

She indicated for him to stand back and give her some room. She started to move her hips around and around in circles, in a slow and deep pull. Donny was definitely intrigued. His jaw dropped when he saw coins and paper clips inch their way towards her across the tabletops. He cracked up in delight when he saw the refrigerator walk its way across the kitchen. She kept the movement going and tried to make it as small as possible. "I'm going to have to keep this up for a long time," she mouthed.

Once she had built up to this point, as long as she kept her pelvis moving, she would be jamming the signals coming from her chip and, she prayed, her anklet. She pointed to the door. Donny picked up her luggage and walked out, turning back to her as she hung there in the doorway. She met his eyes; she took a breath… and stepped through. No harm. Nothing. They both laughed in relief. He grabbed her hand and closed the door behind them for good.

It's not so easy to gyrate and walk for any great distance. It's not a forward moving strategy, really. It required moving very slowly which was not helpful in urgent moments of escape. Donny hurried her towards the car, but if she dropped out of the rhythm, even if she could avert the painful shock up her leg, it would alert those who watched her that she was on the move. So it took some time to reach the vehicle and flee.

Thor and Daisy had the car idling, ready for those two to get in and go. Donny had wanted Thor and Daisy to come along because they all needed someone else besides Lindey who actually knew how to survive in the outdoors. Daisy had finally decided to take a spiritual name. She chose Tarene, Thor's counterpart. It made sense.

Donny drove La Cienega to the airport in a new rental. He felt more nimble on the city streets and off the freeway. Ursula insisted no one speak a word. All the while he was driving, she was circulating those hips in the back seat, while Thor worked to remove her anklet with some tricky, all-in-one tool he'd brought along. He needed her to keep still so he could disable the mechanism, but she couldn't stop or it would shock them both. So he found a way to move with her in the same circles to maintain a consistent relationship to the wires. Finally snip, snip, he cut the connection, click, click, unlocked the clasp, and she was free. There was a whoop of gleeful triumph from everyone when Donny pulled over to the side of the road, and Thor hurled the monstrous anklet out into the street.

Donny kicked on the radio, pressed on the gas, and raced to the airport. Ursula tapped Thor and frantically indicated her upper arm. She wrote, *Listening device. Get it out!* She now had figured out how to keep her hips going in a much more subtle manner, but she was sure she could not get through airport security with this device in her arm. Something would go off, either in the airport or within her.

Thor mouthed that he'd been a medic in the Gulf War and had removed all sorts of shrapnel and other foreign bodies. If she would let him, he would remove her device. From the looks of it, it could be a simple cut. Donny quickly made the turn into a warehouse parking lot and parked way towards the back. Thor had no anesthesia, and no surgeon's tools, but he also had no choice; and Ursula was brave. Donny crawled in the back seat with her, held her hand, and covered her eyes as Thor washed his hunting knife with the fifth of scotch Donny brought along. He poured the scotch all over her arm and made her drink the rest.

Thor was careful, and mostly quick. He sliced an incision in her upper arm, fished around a little with the blade of his knife and tried to lift the chip out. It was holding hard. He tried to jiggle it loose. Ursula clenched against the pain, but it was lodged in there. He pressed back the tissue surrounding the chip. He could see it was square, metal, and compact; but it was already spreading roots, tiny electronic tentacles, reaching down towards her bone. He had seen things like this before in the war—bio-metal that actually grew into the body, and took over functions. Creepy shit. Some kind of military experiment nobody was supposed to talk about, but he'd seen enough of it to know it wasn't nice. He caught Donny's eye and conveyed to him the dire need to act now.

Donny got Ursula to look him straight in the face. He locked eyes with her, though hers were swimming in soft focus. He held her arm down with one hand, her face firmly in his other. He would not let her out of his sight, or grip—not for anything.

Thor grabbed that devil thing with a small tweezers, twisted and yanked. It wouldn't come. Ursula writhed and shot up, biting back her scream. Donny pressed her down harder. Thor got hold of it again. He had to dig even deeper. Blood was everywhere. She was breathing rapidly, trying to break free. Thor bore down, twisted the chip in the other direction, and yanked with all his might. As it came free, a high screeching sound nearly pierced their ears. Thor threw that damn chip out of the car and hammered it to smithereens.

Donny put pressure on the wound to stop the blood. He never took his eyes away from hers. Ursula breathed, breathed, breathed. Then she cried. Donny cried, too.

They were late for their plane; the surgery was far worse than Thor had anticipated. He told Donny to find the nearest drug store. He dashed in, grabbed bandages, iodine, some hand sanitizer, and whatever other anti-bacterial agents he could find to prevent infection, and a needle and thread.

He treated the wound as best he could, but they had to go. They suspected that even smashed, the chip still gave off a signal that had alerted Homeland Security to come find them.

Paul and Lindey were waiting for them outside the terminal. They'd all been planning on going through the airport from the baggage claim up, but

Ursula was still so inebriated and exhausted that she had to be pushed in a wheelchair through security. Thor wrapped Ursula's arm in a sling and put a bandage around her foot to make her look the part of needing assistance. They had to regroup, move items from carry-on into checked luggage and vice versa, careful not to carry with them anything that would sound the alarm. Donny and Ursula had newly created passports. The other four's IDs had already passed through many airports, so they were confident there.

Airport Security always seems to go easier on people in wheelchairs, so they all tried to go through the handicap line, as extended family. But the TSA would only let Donny go through with Ursula, and moved the others on to regular security after they had checked in at the ticket counter. They would all have to meet up at the gate.

Waiting for the next ticket agent, Donny nervously passed the documents back and forth in his hands to keep his mind from thinking too much. It occurred to him he hadn't even looked at them, he'd been so hurried all day. Jake had his "guy" rush them over to Sid to book the tickets. When Donny finally opened the passports—he thought he'd shit. It was too late. The wheelchair was on the move to the ticket stand. Donny handed the ticket agent their documents.

"OK, let's see…" the ticket agent said as he opened Donny's passport. "Captain Donald Marvel. Captain Marvel. Seriously?"

Donny kept a straight face. "Reserves."

"And this is Mrs. Marvel?"

Ursula gave a slight wave.

Jake, you asshole! Donny thought.

"What is the purpose of your trip to Quito?"

"Second Honeymoon."

Donny gave Ursula a sweet smile.

The agent paused, looked at them carefully. "That's quite a name. Ever get…"

"All the time," Donny interrupted trying to move things along.

Ursula just nodded and smiled.

The TSA agent checked the tickets against the passports. Checked again. Then he handed them back the documents. "Enjoy your flight."

That was close. It wasn't until they were on the other side of security that Donny could breathe normally. But he did notice, as nerve racking as that had been, his palms were dry. Hmmm. Maybe Captain Marvel after all.

As Ursula was wheeled toward the gate, she held Donny's hand and sighed as she took a last look around the airport she had passed through so many times—such a familiar friend that she would never see again.

103 | FLYING

Well, here's what happened next. Maybe it was M. Earth's fiddling with herself out of boredom; maybe it was Ursula's electromagnetic *gyrutations*, or both; but The Earth began a low, imperceptible rumble. Imperceptible to humans, but very apparent to toads, canaries, cats, dogs, whales, and to the grasshoppers—whose eggs hatched, and who were frenzied enough by the vibration to swarm.

Locusts moved out across the land, across the corners of the world. And after they ate their fill, there were other waves of locusts right behind them to reproduce and swarm some more. You see, something in the genetically modified corn, soy, and rice they had devoured kept their cycle perpetually in a swarming frenzy and on the attack. The gene for the shut-off mechanism, by which the population of locusts would naturally revert to grasshoppers once the plague has been satiated, had become modified. These creatures were forever hungry and forever ravaging—and they passed their appetites on to their children.

Great.

Normally, after such a devastation of crops, some uneaten seeds remain behind and fall to the soil to grow again. But not these seeds; these were AgriNu's one-shot wonders.

What AgriNu lacked in imagination and vision, they made up for in hubris. They were so humanly foolish as to believe there was no power larger than their own. But here it was.

In one season's time, there simply would be nothing to eat.

Great.

And don't look to the seed banks. They've been raided... and the seeds reportedly taken by large hairy men in capes and long johns.

This tremor was a wakeup call to swarm and take to the sky—and many heeded: cicadas and bees, beetles and gnats…

It was a wonder our merry band's plane could even land.

104 | WHERE DO WE GO NOW?

Ernesto was waiting for them at the Quito airport. He had two jeeps and a truck parked outside, filled with tools, building supplies, food, and water. Weapons too, which brought a smile to Thor and Paul.

As they headed out of the city, in caravan towards the rainforest, it was a sci-fi nightmare, only for real. Curtains of locusts moved towards them. At closer look, if you dared, mixed in were some fearless flies and wild-eyed ladybugs, which are really not so cute in large numbers and at great velocity. Fires burned in the open fields, with no effect on this plague.

They moved ahead cautiously, understanding that sitting still would yield the same result.

Before they knew it, the swarm was upon them. It was like riding through a car wash. Thousands of voracious insects hurled themselves against the car and windshield. The road ahead completely obscured, they had to stop and wait it out.

Hours passed. No one dared get out, not even to pee. The sheer force of all those insects buffeted the cars and truck like crazy, sounding like a giant hailstorm against the metal and glass. Some of the smaller flies made their way through the air vent in Paul, Lindey, and Ernesto's jeep. You never heard so much cursing since Paul's tent collapse. Ursula was fascinated—she was still loopy from too much alcohol and Advil for the pain in her arm. Donny was completely creeped out, but distracted himself by marveling at his dry palms. Thor and Tarene used the time to fool around.

As all storms do, the tempest began to pass. Though the locusts and friends were still around them, they were thinning out. Ernesto gave the signal for them to move. But they couldn't. The bug splatter against the windshields was so thick, they had to wrap bandanas around their faces and chisel off the carcass plaque with shovels, while knee deep in insect debris. Not to mention how the grillwork had to be cleared out with their hands in order to start the vehicles. Yuck.

As they drove closer to the rainforest, the terrain became more and more vegetated. Once they reached the edge of the jungle, they seemed to pierce a veil as they drove through—not one locust was on this side. Oh, there was an absolute flurry of parading ants, termites, and worms, preparing the soil for something… The heavy, musty smell of mushrooms was in the air.

105 | THE BIG PICTURE

Meanwhile, Sean and Sheerah could feel the rumble rebooting into action. They traveled to a cave in New Mexico, and plugged in for the Big Picture. They wondered, if they were to just stay this way, would they somehow completely dissolve into the field they were now such a part of, and not have to return to these bodies? They would remain in this position until the world proved otherwise. What else was there to do?

106 | M. EARTH'S TURN

No matter whether or not you had left the dishes in the sink, had a mini panic over who was supposed to pick up Billy from school, stressed over the pile up of unpaid bills, or even your recent cancer diagnosis that consumed your family with grief—all these concerns and procrastinations, anxieties and sorrows were leveled in one moment. Disappeared completely, along with the entire kitchen, your heavily mortgaged house, the neighborhood… you, your family… All concerns gone with one heavy sigh.

To M. Earth it was a shrug, a yawn, a roll over in bed. And for you, too, it was a relief and release—of all the troubles, worries, and petty concerns that had been strangling your entire life.

The jolt was so sudden and fierce it brought down entire cities and civilizations in an instant. Massive tidal waves and tsunamis engulfed the coastline of just about everywhere. Volcanoes took it as their cue to blow their tops—even ancient ones who thought they no longer had it in them.

All the continents, nearly all the people… M. Earth may be many things, but she's not sentimental. She doesn't pick favorites.

All those seismic events occurring together caused the entire earth's surface to quiver—like a giant vibrator on the clitoris of the world.

This quiver amplified over every inch. In many places, it trembled and toppled what had been. In some places, it signaled a wakeup. It rocked the sleeping seeds in their cradles. It jiggled the mushrooms to reach out in all directions and hook up. It swayed the frightened surviving animals to soothe them. And just like you snap a tablecloth free of crumbs, it shook any remaining humans free of their fabric of security.

In all honesty, it's a relief that all this happened, since most people would have nothing to eat in a short time, thanks to AgriNu. No crops, no more seeds to reproduce themselves. No life cycle. All gone. M. Earth doesn't pick favorites, nor is she into prolonged suffering.

This is not an apocalypse. Not the fulfilled prediction of the fiery End of Days. It's simply M. Earth pressing the reset button, as it happens from time to time every few million years or so. By her pressing the reset button all you people were spared the agonizing cancer you would be dying from as a result of the continuous eating of the untested GMO food. And spared the cruel and bloody survivalist wars over scant resources. Really, it's a blessing.

Humans, while very important to themselves, were ever only a small part of the picture. M. Earth says, "I'm staying right here; it's you fools who need a new address."

Whether it was humans' fault or not, whether you call this global warming through short sighted excess, or whether it was simply part of a larger cycle—like the cicadas and the locusts—it would be happening anyway.

The end of a season.

The real mushrooms say, "Thank you, job well done," because now they'll have more room to spread out and thrive. They and the cicadas and the cockroaches, or whatever they morph into in the next million years. Unimpeded, the mushrooms will have century after century of undisturbed propagation, allowing their underground network to form the true Internet clear around the globe, and create, perhaps, a more intelligent order. They'll have plenty of remains to feast upon.

Who knows, with all the loose debris and garbage now floating around, the Northern Pacific Gyre might gather the new Super Continent. Fungi could do wonders with that dump.

Thanks to the mushrooms, over time, M. Earth might even get her fertile topsoil back, and maybe, somewhere, there will be farmers again. Or creatures just like them. Because somewhere in small pockets, all around the globe, seeds planted by superheroes will be sprouting, and there might be a few earthlings left to eat them. But we will never know who killed JFK.

Over time, the mushrooms might even be able to rehabilitate the GMO seeds that had gone haywire. Return them to Nature, and to their original nature. You'll be happy to know that even now, there are fairy rings of fungi sprouting up around all those seeds that Ursula and Donny and then Señor Montenegro planted, the ones Kombucha had failed. Wow.

The plan now completed, who knew whose world Donny and Ursula were saving and why? No matter. They were proud to play their part. And M. Earth was proud of them.

Just so you know, the masterminds of AgriNu were among the first to perish. Not because their corporate headquarters was situated directly over some sort of epicenter and their buildings would have collapsed with the first tremors. No, just before that… something else.

Seems al-Qaeda really was mostly into big explosions, and took offense that their good name was being used to front AgriNu's shameless attacks on food. So they blasted them, *Boom*—up to the heavens, in that big jihad ejaculation they'd all been working towards.

Mr. Ed met with an even crueler end.

One day before the tremors, after his many days in England, Daphne finally consented to meet him. Said she had something good to tell him—maybe she had changed her mind, maybe she did love him after all? She asked that they meet on the patio outside her favorite pub. His heart was racing in anticipation of all the possibilities as he sat down to wait for her.

He heard it before he saw it—a tremendous buzzing that pulsed the air, growing louder and louder as it approached. People ran from the streets, taking cover wherever they could find it, but Mr. Ed remained in his seat waiting for his love. Too bad, because then, a giant swarm of frenzied bees and mosquitoes were upon him… They stung him all over first, then they devoured him… and that was that. In there were a couple of vengeful butterflies.

Oh, well.

107 | ADAM AND EVE

M. Earth may not be sentimental, but she does like to show her gratitude.

Where Donny and Ursula had gone was safely hidden away from even the awareness of what had happened to the rest of the planet. They knew they would be off the grid, just didn't know there wouldn't be one anymore.

This Eden had been prepared for them by the native plant-keepers who lived down the "road" in the jungle. Our heroes had everything they would need—food, shelter, friends, and a connection with the ancients. Funny how essential things can become.

Ursula sat on the makeshift covered porch watching the warm rain as it splattered on the planted field, courted the furrows of turned soil, and slipped down in. They had planted in time. Before the heavy rains. Even in this downpour she could sense a hazy hint of green beginning to appear on the rows. The seeds were sprouting. Some of them were spinach.

Each seed had been planted with the mushrooms, the real ones. This time they were flourishing.

And that's not all that's growing… Paul and Lindey were growing a little something of their own, the tip of Florida starting to spread out across her belly. Paul had been right about wanting women of good reproductive strength. If there was a future, this was the beginning of the new world.

Thor and Tarene were working day and night to do their part, and undoubtedly would catch up.

Ursula could feel the stirring of a new world inside her, as she took Donny by the hand and led him away to the soft clearing that she had draped with the few colorful cloths she had packed with her. He was surprised and delighted. She sat, and gently pulled him down beside her.

The holding, stroking, caressing, kissing, licking, tickling preamble to their making love must have been a doozy, because it built and built to an outrageous climax that peaked on and on and on. One, two, three, four in a row… Ursula lost count as she heard her open throated voice sing out from her deepest deep. Donny was right with her every bit of the way. Five, six, seven… her voice exploded… eight, nine, ten… and showered over them like a million sparkles laughing.

"Wow," she said, sitting up.

"What did you say?" Donny popped up. She hadn't spoken for months, and now she just did.

"Wow. I guess I just said, wow." She giggled. Donny engulfed her in his arms and kissed her.

"Wow," he said.

Wow! She couldn't believe how good she felt, and how potent. How far could it go? 50? 100? 500?

Wow! He couldn't believe how ecstatically happy he was. She got it back, her voice, her orgasm, all of it. And he had been her champion.

He started to cry. He couldn't quite believe that either—or the things that had happened to him in the last few months, or even the last forty-eight hours. He told himself the tears were from exhaustion, but really, her returned orgasm and voice were the signals that it was all over… and they were safe.

Ursula cried, too. All that fear… no, all that *trust* in the face of the fear, had transformed them into rebel lovers beyond their imagination. Looking back, she saw how one awakening inside her had led to another—leading to the unimpeded opening of her heart in this very moment. What could be next?

Donny laid his head gently on Ursula's belly. She sweetly stroked his hair. *A farmer,* he mused. *Now I'm a farmer?* Who would believe this outcome? In time, when these plants have grown tall and he and Ursula have six barefoot little kids running around, and they grow up and marry Paul's little mongrels, and their houses are built and their needs are taken care of…

There may not be a happily ever after. The world is too cynical, cyclical, and precarious… but there is a happy for now.

108 | IN THE END

When Donny and Ursula made crazy love on the rainforest floor, her streaming orgasm spread out through the network of mycelia, lighting up the entire switchboard, causing fruiting bodies of mushrooms to thrust up from the earth everywhere, spraying their spores in their own orgasmic explosion…

If one could see down from the widest zoom out of the Google Earth satellite still beaming signals down to The Earth they could read this glowing banner, flashing on and off, clear around the equator:

DON'T WORRY BE HAPPY. DON'T WORRY BE HAPPY. DON'T WORRY BE HAPPY…

M. Earth sings that song by R.E.M. The mushrooms all hum along…

It's the end of the world as we know it… and I feel fine.

Was it good for you?

THE END

FINAL NOTE

This story is a fiction, thank God. Some kooky thing the author dreamed up, or was told by other intelligent creatures.

But if any of it sounds like something you know, even if only in your wildest paranoid imagination, here are some things you can do:

1. Stay Awake.
2. Read labels. Insist that the government label GMO foods, and while you still can—don't buy them.
3. Buy organic. Support local, organic farms.
4. Plant your own garden. Tend your own soil.
5. Buy your seed from organic seed-savers.
6. Love with all your might.
7. Don't worry, be happy!

JOIN THE DONNY & URSULA MOVEMENT

Become part of our Wall of Strangers.

What is our Wall of Strangers, you ask? It's the place where all us like-minded, Eros-inspired, seed-saving outlaw defenders of M. Earth can join up and watch our numbers grow.

It's also the place where you can connect with real activists working on all these issues. Go to **donnyandursula.com** to post your photo and receive your instructions.

ACKNOWLEDGEMENTS

A story is a field that gathers to itself what it needs in order to be told—characters, ideas, and lots and lots of details. It also gathers to itself allies; helpful, gracious, smart, supportive people without whose contribution, it simply would not exist—nor would there be the courage to bring it forward. And with their contributions, both seen and unseen, they have become part of its constellation.

I have many allies to thank.

First of all, I want to thank Deena Metzger and the Wednesday Night Writing Group, who have held this story with me for all these years. This is where Donny and Ursula first showed their faces and became like good friends. Especially the early circle of Carmen Tolivar, Amanda Foulger, Jeanne James, Lynne Littman, and Deborah Behrens. And I hold a deep appreciation to MJ Roberts, then and now, for her fierce, ongoing writer-friendship.

A special thanks to Danelia Wild, research hound extraordinaire, who for years fed this field with fact. In the beginning, the ideas and dangers in this story seemed outrageous, but in far too short a time, have been proven more than true.

My appreciation goes to my early readers, Patricia Childs, Deena, MJ, and Ann Sheree Greenbaum, whose enthusiasm and insightful comments encouraged me. Then to Clarke Gallivan, Emilie Conrad, Camille Maurine, Robert Litman, Helen Luce, Loree Gold, Diane Schuman, Pam Arnold, Carole Burstein, Michael Lerner, and Renee Hayes, who next stepped into D and U's world and helped me go the next steps.

And always to Coke Sams, who held a space for this story long before he'd even read it, who saw me naked in my work and didn't laugh, and whose comments on every draft gave me incredible guidance to see what I could not yet see.

I stand, lifted upon the shoulders of my Nashville homies.

My heartfelt thanks to Emilie Conrad and Continuum who've taught me everything I know about bio-intelligence, the life force of full-bodied Eros, and how to enter its matrix.

To my editor, the smart and sharp-witted Cyra McFadden, who kept this crazy narrator from tripping all over herself, but let her speak in her own voice—only better.

Again to Patricia Childs for her vision and responsiveness, for how she hears the music of words, and for being the last eyes on the manuscript.

To Rachel Lang, without whose brilliant marketing and design creativity, this book would not be in your hands.

To those who expanded the story into visuals, David Yepiz and Robin Keyser of The Live Box for the incredible website, and Valerie Madden for the book's dynamic cover and design.

To my comrades at The Lia Fund, Chela Blitt, Eleanore Despina, Bing Gong, Beth Rosales, Cornelia Durrant, Claire Greensfelder, Angela Johnson Peters, Renee Hayes, Penny Livingston, James Stark, Michael Stocker, and Jacques Verduin, who, through their dedication, have taught me about being a voice for change in the world. This book has grown from my knowing them. And to my sister, Randy Lia Weil, for starting it all.

Abundant thanks to Lesley MacKinnon, Reyna Monterroso, Emma Destrube, Terri Talbert, and Ruth Weil for the support they give to my life.

And I really must pay tribute to Anaïs Nin, who lived boldly and unabashedly in her senses, and wrote beautifully about it. Her Balinese sarong hangs over the back of my chair as I write, given to me by Deena Metzger who had received it from Anaïs. When Deena presented it to me on my 40th birthday, I was placed in a legacy I am only now beginning to realize.

My thanks to all who have jumped in and wanted to play, contributing talent, ideas, resources, connections, and enthusiasm. That could even be you.

We are all part of this web of awakening.

SHARON WEIL is an award-winning screenwriter, producer and director. Donny and Ursula Save the World *is her first novel. It grows out of her love of nature, her concerns for the world, and her ability to find depth and humor in everything.*

Visit her at www.passing4normal.com.